Miranda of the Balcony

Miranda of the Balcony

A Story

A.E.W. Mason

MINT EDITIONS

Miranda of the Balcony: A Story was first published in 1899.

This edition published by Mint Editions 2021.

ISBN 9781513281292 | E-ISBN 9781513286310

Published by Mint Editions®

MINT
EDITIONS

minteditionbooks.com

Publishing Director: Jennifer Newens
Design & Production: Rachel Lopez Metzger
Project Manager: Micaela Clark
Typesetting: Westchester Publishing Services

Contents

I

In Which a Short-Sighted Taxidermist from Tangier Makes a Discovery Upon Rosevear

The discovery made a great stir amongst the islands, and particularly at St. Mary's. In the square space before the Customs' House, on the little stone jetty, among the paths through the gorse of the Garrison, it became the staple subject of gossip, until another ship came ashore and other lives were lost. For quite apart from its odd circumstances, a certain mystery lent importance to Ralph Warriner. It transpired that nearly two years before, when on service at Gibraltar, Captain Warriner of the Artillery had slipped out of harbour one dark night in his yacht, and had straightway disappeared; it was proved that subsequently he had been dismissed from the service; and the coroner of St. Mary's in a moment of indiscretion let slip the information that the Home Office had requested him to furnish it with a detailed history of the facts. The facts occurred in this sequence.

At seven o'clock of a morning in the last week of July, the St. Agnes lugger which carries the relief men to and fro between the Trinity House barracks upon St. Mary's and the Bishop Lighthouse in the Atlantic, ran alongside of St. Mary's pier. There were waiting upon the steps, the two lighthouse men, and a third, a small rotund Belgian of a dark, shiny countenance which seemed always on the point of perspiring. He was swathed in a borrowed suit of oilskins much too large for him, and would have cut a comical figure had he not on that raw morning looked supremely unhappy and pathetic. M. Claude Fournier was a taxidermist by profession and resided at Tangier; he was never backward in declaring that the evidences of his skill decorated many entrance-halls throughout Europe; and some three weeks before he had come holiday-making alone to the islands of Scilly.

He now stood upon the steps of the pier nervously polishing his glasses as the lugger swung upwards and downwards on the swell. He watched the relief men choose their time and spring on board, and just as Zebedee Isaacs, the master of the boat, was about to push off with his boat-hook, he nerved himself to speak.

"I go with you to the Bishop, is it not?"

Isaacs looked up in surprise. He had been wondering what had brought the little man out in this dress and on this morning.

"There'll be a head-wind all the way," he said discouragingly, "and wi' that and a heavy ground sea we'll be brave an' wet before we reach the Bishop, brave an' wet."

"I do not mind," replied M. Fournier. "For the sea, I am *dévot*;" but his voice was tremulous and belied him.

Isaacs shook his head.

"It's not only the sea. Look!" And he stretched out his arm. A variable fog rolled and tumbled upon a tumbling wilderness of sea. "I'ld sooner have two gales lashed together than sail amongst these islands in a fog. I'ld never go to-day at all, but the boat's more'n three weeks overdue."

Indeed, as M. Fournier looked seawards, there was no glimpse of land visible. A fortnight of heavy weather had been followed by a week of fog which enveloped the islands like a drenched blanket. Only to-day had it shown any signs of breaking, and the St. Agnes lugger was the first boat, so far as was known, to run the hazard of the sea. It is true that two days before one man had run in to the bar of Tregarthen's Hotel and told how he had stood upon the top of the Garrison and had looked suddenly down a lane between two perpendicular walls of mist, and had seen the water breaking white upon Great Smith Rock, and in the near distance an open boat under a mizzen and a jib, beating out through the heavy swell towards the west. But his story was in no wise believed.

To all of Isaacs's objections M. Fournier was impervious, and he was at last allowed to embark.

"Now!" cried Zebedee Isaacs, as the lugger rose. M. Fournier gave a pathetic look backwards to the land, shut his eyes and jumped. Isaacs caught and set him upon the floor of the boat, where he stood clutching the runners. He saw the landing-steps dizzily rush past him up to the sky like a Jacob's ladder, and then as dizzily shut downwards below him like a telescope.

The boat was pushed off. It rounded the pier-head and beat out on its first tack, across the Road. M. Fournier crouched down under the shelter of the weather bulwark.

"As for the sea I am *dévot*," he murmured, with a watery smile.

In a little the boat was put about. From Sour Milk Ledge it was sailed on the port tack towards Great Minalto, and felt the wind and felt the sea. It climbed up waves till the red lug-sail swung over M. Fournier's head like a canopy; and on the downward slope the heavy bows took the water with a thud. M. Fournier knelt up and clung to the stays. At all costs he must see. He stared into the shifting fog at the rollers which came hopping and leaping towards him; and he was very silent and very still, as though the fascination of terror enchained him.

On the third tack, however, he began to resume his courage. He even smiled over his shoulder towards Zebedee Isaacs at the tiller.

"As for the sea," he began to say, "I am—" But the statement, which he was not to verify on this day, ended in a shriek. For at that moment a great green wave hopped exultingly over the bows, and thenceforward all the way to the Bishop the lugger shipped much water.

M. Fournier's behaviour became deplorable. As Isaacs bluntly and angrily summarised it, "he lay upon the thwarts and screeched like a rook;" and in his appeals to his mother he was quite conventionally French.

He made no attempt to land upon the Lighthouse. The relief men were hoisted up in the sling, the head-keeper and one of his assistants were lowered, and the lugger started upon its homeward run before the wind. The fog thickened and lightened about them as they threaded the intricate channels of the western islands. Now it was a thin grey mist, parting here and there in long corridors, driven this way and that, twirling in spires of smoke, shepherded by the winds; now again it hung close about them an impenetrable umber, while the crew in short quick tones and gestures of the arms mapped out the rocks and passages. About them they could hear the roar of the breaking waves and the rush of water up slabs and over ledges, and then the "glumph glumph" as the wave sucked away. At times, too, the fog lifted from the surface and hung very low, massed above their heads, so that the black hillocks of the islets stood out in the sinister light like headstones of a cemetery of the sea, and at the feet of them the water was white like a flash of hungry teeth.

It was at one such moment, when the boat had just passed through Crebawethan Neck, that M. Fournier, who had been staring persistently over the starboard bulwark, suddenly startled the crew.

"There's a ship on shore. *Tenez*—look!" he cried. "There, there!" And as he spoke the mist drove between his eyes and what he declared that he saw.

Zebedee Isaacs looked in the direction.

"On Jacky's Rock?" he asked, nodding towards a menacing column of black rock which was faintly visible.

"No, no—beyond!—There!" And M. Fournier excitedly gesticulated. He seemed at that moment to have lost all his terror of the sea.

"On Rosevear, then," said the keeper of the lighthouse, and he strained towards Rosevear.

"I see nothing," he said, "and—"

"There's nothing to see," replied Isaacs, who did not alter his course.

"But it's true," exclaimed the little Belgian. "I see it no more myself. But I have seen it, I tell you. I have seen the mast above the island—"

"You!" interrupted Isaacs, with a blunt contempt; "you are blind!" And M. Fournier, before anyone could guess his intention, flung himself upon Isaacs and jammed the tiller hard over to port. The boat came broadside to the wind, heeled over, and in a second the water was pouring in over the gunwale. Zebedee wrenched the main sheet off the pin, and let the big sail fly; another loosed the jib. The promptitude of these two men saved the boat. It ran its head up into the wind, righted itself upon its keel, and lay with flapping sails and shivered.

Isaacs without a word caught hold of M. Fournier and shook him like a rat; and every man of the crew in violent tones expounded to the Belgian the enormity of his crime. Fournier was himself well-nigh frantic with excitement. He was undaunted by any threats of violence; neither the boat, nor the sea, nor the crew had any terrors for him.

"There is a ship!" he screamed. "The fog was vanished—just for a second it was vanished, and I have seen it. There may be men alive on that rock—starving, perishing, men of the sea like you. You will not leave them. But you shall not!" And clinging to the mast he stamped his feet. "But you shall not!"

"And by the Lord he's right," said the lighthouse-keeper, gravely—so gravely that complete silence at once fell upon the crew. One man stood up in the bows, a second knelt upon the thwarts, a third craned his body out beyond the stern, and all with one accord stared towards Rosevear. The screen of haze was drawn aside, and quite clear to the view over a low rock, rose the mast and tangled cordage of a wreck.

The sheets were made fast without a word. Without a word, Zebedee Isaacs put the boat about and steered it into the Neck between Rosevear and Rosevean. As they passed along that narrow channel, no noise was heard but the bustle of the tide. For at the western end they

A.E.W. MASON

saw the bows of a ship unsteadily poised upon a ledge. There was a breach amidships, the stern was under water, only the foremast stood; and nowhere was there any sign of life.

Isaacs brought the boat to in a tiny creek, some distance from the wreck.

"We can land here," he said, and the lighthouse-keeper and Fournier stepped ashore.

On the instant that quiet, silent islet whirred into life and noise. So startling was the change that M. Fournier jumped backwards while his heart jerked within him.

"What's that?" he cried, and then laughed as he understood. For a cloud of puffins, gulls, kittiwakes and shearwaters whirled upwards from that nursery of sea-birds and circled above his head, their cries sounding with infinite melancholy, their wings flickering like silver in that grey and desolate light.

"It's so like your Robinson Crusoe," said M. Fournier.

"It is more like our islands of Scilly," said the lighthouse-keeper, as he looked towards the wreck.

They climbed over the low rocks and walked along the crown of the island towards the wreck. There was no tree or shrub upon the barren soil, only here a stretch of sandy grass, there a patch of mallows— mallows of a rusty green and whitened with salt of the sea. In the midst of one such patch they came upon the body of a man. He was dressed in a pilot coat, sea boots and thick stockings drawn over his trousers to the hips, and he lay face downwards with his head resting upon his arms in a natural posture of sleep.

Fournier stood still. The lighthouse-keeper walked forward and tapped the sleeper upon the shoulder. But the sleeper did not wake. The lighthouse man knelt down and gently turned the man over upon his back; as he did so, or rather just before he did so, Fournier turned sharply away with a shudder. When the sailor was lying upon his back, the keeper of the lighthouse started with something of a shudder too. For the sailor had no face.

The lighthouse man drew his handkerchief from his pocket and gently covered the head. It seemed almost as if Fournier had been waiting, had been watching, for this action. For he turned about immediately and stood by the lighthouse-keeper's side. Above the lonely islet the sea-birds circled and called; on the sea the mist was now no more than a gauze, and through it the glow of the sun was faintly diffused.

"Strange that, isn't it?" said the lighthouse-keeper, in a hushed voice. "The sea dashed him upon the rocks and drew him down again and threw him up again until it got tired of the sport, and so tossed him here to lie quietly face downwards amongst the mallows like a man asleep."

Then he sat back upon his heels and measured the distance between the mallows and the sea with some perplexity upon his forehead— and the perplexity grew.

"It's a long way for the sea to have thrown him," he said, and as Fournier shifted restlessly at his side, he looked up into his face. "Good God, man, but you look white," he said.

"The sight is terrible," replied Fournier, as he wiped his forehead.

The lighthouse-keeper nodded assent.

"Yes, it's a terrible place, the sea about these western islands," he said. "Did you ever hear tell that there are sunken cities all the way between here and Land's End, the sunken cities of Lyonnesse? Terrible sights those cities must see. I often think of the many ships which have plunged down among their chimneys and roof-tops—perhaps here a great Spanish galleon with its keel along the middle of a paved square and its poop overhanging the gables, and the fishes swimming in and out of the cabins through the broken windows; perhaps there a big three-decker like Sir Cloudesley Shovel's, showing the muzzles of her silent guns; or a little steam-tramp of our own times, its iron sides brown with rust, and God knows what tragedy hidden in its tiny engine-room. A terrible place—these islands of Scilly, dwelling amongst the seas, as the old books say—dwelling amongst the seas."

He bent forward and unfastened the dead sailor's pilot jacket. Then he felt in his pocket and drew out an oilskin case. This he opened, and Fournier knelt beside him.

There were a few letters in the case, which the two men read through. They were of no particular importance beyond that they were headed "Yacht The Ten Brothers," and they were signed "Ralph Warriner," all of them except one. This one was a love-letter of a date six years back. It was addressed to "Ralph," and was signed "Miranda."

"Six years old," said the lighthouse-keeper. "For six years he has carried that about with him, and now it will be read out in court to make a sorry fun for people whom he never knew. That's hard on him, eh? But harder on the woman."

At the words, spoken in a low voice, M. Fournier moved uneasily and seemed to wince. The lighthouse-keeper held the letter in his hands and thoughtfully turned over its pages.

"I have a mind to tear it up, but I suppose I must not." He returned the papers to the oilskin case, and going back to the boat called for two of the crew to carry the body down. "Meanwhile," said he to Fournier, "we might have a look at 'The Ten Brothers.'"

They could not approach the bows of the ship, but overlooked them from a pinnacle of rock. There was, however, little to be remarked.

"She is an old boat, and she has seen some weather from the look of her," said the lighthouse-keeper. That, indeed, was only to be expected, for "The Ten Brothers" had been a trader before Ralph Warriner bought her, and two years had elapsed between the night when he slipped from Gibraltar Harbour, and the day when this boat came to its last moorings upon Rosevear.

The mist cleared altogether towards sunset. The sun shone out from the edge of the horizon a ball of red fire, and the lugger ferried the dead body back to St. Mary's over a sea which had the colour of claret, and through foam ripples which sparkled like gold.

The Miranda who wrote the love-letter was Miranda Warriner, Ralph Warriner's wife. Miranda Bedlow she had been at the date which headed the letter. She was living now at Ronda in the Andalusian hills, a hundred miles from Algeciras and Gibraltar, and had lived there since her husband's disappearance. To Ronda the oilskin case was sent. She heard the news of her Ralph's death with a natural sense of solemnity, but she was too sincere a woman to assume a grief which she could not feel. For her married life had been one of extraordinary unhappiness.

II

Presents the Hero in the Unheroic Attitude of a Spectator

It was Lady Donnisthorpe who two years later introduced Luke Charnock to Mrs. Warriner. Lady Donnisthorpe was an outspoken woman with an untameable passion for match-making, which she indulged with the ardour and, indeed, the results of an amateur chemist. Her life was spent in mingling incompatible elements and producing explosions to which her enthusiasm kept her deaf, even when they made a quite astonishing noise. For no experience of reverses could stale her satisfaction when she beheld an eligible bachelor or maid walk for the first time into her parlour.

She had made Charnock's acquaintance originally in Barbados. He sat next her at a dinner given by the Governor of the Island, and took her fancy with the pleasing inconsistency of a boyish appearance and a wealth of experiences. He was a man of a sunburnt aquiline face, which was lean but not haggard, grey and very steady eyes, and a lithe, tall figure, and though he conveyed an impression of activity, he was still a restful companion. Lady Donnisthorpe remarked in him a modern appreciation of the poetry of machinery, and after dinner made inquiries of the Governor.

"He is on his way homewards from Peru," answered the latter. "He has been surveying for a railway line there during the last two years. What do you think of him?"

"I want to know what you think."

"I like him. He is modest without diffidence, successful without notoriety."

"What are his people?" asked Lady Donnisthorpe.

"I don't believe he has any. But I believe his father was a clergyman in Yorkshire."

"It would sound improper for a girl without visible relations to say that she was the daughter of a clergyman in Yorkshire, wouldn't it?" said her ladyship, reflectively. "But I suppose it's no objection in a man;" and in her memories she made a mark against Charnock's name. She heard of him again once or twice in unexpected quarters from the lips of the men who from East to West are responsible for the work that is done; and once or twice she met him, for she was a determined traveller. Finally, at Cairo, she sat next to Sir John Martin, the head partner of a great Leeds firm of railway contractors.

"Did you ever come across a Mr. Charnock?" she asked.

The head partner laughed.

"I did; I knew his father."

"It's a strange thing about Mr. Charnock," said she, "but one never hears anything of what he was doing before the last few years."

"Why not ask him?" said the North-countryman, bluntly.

"It might sound inquisitive," replied Lady Donnisthorpe, "and perhaps there's no need to, if you know."

"Yes, I know," returned Sir John, with a great deal of provoking amusement, "and, believe me, Lady Donnisthorpe, it's not at all to his discredit."

Lady Donnisthorpe began thereafter to select and reject possible wives for Charnock, and while still undecided, she chanced to pass one December through Nice. The first person whom she saw in the vestibule of the hotel was Luke Charnock.

"What in the world are you doing here?" she asked.

"Taking a week's holiday, Lady Donnisthorpe. I have been in Spain for the last two years, and shall be for the next nine months."

"In Spain?"

"I am making a new line between Cadiz and Algeciras."

"God bless the man, and I never thought of it!" exclaimed Lady Donnisthorpe. "I think you will do," she added, looking him over, and nodding her head.

"I hope so," replied Charnock, cheerfully. "It's a big lift for me."

"In a way, no doubt," agreed her ladyship. "Though, mind you, the land isn't what it was."

"The railway will improve it," said Charnock.

They happened to be talking of different subjects. Lady Donnisthorpe pursued her own.

"Then you won't be in England for a year?" she said regretfully.

"The company building the line is an English one," replied Charnock. "I shall have to see the directors in June. I shall be in London then."

"Then you must come and see me. Write before you leave Spain. Promise!" said Lady Donnisthorpe, who was now elated.

Charnock promised, and that day Lady Donnisthorpe wrote to her cousin, Miranda Warriner, at Ronda, who was now at the end of the first year of her widowhood, and of the third year of her ridiculous seclusion at that little hill-town of Spain. Miranda was entreated, implored, and commanded to come to London in May. There was the season, there was Miranda's estate in Suffolk, which needed her attention. Miranda reluctantly consented, and so Lady Donnisthorpe was the instrument by which Charnock and Mrs. Warriner became acquainted. But the foundations of that acquaintanceship were laid without her ladyship's agency, and indeed without the knowledge of either Charnock or Miranda.

A trifling defect in the machinery of a P. and O. boat began it. The P. and O. stayed for four days at Aden to make repairs, and so Charnock had four days to wait at Gibraltar before he could embark for England. He did not, however, spend more than two of those four days at Gibraltar, but picking up a yellow handbill in the lounge of the hotel, he obeyed its advice, and crossing the sunlit straits early the next morning saw the jealous hills about Tangier unfold and that cardboard city glitter down to the sea.

He was rowed ashore to the usual accompaniment of shouts and yells by a villainous boat's crew of Arabs. A mob of Barbary Jews screamed at him on the landing-stage, and then a Moorish boy with a brown roguish face who was dressed in a saffron jellabia, pushed his way forwards and in a conversational voice said, "You English? God damn you, give me a penny!"

Charnock hired that boy, and under his guidance sauntered through Tangier where the East and the West rub shoulders, where the camel snarls in the Sôk with an electric arc-lamp for a night-light, and all the races and all the centuries jostle together in many colours down the cobbles of its narrow streets. Charnock was shown the incidentals of the Tangier variety entertainment: the Basha administering more or less justice for less or more money at his Palace gate; the wooden peep-hole of the prison where the prisoners' hands come through and clutch for alms; a dancing-room where a Moorish woman closely veiled leaned her back against a Tottenham Court Road chest of drawers under a portrait of Mrs. Langtry, and beat upon a drum while another stamped an ungainly dance by the light of a paraffin lamp; and coming out again into the sunlight, Charnock cried out, "Hamet, take me somewhere where it's clean, and there's no din, and there are no smells."

Hamet led the way up the hills, and every now and then, as he passed a man better dressed than his fellows he would say in a voice of awe:

"That's a rich." He invariably added, "He's a Juice."

"Look here, Hamet," said Charnock, at length, "can't you show me a rich who isn't a Jew?"

"These are the loryers," observed Hamet, after the fashion of the March Hare when posed with an inconvenient question. He pointed to a number of venerable gentlemen in black robes who sat in wooden hutches open to the street. "I will show you," he continued, "a Moor who was the richest man in all Tangier."

The pair walked up out of the town towards the Mazan, and came to a lane shadowed by cedars and bordered with prickly pears. Here the resounding din of the streets below was subdued to a murmurous confusion of voices, from which occasionally a sharp cry would spirt up clear into the air like a jet of water. Only one voice was definite and incessant, and that voice came down to them from the trees higher up the lane—a voice very thin, but on that hot, still afternoon very distinct—a voice which perpetually quavered and bleated one monotonous invocation.

"Hassan Akbar," said Hamet.

The invocation became articulate as they ascended. "Allah Beh!" the voice cried, and again "Allah Beh!" and again, until the windless air seemed to vibrate with its recurrence.

They came upon the Moor who uttered this cry at the gate of the Moorish cemetery. A white, stubbly beard grew upon his chin and lips, but his strength was not diminished by his years, and with every movement of his body the muscles beneath the tough skin of his bare legs worked like live things. He sat cross-legged in the dust with a filthy sack for his only garment; he was blind, and his eyes stared from their red sockets covered with a bluish film as though the colours of the eyeballs had run.

"Allah Beh!" he cried, swaying his body backwards and forwards with the regularity of an automaton and an inimitable quickness. He paid no heed whatever to Charnock and the boy as they halted beside him. "Allah Beh!" he cried, and his chest touched the cradle of his knees. He marked the seconds with the pendulum of his body; he struck them with his strident invocation.

"He was the richest man in Tangier," said Hamet, and he told Hassan Akbar's story as though it was an affair of every day. Hassan had not secured the protection of any of the European Legations. He had hoped to hide his wealth by living poorly, and though he owned a house worth three thousand dollars in Tangier, he did not dwell in it. But no concealments had availed him. Someone of his familiars had told, and no doubt had made his profit from the telling. The Basha had waited his opportunity. It came when blindness left Hassan defenceless. Then the Basha laid hands upon him, forced him to give up the gains of a lifetime's trade, and so cast him out penniless to beg for copper flouss at the gate of the cemetery.

"And Europe's no more than seven miles away," cried Charnock. Even where he stood he could see the laughing water of the Straits, and beyond that, the summit of Gibraltar. "Who was it that told?" he asked.

"That is not known."

Charnock dropped some money into the blind man's lap, but Hassan did not cease from his prayer to thank him.

"He is very strong," said Hamet, who saw nothing strange in the story he had told. "He swings like this all day from seven in the morning to five at night. He never stops." And at that moment, upon the heels of Hamet's words, as though intentionally to belie them, Hassan Akbar suddenly arrested the motion of his body and suddenly ceased from his pitiable cry.

His silence and immobility came with so much abruptness that Charnock was fairly startled. Then Hamet held up a finger, and they both listened. Maybe the blind man was listening too, but Charnock could not be certain. His face was as blind as his eyes, and there was no expression in the rigid attitude of his body.

Charnock heard a faint sound higher up the lane. The sound became louder and defined itself. It was the slap-slap of a pair of Moorish slippers. Charnock drew Hamet back by the trunk of a tree, which sheltered them both from the view of anyone who came down the hill. He left the lane free, and into the open space there came a man who wore the dress of a Moor of wealth, serwal, chamir, farajia, and haik, spotless and complete. In figure he was slight and perhaps a trifle under the middle height, and the haik was drawn close over his forehead to shield him from the sun.

Hassan was seated in the dust with the sun beating full upon his head. In front of him the newcomer stopped. "Peace be with you," he said, as Charnock, who had some knowledge of Arabic, understood. But the beggar made no answer, nor gave any sign that he heard. He sat motionless, impassive, a secret figure of stone.

The newcomer laughed lightly to himself, and the laughter, within view of the rags and misery of the once rich man, sounded unpleasant and callous. Hamet shifted a foot at Charnock's side, and Charnock, whose interest in this picturesque encounter was steadily growing, pressed a hand upon the boy's shoulder to restrain him.

The stranger, however, had noticed neither of the two spectators. He was still laughing softly to himself as he watched the beggar, and in a little he began to hum between his teeth a tune—a queer, elusive tune of a sweet but rather mournful melody; and it seemed to Charnock by some indefinable hint of movement that Hassan Akbar was straining his ears to catch and register that tune.

The stranger advanced to Hassan and dropped a coin in his lap. The coin was not copper, for it sparkled in the air as it fell. Then with another easy laugh he turned to go down into Tangier. But as he turned he saw Charnock watching him. On the instant his hand went to his hood and drew it close about his cheeks, but not before Charnock had seen a scared face flashed at him for a moment, and immediately withdrawn. The Moor went down the lane.

"Perhaps it was he who told?" said Charnock.

Hamet disagreed.

"He would not know. His beard was fair, so he comes from Fez." Charnock, too, had remarked that the man was fair-haired. But nevertheless this encounter of the rich Moor and the beggar remained in his thoughts, and he allowed his imagination lazily to fix a picture of it in his mind. Thus occupied, he walked through the cemetery, taking in that way a short cut to the Sôk. But he was not half-way across the cemetery when he turned sharply towards Hamet.

"Do you remember the tune the Moor hummed?"

Charnock's ear was slow to retain the memory of music. Hamet, however, promptly whistled the melody from beginning to end, while Charnock stood and took count of it.

"I shall have forgotten it to-morrow," said Hamet.

"I think now that I shall recollect it tomorrow," said Charnock, and he walked on.

But in a moment or two he stopped again as though some new perplexity was present to his mind.

"Hamet," he said, "before the Moor appeared at all, while his footsteps were still faint, certainly before he spoke, Hassan Akbar stopped his prayer, which you say he never stops. He knew then who was coming. At all events he suspected. How did he know? How did he suspect?"

"There is the Sôk," replied Hamet.

They had passed round the bend of the hill up which the cemetery slopes, and were come within view of the market-place. Charnock was puzzled by his unanswered question, and the question was forced to his notice again that afternoon, and with yet greater force.

It was market-day. Charnock beheld stretched out beneath him a great field, or rather a great plain, (for the grass was long since trampled into mud,) which curved down to the yellow sun-baked wall of the city, and whereon an innumerable throng, Negroes from Timbuctoo, Arabs, Jews, and Moors, in all manner of raiment, from rags to coloured robes, jostled and seethed, bawled and sweated, under a hot sun and in a brilliant air. Here an old hag screamed aloud the virtues of her merchandise, a few skinny onions and vegetables; there two men forced a passage with blows of their sticks, and behind them a stately train of camels brought in from the uplands their loads of dates. A Riffian sauntered by with an indifferent air, his silver-mounted gun upon his back, a pair of pistols in his belt, and a great coarse tail of hair swinging between his shoulders. He needed no couriers to prepare his way. At one spot a serpent-charmer thrust out his tongue, from which a snake was hanging by the fangs; at another a story-teller, vivid in narration, and of an extraordinary aptness in his gestures, held an audience enchained. From every side the din of human voices rose into the air, and to the din was added the snarling of camels, the braying of donkeys, the bleating of sheep, the lowing of oxen, and all manner of squeals and grunts, so that it seemed the whole brute creation had combined to make one discordant orchestra.

Into this Babel Charnock descended.

"Those are the shoemakers," said Hamet. He pointed to a cluster of tiny grimed gunny-bag tents in a corner of the highest part of the Sôk. In the doorways of the tents a few men sat cobbling; one or two wood fires crackled in the intervals between the tents; and in close proximity a dead mule took its last unsavoury sleep.

"Hassan Akbar sleeps in the mud near to the tents," continued Hamet. "Every evening he comes down to the Sôk, buys milk and bread from the shoemakers, and sleeps—"

"Near to that mule!" interrupted Charnock. "And he was the richest man in all Tangier."

A moment later there was shown to him the second picture which he was to carry away from Tangier. Down the Sôk, through the crowd,

A.E.W. MASON

came the Moor, in his spotless robes, and a few yards behind him, striding swiftly and noiselessly, the blind gaunt beggar of the cemetery gate followed upon his trail. In and out amongst the shifting groups he threaded and wound, and never erred in his pursuit. The man in whose track he kept never spoke when all were shouting, yet Hassan never faltered. The sound of his footsteps was lost in a multitude of the like sounds, yet Hassan was somehow sensible of it, somehow to his ears it emerged distinct.

Charnock was amazed; in a way too he was chilled. It seemed uncanny that this sightless creature of the impassive face should be able to follow, follow, follow relentlessly, unswervingly, one silent man amongst the noisy hundreds. Charnock walked for a few yards by Hassan Akbar's side, keeping pace with him. Even with his eyes fixed upon the Moor in front, even though he saw his feet tread the ground, he could not distinguish his footfalls. How then could Hassan?

Tracker and Tracked passed from the Sôk under the archway of the gate, and Charnock dismissing Hamet walked down towards his hotel near the waterside. However, he missed his road. He turned through the horse market, descended the steep street, past the great Mosque, and walked along a narrow, crooked alley between blank and yellow walls, which ended in a tunnel beneath over-arching houses. Almost within the mouth of this tunnel there was a shop, or so it seemed, for a stuffed jackal swung above the door as a sign. Before this shop Charnock halted with a thrill of excitement. The door of the shop was shut, the unglazed window was shuttered. It was not on that account that Charnock stopped; but underneath the shuttered window, his head almost touching the sill, Hassan squatted on the cobbles fingering now and then a silver dollar.

Inside the door a bolt grated, the door opened, and a stout, undersized European appeared in the entrance, polished a pair of glasses, set them upon his nose, glanced up and down the street, closed the door behind him, and taking no heed whatever of the blind man under his window, walked briskly into the tunnel. He walked with a short, tripping, and jaunty step.

Charnock waited while the echo of it diminished and ceased, and the moment it had ceased he saw Hassan, without any hurry, without any sign of expectation or excitement, rise slowly to his feet and move along the house wall towards the door. His right elbow scraped the plaster; then his elbow touched nothing. He had come to the recess of the door, and he stopped.

It flashed upon Charnock that he had not heard the bolt again grate into its socket. The door was then only latched and—was Hassan's quarry behind its panels?

The affair had ceased to be a toy with which Charnock's imagination could idly play. He strode across the alley and planted himself face to face with Hassan. Hassan quietly and immediately murmured a request for alms and stretched out his left hand, a supple, corded hand, with long sinuous fingers, a hand of great strength. But as he spoke he drew within the recess of the door, and Charnock noticed his right hand steal up the panels feeling for the latch.

Made by this seemingly passionless and apathetic man, the secret movement shocked Charnock. It seemed to him at that moment so cold-blooded as to be almost inhuman.

"Look out!" he shouted through the door and in broad English, forgetting that the man for whom his warning was intended was a Moor. But the warning had its effect. There was a heavy blow upon the door, as though a man's shoulder lurched against it, and then the bolt grated into the socket. Hassan Akbar walked on repeating his prayer for alms, as if his hand had never for an instant stolen up the panel and felt for the latch.

Charnock, to make his warning the more complete, rapped on the door for admission, once, twice, thrice. But he got no answer. He leaned his ear to the panel. He could detect not so much as a foot stirring. Absolute silence reigned in that dark and shuttered room.

Charnock walked back to his hotel. On the way he passed the end of the pier, where he saw the little Frenchman bargaining with the owner of a felucca. His excitement gradually died down. It occurred to him that there might have been no grounds at all for any excitement. Hassan Akbar might have been following through the Sôk by mere accident. He might have tried the door in pursuit of nothing more than alms; and in a little the whole incident ceased to trouble his speculations. He crossed the Straits to Gibraltar the next morning, and waited there for two days until the P. and O. came in. It was on the P. and O. that he first fell in with Major Wilbraham.

A.E.W. MASON

III

Treats of a Gentleman with an Agreeable Countenance, and of a Woman's Face in a Mirror

Major Ambrose Wilbraham had embarked at Marseilles, and before the boat reached Gibraltar he had made the acquaintance of everyone on board, and had managed to exchange cards with a good many. The steamer was still within sight of Gibraltar when he introduced himself to Charnock with a manner of effusive jocularity to which Charnock did not respond. The Major was tall and about forty years of age. A thin crop of black hair was plastered upon his head; he wore a moustache which was turning grey; his eyebrows were so faultlessly regular that they seemed to have been stencilled on his forehead, and underneath them a pair of cold beady eyes counterfeited friendliness. Charnock could not call to mind that he had ever met a man on whom geniality sat with so ill a grace, or one whose acquaintance he less desired to improve.

Major Wilbraham, however, was not easily rebuffed, and he walked the deck by Charnock's side, talkative and unabashed.

Off the coast of Portugal the boat made bad weather, and she laboured through the cross-seas of the Bay under a strong south-westerly wind. Off Ushant she picked up a brigantine which Charnock watched from the hurricane deck without premonition, and indeed without more than a passing curiosity.

"Fine lines, eh, Charnock old fellow!" said a voice at his elbow.

The brigantine dipped her head into a roller, lifted it, and shook the water off her decks in a cascade of snow.

"I have seen none finer," answered Charnock, "except on a racing-yacht or a destroyer."

"She's almost familiar to me," speculated the Major.

"She reminds me of some boats I saw once at the West Indies," returned Charnock, "built for the fruit-trade, and so built for speed. Only they were schooners—from Salcombe, I believe. The Salcombe clippers they were called."

"Indeed!" said the Major, with a sharp interest, and he leaned forward over the rail. "Now I wonder what her name is."

Charnock held a pair of binoculars in his hand. He gave them to the Major. Wilbraham raised them to his eyes while the P. and O. closed upon the sailing-boat. The brigantine slid down the slope of a wave and hoisted her stern.

"The 'Tarifa,'" said the Major, and he shut up the binoculars. "What is her tonnage, do you think?"

"About three hundred, I should say."

"My notion precisely. Would it be of any advantage to alter her rig, supposing that she was one of the Salcombe schooners?"

"I should hardly think so," replied Charnock. "I rather understood that the schooners were noted boats."

"Ah, that's interesting," said Wilbraham, and he returned the binoculars. The steamer was now abreast of the brigantine, and in a little it drew ahead.

"By the way, Charnock, I shall hope to see more of you," resumed Major Wilbraham. "I haven't given you a card, have I?"

He produced a well-worn card-case.

"It's very kind of you," said Charnock, as he twirled the card between his forefinger and his thumb. "Don't you," he added, "find cards rather a heavy item in your expenses?"

Major Wilbraham laughed noisily.

"I take you, dear friend," he exclaimed, "I take you. But a friend in this world, sir, is a golden thread in a very dusty cobweb."

"But the friendship is rather a one-sided arrangement," rejoined Charnock. "For instance, the cards you give, Major Wilbraham, bear no address, the cards you receive, do." And while showing the card to his companion, he inadvertently dropped it into the sea.

Major Wilbraham blamed the negligence of a rascally printer, and made his way to the smoking-room.

The P. and O. boat touched at Plymouth the next morning, and landed both Major Wilbraham and Charnock. The latter remained in Plymouth for two days, and on the morning of the third day hired a hansom cab, and so met with the last of those incidents which were to link him in such close, strange ties with the fortunes of men and women who even in name were then utterly unknown to him.

A yellow handbill had led Charnock across the Straits to Tangier, and now it was nothing more serious than a draft upon Lloyd's bank which took him in a hansom cab through the streets of Plymouth. Spring was in the air; Charnock felt exceedingly light-hearted and cheerful. On the way he unconsciously worked his little finger into the eye of the brass bracket which juts inwards on each side of the front window at the level of the shoulder; and when the cab stopped in front of the bank he discovered that his finger was securely jammed.

Across the road he noticed a chemist's shop, and descending the steps of the bank a fair-haired gentleman of an agreeable countenance, who, quite appropriately in that town of sailors, had something of a nautical aspect.

"Sir," began Charnock, politely, as he leaned out of the window, "I shall be much obliged—"

To Charnock's surprise the good-natured gentleman precipitately sprang down the steps and began to walk rapidly away. Charnock was sufficiently human and therefore sufficiently perverse to become at once convinced that although there were others passing, this reluctant man was the only person in the world who could and must help him from his predicament.

So he leaned yet farther out of the cab.

"Hi, you sir!" he shouted, "you who are running away!"

The words had an electrical effect. The man of the agreeable countenance stopped suddenly, and so stood with his back towards Charnock while gently and thoughtfully he nodded his head. It seemed to Charnock that he might perhaps be counting over the voices with which he was familiar.

"Well," cried Charnock, who was becoming exasperated, "my dear sir, am I to wait for you all day?"

The street was populous with the morning traffic of a business quarter. Curious people stopped and attracted others. In a very few moments a small crowd would have formed. The stranger thereupon came slowly back to the hansom, showing a face which was no longer agreeable. He set a foot upon the step of the cab, and fixed a blue and watchful eye upon Charnock.

"I am afraid," said the latter, with severity, "that my first impression of you was wrong."

An indescribable relief was expressed by the other, but he spoke with surliness.

"You mistook me for someone else?"

"I mistook your disposition for something else," Charnock affably corrected. "I expected to find you a person of great good-nature."

"You hardly made such a point of summoning a perfect stranger," and here the blue eyes became very wary, "for no other reason than to tell him that."

"Certainly not," returned Charnock; "I would not trespass upon your time, which seems to be extremely valuable, without a better reason. But my finger is fixed, as you can see, in this brass ring, and I cannot withdraw it. So if you would kindly cross over to the chemist and buy me a pennyworth of vaseline, I shall be more than obliged." And with the hand which was free he felt in his pocket for a penny and held it out.

A look of utter incredulity showed upon the listener's face.

"Do you mean to tell me—" he blurted out.

"That I ask you to be my good Samaritan? Yes."

The stranger's face became suddenly vindictive. "Vaseline!" he cried.

"A pennyworth," said Charnock, again offering the penny.

The man of the agreeable countenance struck Charnock's hand violently aside, and the penny flew into a gutter. He stood up on the step and thrust his face, which was now inflamed with fury, into the cab.

"I tell you what," he cried, "you are a fair red-hotter, you are. Buy you vaseline! I hope your finger will petrify. I hope you'll just sit in that cab and rot away in your boots, until you have to ante up in kingdom come." He added expletives to his anathema.

"Really," said Charnock, "if I was a lady I don't think that I should like to listen to you any longer."

But before Charnock had finished the sentence, the good Samaritan, who was no Samaritan at all, had flung himself from the cab and was striding up the street.

"After all," thought Charnock, "I might just as well have driven across to the chemist, if I had only thought of it."

This he now did, got his finger free, cashed his draft, and took the train to London.

During this journey the discourteous stranger occupied some part of his thoughts. Between Charnock's eyes and the newspaper, against the red cliffs of Teignmouth, on the green of the home counties, his face obtruded, and for a particular reason. The marks of fear are unmistakable. The man whom he had called, had been scared by the call, nor had his fear quite left him when he had come face to face with Charnock. Set features which strove to conceal, and a brightness of the eye which betrayed emotion, these things Charnock remembered very clearly.

In London he dined alone at his hotel, and over against him the stranger's face bore him company. He went out afterwards into the street, and amidst the myriad ringing feet, was seized with an utter sense of loneliness, more poignant, more complete, than he had ever experienced in the waste places of the world. The lights of a theatre attracted him. He paid his money, took a seat in the stalls, and was at once very worried and perplexed. He turned to his neighbour, who was boisterously laughing.

"Would you mind telling me what this play is?" he asked.

"Oh, it's a musical comedy."

"I see. But what is it about?"

Charnock's neighbour scratched his head thoughtfully.

"I ought to remember," he said, "for I saw the piece early in the run."

Charnock went out, crossed a street, and came to another theatre, where he saw a good half of the tragedy of *Macbeth*. Thence he returned to his hotel and went to bed.

The hotel was one of many balconies, situated upon the Embankment. From the single window or his bedroom Charnock looked across the river to where the name of a brewery perpetually wrote itself in red brilliant letters which perpetually vanished. It was his habit to sleep not merely with his window open, but with the blinds drawn up and the curtains looped back, and these arrangements he made as usual before he got into bed.

Now, the looking-glass stood upon a dressing-table in the window, with its back towards the window-panes; and since the night was moonless and dark, this mirror, it should be remembered, reflected nothing of the room or its furniture, but presented only to the view of Charnock, as he lay in bed, a surface of a black sheen.

Charnock recurred to his adventure of the morning, and thus the abusive stranger was in his thoughts when he fell asleep. He figured also in his dreams.

For, after he had fallen asleep, a curtain was raised upon a fantastic *revue* of the past week. Hassan Akbar strode quickly and noiselessly behind his quarry, tracking him by some inappreciable faculty, not through the muddy Sôk, but across the polished floor of the ball-room in the musical comedy. Again Charnock shouted "Look out!" and the Moor with one bound leapt from the ball-room, which was now become a landing-stage, into a felucca. The crew of the felucca, it now appeared, was made up of Charnock, Lady Macbeth, and Hassan

Akbar, and by casting lots with counters made of vaseline, Charnock was appointed to hold the tiller. This duty compelled extraordinary care, for the felucca would keep changing its rig and the bulk of its hull swelled and dwindled. At last, to Charnock's intense relief, the boat settled into a Salcombe clipper with the rig of a P. and O., but with immeasurably greater speed, so that within a very few seconds they sailed over a limitless ocean and anchored at Tangier. At once the crew entirely vanished. Charnock was not distressed, because he saw a hansom cab waiting for him at the Customs, though how the hansom was to pass up those narrow cobbled streets he could not think. That however was the driver's business.

"I hope your horse is good," said Charnock, springing into the cab.

"She comes of the great Red-hotter stock," replied the cabman, and lifting the trap in the roof he showered packets of visiting cards, which fell about Charnock like flakes of snow.

Charnock had not previously noticed that the cabman was Major Wilbraham.

The cab shot up the hill through the tunnel, past the closed shop. A figure sprang from the ground and thrust a face through the window of the cab. The man was in Moorish dress, but the face was the face of the abusive stranger of Plymouth—and all at once Charnock started up on his elbow, and in the smallest fraction of a second was intensely and vividly awake. There was no sound at all within the room. But in the black sheen of the mirror he saw a woman's face.

He saw it quite clearly for perhaps five seconds, the face rising white from the white column of the throat, the dark and weighty coronal of the hair, the curved lips which alone had any colour, the eyes, deep and troubled, which seemed to hint a prayer for help which they disdained to make—for five seconds perhaps the illusion remained, for five seconds the face looked out at him from the black mirror, lit palely, as it seemed, by its own pallor, and so vanished.

Charnock remained propped upon his elbow. A faint twilight from the stars crept timidly through the open window as though deprecating its intrusion. Charnock looked into the dark corners of the room, but nowhere did the darkness move. Nor could he hear any sound. Not even a board of the floor cracked, and outside the door there was no noise of a footstep on the stairs. Then from a great distance the jingle of a cab came through the open window to his ears with a light companionable lilt. Gradually the sound ceased, and again the silence breathed about him. Charnock struck a match and looked at his watch. It was a few minutes after three.

Charnock lay back in his bed wondering. For he had seen that face once, he had once exchanged glances with those eyes, once only, six years ago, and thereafter had entirely forgotten the incident—until this moment. He had stopped for a night at Monte Carlo and had seen—the girl—yes, the *girl*, though it was a woman's face which had gleamed in the depths of his mirror—standing under the green shaded lamps in the big gambling-room. His attention, he now remembered, had been seized by the contrast between her amused indifference and the feverish haste of the gamblers about the table; between her fresh, clear looks and their heated complexions,—even between her frock of lilac silk and their more elaborate toilettes. The girl was entirely happy then, the red lips smiled, the violet eyes laughed. Why should her face appear to him now, after these years, and paled by this distress?

A queer fancy slipped into his mind—a fancy at the extravagance of which he knew very well he should laugh in the sane light of the morning, though he indulged it now—that somehow, somewhere, this woman needed help, and that it was thus vouchsafed to her, a stranger, to make her appeal to him in this way, which spared her the humiliation of making any appeal at all. Charnock fell asleep convinced that somehow, somewhere, he was destined to meet and know her. As he had foreseen, he laughed at his fancies in the morning, but nevertheless, he did meet her. It had, in fact, already been arranged that he should. For the face which he saw in the mirror was the face of Miranda Warriner.

IV

TREATS OF THE FIRST MEETING BETWEEN CHARNOCK AND MIRANDA

Lady Donnisthorpe, with a sigh of relief, retired from her position at the head of the stairs, and catching Charnock in the interval between two dances:—

"You kept some dances free," she said, "didn't you? I want to introduce you to a cousin of mine, Miranda Warriner, because she lives at Ronda."

"At Ronda. Indeed?"

"Yes." Her ladyship added with a magnificent air of indifference, "She is a widow," and she led Charnock across the ball-room.

Miranda saw them approaching, noticed an indefinable air of expectation in Lady Donnisthorpe's manner, and smiled. A few excessively casual remarks concerning one Mr. Charnock, which Lady Donnisthorpe had dropped during the last few days, had not escaped the notice of Miranda, who was aware of her cousin's particular weakness. This was undoubtedly Mr. Charnock. She raised her eyes towards him, and had her ladyship been less fluttered, she might have remarked that Miranda's eyes lit up with a momentary sparkle of recognition.

"Mrs. Warriner—Mr. Charnock."

Lady Donnisthorpe effected the momentous introduction and felt immediately damped. She had not indeed expected that her two newest victims would at once and publicly embrace. But at all events she had decked out her ball-room as the sacrificial altar, and had taken care that a fitting company and cheerful music should do credit to the immolation. This tame indifference was less than she deserved.

Miranda, to whom Lady Donnisthorpe was looking, made the perfunctory dip of the head and smiled the perfunctory smile, and Charnock—why in the world did he not move or speak? Lady Donnisthorpe turned her eyes from Miranda to this awkward cavalier, and was restored to a radiant good-humour. "Dazzled," she said to herself, "absolutely dazzled!" For Charnock stood rooted to the ground and tongue-tied with amazement.

It was fortunate for Lady Donnisthorpe that at this point she thought it wise to withdraw. Otherwise she would surely have remarked an unmistakable look of disappointment which grew within Charnock's eyes and spread out over his face. Then the disappointment vanished, and as he compared programmes with Miranda, he recovered his speech.

Four dances must intervene before he could claim her, and Charnock was glad of the interval to get the better of his bewilderment. Here was the woman whom his mirror had shown to him! After all, his nocturnal fancy was fulfilled, or rather part of it, only part or it. He had met her, he was to dance with her. Some miracle had brought them together. From the corner by the doorway he watched Miranda, he remarked an unaffected friendliness in her manner towards her partners. Candour was written upon her broad white forehead and looked out from her clear eyes. He had no doubt it was fragrant too in her hair. There were heavy masses of that hair, as he knew very well from his mirror, but now the masses were piled and woven about her head with a cunning art, which to be sure they deserved. There was a ripple in her hair, too, which caught the light—a most taking ripple. Here was a woman divested of a girl's wiles and vanities. Charnock, without a scruple, aspersed all girls up to the age of say twenty-four, that he might give her greater praise.

He fell to wondering, not how it was that her face had appeared to him, nor by what miracle he was now enabled to have knowledge of her, but rather by what miracle of forgetfulness he had allowed her face, after he had seen it that one time six years ago, ever to slip from his thoughts, or her eyes after that one time he had exchanged a glance with them.

The whirl of the dance carried her by his corner. She swung past him with the lightest imaginable step, and he was suddenly struck through and through with a chilling apprehension that by some unconscionable maladroitness he would surely tread upon her toes.

At once he proceeded to count over the dances in which he had borne himself with credit. He had danced with Spanish women, he assured himself, and they had not objected. He was thus consoling himself when the time came for him to lead her out. And the touch of her hand in his, he remembers, turned him into a babbling idiot.

He recollects that they danced with great celerity; that they passed Lady Donnisthorpe, who smiled at him with great encouragement, and that he was dolefully humorous concerning Major Wilbraham and his exchanges of cards, though why Major Wilbraham should have thrust his bald head into the conversation, he was ever at a loss to discover. And then Miranda said, "Shall we stop?"

"Oh, I didn't, did I?" exclaimed the horror-stricken Charnock, as he looked downwards at her toes.

"No, you didn't," Miranda assured him with a laugh. "Do you usually?"

"No," he declared vehemently, "believe me, no! Never, upon my word! I have danced with Spanish women,—not at all,—no—no—no—no."

"Quite so," said Miranda.

And they laughed suddenly each to the other, and in a moment they were friends. Conversation came easily to their tongues, and underneath the surface of their light talk, the deeps of character called steadily like to like.

"I have seen you once before, Mrs. Warriner," said Charnock, as they seated themselves in an alcove of the room.

"Yes," she returned promptly, "at Monte Carlo, six years ago," and her face lost its look of enjoyment and darkened with some shadow from her memories. The change was, however, unremarked by Charnock.

"It seems strange," he said in an absent voice, "that we should meet first of all in a gambling-room, and the next time at a ball."

"Why?"

The question could not be answered. Charnock had a real but inexplicable feeling that Miranda and he should have met somewhere amidst the grandeur of open spaces, in the centre of the Sahara, and for the moment he forgot to calculate the effect of the sand upon Miranda's eyes. This feeling, however, he could hardly express at the present point of their acquaintanceship; and, indeed, he immediately ceased to be aware of it.

"Do you actually remember our meeting in that way six years ago?" he exclaimed. "How wonderful of you!"

"Why?" again asked Mrs. Warriner. "Why is it wonderful, since you remember it?"

"Ah, but I didn't remember it until"—he paused for a second or two—"until I saw your face in a looking-glass."

Miranda glanced at him in considerable perplexity. Then she said with a demure smile, "I have at times seen it there myself."

"No doubt," he replied with a glance at the cunning arrangement of her hair.

"My maid does that," said she, biting her lip.

"No doubt, but you sit in front of the glass at the time. You're in the room," he continued hastily; "but when I saw your face in my mirror, you couldn't be. I was in bed,—I mean,—let me tell you!" He stopped, overwhelmed with embarrassment. Miranda, with an air of complete unconsciousness, carefully buttoned her glove; only the glove was already buttoned, and her mouth twitched slightly at the corners.

"It was just a week ago to-day," Charnock began again. "I got home to my hotel late."

"Ah!" murmured Mrs. Warriner, as though the whole mystery was now explained to her.

"I assure you," he retorted with emphasis, "that I dined in the train and drank nothing more serious than railway claret."

"I made no accusation whatever," Miranda blandly remarked, and seemed very well pleased.

"After I had fallen asleep, I began to dream, but not about you, Mrs. Warriner; that's the strange feature of the business. It wasn't that I had been thinking of you that evening, or indeed, that I had ever been at all in the habit of thinking—" Again Charnock was utterly confused. "I don't seem to be telling the story with the best taste in the world, do I?" he said ruefully.

"Never mind," she said in a soothing voice.

"Of course, I could have turned it into a compliment," he continued. "Only I take it you have no taste for compliments, and I lack the experience to put them tactfully."

"For a novice," said she, "you seem to be doing very well." Charnock resumed his story. "I dreamt solely of people I had seen, and incidents I had witnessed during the last week, at Tangier and at Plymouth. I dreamed particularly of a man I quarrelled with at Plymouth, and I suddenly woke up and saw your face in the mirror."

"As you fancied."

"It was no fancy. It was no dream-face that I saw—dream-faces are always elusive. It was no dream-face, it was yours."

"Or one like mine."

"There cannot be two."

"For a novice," repeated Miranda, with a smile, "you *are* doing very well."

Charnock had watched her carefully while he told his story, on the chance that her looks, if not her lips, might give him some clue to the comprehension of his mysterious vision. But she had expressed merely an unconcerned curiosity and some amusement.

"Shall I explain your vision?" said she. "You must have seen me in London during the day: the recollection that you had seen me must have lain latent, so that when you woke up you saw me in your mirror and did not remember that you had seen me during the day."

"Were you at any theatre this day week?"

"No," said Miranda, after counting over the days.

"You did not see *Macbeth* that night?"

"No."

"Then it is impossible I should have seen you. For I came up from Plymouth only that afternoon. I drove from Paddington to my hotel; from the hotel I went to the theatre; from the theatre I walked back to the hotel. It is impossible."

"It is very strange," said Miranda, whose interest was increasing, and whose sense of amusement had vanished; for she saw that her companion was moved by something more than curiosity. It was evident to her from his urgent tones, from the eagerness of his face, that he had some hidden reason for his desire to fathom the mystery. It seemed to her that he nourished some intention, some purpose in the back of his mind, which depended for fulfilment upon whether or no there was any feasible solution.

"Tell me your dream," she said.

"It was the oddest jumble,—it had neither sense nor continuity. Moors figured in it, ships, Lady Macbeth, the Major with his card-case, and the stranger who swore at me through the cab-window at Plymouth. The phrases that man used came into it."

"What phrases?"

"I couldn't repeat to you the most eloquent. There were milder ones, however. He called me a fair red-hotter amongst other things," said Charnock, laughing at his recollections, "and expressed a wish that I might—well, sit in that cab until I ante'd up in kingdom come."

Miranda leaned back in her seat and opened and shut her fan. "He was a stranger to you, you say?"

"Quite."

"You are sure?"

"Quite."

"You had never seen him anywhere—anywhere? Think!"

Charnock deliberated for a few seconds. "Never anywhere," he replied.

There was a moment's silence. Mrs. Warriner gently fanned herself as she leaned back in the shadow of the alcove. "Describe him to me," she said quietly.

"A man of a slight figure, a little under the middle height, fair hair, bright blue eyes, an open, good-natured face, and I should say a year or so under forty. I took him to be a sailor."

The fan stopped. Miranda let it fall upon her lap. That was the only movement which she made, and from the shadow of the recess, she said: "There is no explanation."

Charnock drew a breath and leaned forward, his hands clasped, his elbows on his knees. It seemed he had been waiting for just that one sentence. As he sat now his face was in the light, and Miranda remarked a certain timidity upon it, as though now that he had heard the expected words, he dared not after all reply to them. He did not look towards her. He stared at the dancers, but with vacant eyes. He saw nothing of their jewels, or their coloured robes, or the flash of their silver feet, and the noise of their chatter sounded very dimly in his ears. He was quite occupied, indeed, with the hardihood of what he had it on his tongue's tip to say—when he had gained sufficient courage.

Miranda moved restlessly, unbuttoned a glove, drew it off her wrist unconsciously, and then was still as Charnock began to speak.

"Is there no explanation?" he asked. "I imagined one. You know how fancies come to one in the dark. That night I imagined one. I laughed at it the next morning, but now, since I have talked with you, I have been wondering whether by any miracle, it might be true. And if there's an infinitesimal chance that it's true, I think that I ought to tell you it, even though it may seem merely ridiculous, even though it may offend you. But I have lived for the most part of my time, since I was a man, in the waste places of the earth, and what may well be an impertinence— for we are only these few minutes acquainted—you will perhaps pardon on that account."

He received no encouragement to continue; on the other hand he received no warning to stop, for Miranda neither spoke nor moved. He did not look at her face lest he should read the warning there; but from the tail of his eye, he could see the fan, the white glove lying idle upon the black satin of her dress. The skirt hung from her knee to her foot without a stir in its folds, nor did her foot stir where it showed beneath the hem. She remained in a pose of most enigmatical quietude.

"The face which my mirror showed to me," he went on, "was your face, as I said; but in expression it was not your face as I see it to-night. It was very troubled, it was very pale; the eyes haunted me because of the pain in them, and because of—something else beside. It was a tortured face I saw, and the eyes seemed to ask—but to ask proudly—for help. Is it plain, the explanation which occurred to me?" His voice sank; he went on, slowly choosing every word with care, and speaking it with hesitation. "I imagined that out of all the millions of women in the world, here was one who needed help—my help, who was allowed to appeal to me for it, without, if you understand, making any appeal at all, and the explanation was not. . . unpleasant. . . to a man who lives much alone. In fact it has been so pleasant, and has become so familiar during this last week, that when I saw you to-night without a care, just as I saw you that night at Monte Carlo," and indeed it seemed to Charnock that the black dress she wore alone marked the passage of those six years,—"I am ashamed to say that I was disappointed."

"Yes," said Miranda. "I noticed the disappointment, but there's a simpler explanation of the troubled face than yours. You had been to *Macbeth* that evening; Lady Macbeth played a part in your dreams. What if Lady Macbeth lent her pallor and her distress to the face which you saw in your mirror?"

Charnock swung abruptly round towards her. It was not the explanation which surprised him, but the altered voice she used. And if her voice surprised him, he was shocked and startled by her looks. She was still leaning back in the shadow of the alcove, and her head rested against the dark wood-panels. She did not move when he looked towards her.

"My God," he said in a hushed and trembling whisper, and she gave no sign that she heard. She might have fainted, but that her eyes glittered out of the shadow straight and steadily into his. She might be dead from the whiteness of her face against the panels, but that her bosom rose and fell.

"What can I do?" he exclaimed.

"Hush!" she replied, and rose to her feet. "Here is Lady Donnisthorpe." She walked abruptly past him across the room to the open window. Charnock remained nailed to the ground, following her with his eyes. For in that alcove, leaning against the dark panels, he had seen not merely the features, but the expression on the features, he had seen exact in every detail the face which he had seen in the polished darkness of his mirror. The sheen of the dark polished panels helped the illusion. His fancy had come true, was transmuted into fact. Somewhere, somehow, he was to meet that woman. He had met her here and in this way, and her eyes and her face uttered her distress as with a piercing cry.

Her eyes! The resemblance was perfect to the last detail. For Charnock ventured to surmise in them the same involuntary appeal which he had seen in the eyes that had looked out from his mirror. What then if the rest were true? What if his explanation was as true as the true facts which it explained? What if it was given to him and to her to stand apart from their fellows in this mysterious relation? . . .

He saw that Miranda was already near the window, that Lady Donnisthorpe was approaching him. He followed instantly in Miranda's steps, and Lady Donnisthorpe, perceiving his attention, had the complaisance to turn aside. For the window opened on to a balcony wherein discreet palms sheltered off a nook. There was one of Lady Donnisthorpe's guests who did not share her ladyship's complacency. A censorious dowager sitting near to the window had kept an alert eye upon the couple in the recess during the last three dances; and each time that her daughter—a pretty girl with hair of the palest possible gold, and light blue eyes that were dancing with a child's delight at all the wonders of a first season—returned to the shelter of her portly frame, the dowager drew moral lessons for her benefit from the text of the oblivious couple. She remarked with pain upon their increasing infatuation for each other; she pointed out to her daughter a hapless youth who tiptoed backwards and forwards before Mrs. Warriner, with a dance-card in his hand, too timorous to interrupt the intimate conversation; and when Mrs. Warriner dropped a glove as she stepped over the window-sill on to the balcony, the dowager nudged her daughter with an elbow.

"Now, Mabel, there's a coquette," she said.

Charnock was close behind, and overheard the triumphant remark.

"I beg your pardon," he said politely, "it was the purest accident."

The dowager bridled; her face grew red; she raised her tortoiseshell glasses and annihilated Charnock with a single stare. Charnock had the audacity to smile. He stooped and picked up the glove. Mrs. Warriner had indeed dropped the glove by accident; but since it fell in Charnock's way and since he picked it up, it was to prove, like the handbill at Gibraltar and the draft on Lloyd's bank, a thing trivial in itself, but the opportunity of strange events.

V

Wherein Charnock and Miranda Improve their Acquaintanceship in a Balcony

Lady Donnisthorpe's house stood in Queen Anne's Gate, and the balcony overlooked St. James's Park. There Charnock found Miranda; he leaned his elbows upon the iron balustrade, and for a while neither of them spoke. It was a clear night of early June, odorous with messages of hedgerows along country lanes and uplands of young grass, and of bells ringing over meadows. In front of them the dark trees of the Park rippled and whispered to the stray breaths of wind; between the trees one line of colourless lamps marked the footpath across the bridge to the Mall; and the carriages on the outer roadway ringed that enclosure of thickets and lawns with flitting sparks of fire.

Charnock was still holding the glove which he had picked up on the window-sill.

"That's mine," said Miranda; "thank you," and she stretched out her hand for it.

"Yes," said Charnock, absently, and he drew the glove through his fingers. It was a delicate trifle of white kid; he smoothed it, and his hand had the light touch of a caress. "Miranda," he said softly but distinctly, and lingered on the word as though the sound pleased him.

Miranda started and then sank back again in her chair with a quiet smile. Very likely she blushed at this familiar utterance of her name, and at the caressing movement of his hand which accompanied and perhaps interpreted the utterance, or perhaps it was only at a certain throb of her own heart that she blushed. At all events, the darkness concealed the blush, and Charnock was not looking in her direction.

The freshness of the night air had restored her, but she was very willing to sit there in silence so long as no questions were asked of her, and Charnock had rather the air of one who works out a private problem for himself than one who seeks the answer from another.

The clock upon Westminster tower boomed the hour of twelve. Miranda noticed that Charnock raised his head and listened to the twelve heavy strokes with a smile. His manner was that of a man who comes unexpectedly upon some memento of an almost forgotten time.

"That is a familiar sound to you," said Mrs. Warriner, and she was suddenly sensible of a great interest in all of the past life of this man who was standing beside her.

"Yes," said Charnock, turning round to her.

"You lived in Westminster, then? At one time I used to stay here a good deal. Where did you live?"

Charnock laughed. "You would probably be no wiser if I named the street; it is not of those which you and your friends go up and down," he replied simply. "Yes, I lived in Westminster for three hard, curious years."

"It's not only the years that are curious," said Miranda, but the hint was lost, for Charnock had turned back to the balustrade. She was still, however, inclined to persist. The details which Lady Donnisthorpe had sown in her mind, now bore their crop. Interested in the man, now that she knew him, she was also interested in his career, in his hurried migratory life, in the mystery which enveloped his youth, and all the more because of the contrast between her youth and his. He had lived for three years in some small back street of Westminster; very likely she had more than once rubbed shoulders with him in the streets on the occasions when she had come up from her home in Suffolk. That home became instantly very distinct in her memories—an old manor-house guarded by a moat of dark silent water, a house or broad red-brick chimneys whereon she had known the roses to bloom on a Christmas-day, and of leaded windows upon which the boughs of trees continually tapped.

"I should like to show you my home," she said with a sudden impulse, and did not check herself before the words were spoken. "Perhaps some day," she continued hurriedly, "you will tell me of those three years you spent in Westminster." And she hoped that he had not heard the first sentence of the two.

"I will make an exchange," said Charnock. "I will exchange some day, if you will, the history of my three years for the history of your trouble." He turned eagerly towards her, but she held up her hand.

"Please, please!" she said in a low, shaking voice, for her distress had come back upon her. She had begun, if not to forget it, at all events to dull the remembrance of it since she had come out upon the balcony. She had, in a word, sought and found a compensation in the new friendship of this man, and a relief in his very *naiveté*. But he had brought her anxieties back to her, as he clearly understood, for he said: "That is the second time this evening. I am sorry."

"The second time?" said Miranda, quickly. "Why do you say that?"

"Am I wrong?" he asked. "Am I wrong in fearing that I myself have brought on you the trouble which I fancied I was to avert? I should be glad to know that I was wrong, for since I have stood here on this balcony, that fear has been growing. Your face so changed at the story I told you. At what point of it I do not know. I was not looking. Did I show you some misfortune you were unaware of, and might still be unaware of, if I had only held my tongue? In offering to shield you, did I only strike at you? I do not know, I am in the dark." He spoke in a voice of intense remorse, pleading for a proof that his fear was groundless, and Miranda did not answer him at all. "I do not ask you to speak freely now," he continued; "but sometime perhaps you will. You see, we shall be neighbours."

"Neighbours!" exclaimed Miranda, and her lips parted in a smile.

"You live at Ronda, Lady Donnisthorpe tells me; my headquarters now are at Algeciras;" and he told her briefly of his business there.

"My cousin did not tell me that," said Miranda.

Lady Donnisthorpe, in the wisdom of her heart, had, in fact, carefully concealed Charnock's place of abode, thinking it best that Miranda should learn it from Charnock's lips, and be pleasantly surprised thereby. That Miranda was pleasantly surprised might perhaps have been inferred by a more experienced man, from the extreme chilliness of her reply.

"Ronda is at the top," she said, "Algeciras at the bottom, and there are a hundred miles of hillside and cork-forest between."

"There are also," retorted Charnock, "a hundred miles of railway."

"Shall we go back into the room?" suggested Miranda.

"If you wish. Only there is something else I am trying to say to you," said Charnock, and at that Miranda laughed, and laughed with a fresh bright trill of amusement. It broke suddenly and spontaneously from her lips and surprised Charnock, who was at a loss to reconcile it with the signs of her distress. He turned towards her. "What is it?" he asked.

"Nothing," she said hastily, "nothing at all."

"You wished to go in?"

"Not now,—not for the world."

She was genuinely amused. Her eyes laughed at him in the starlight. Charnock was very content at the change in her, though he did not at all understand it. It made what he meant to say easier, if he could only find the means to say it. He held the means unwittingly in his hand, for he held Miranda's glove. It was that glove which provoked her amusement. Charnock, with a pertinacity which was only equalled by his absence of mind, was trying to force his hand into Mrs. Warriner's glove. He had already succeeded in slipping the long sleeve of it over his palm; he was now engaged in the more strenuous task of fitting his fingers into its slender fingers, as he leaned upon the balcony.

"You are laughing, no doubt, at my pertinacity, and it is true that our acquaintanceship is very slight," said he.

"In a moment you will irretrievably destroy it," said she, looking at the glove.

"I hope you don't mean that," he answered sadly, as he smoothed the finger-tip of the forefinger down upon his own, and at once proceeded to the other fingers. The little finger in particular needed a deal of strenuous coaxing, and caused him to break up his words with intervals of physical effort. "Because—as I say—we shall be neighbours—there!"—The exclamation "there" meant that he was satisfied with the third finger.—"A hundred miles of hill-side—in a foreign country—on a map a thumb will cover it."

"Will it cover a thumb, though?" asked Miranda, who took a feminine interest in the durability of her glove. She leaned forward in a delighted suspense, as Charnock proceeded to answer her question by experiment.

"There's the railway too," said he, as he struggled with the thumb of the glove, "and as I say, a foreign country. Very likely, we shall be nearer neighbours, though you are at Ronda and I am at Algeciras, than if you lived in this house and I at the house next door. Because after all there's one advantage in trouble of any kind. Trouble is the short foot-path to friendship, don't you think? Like that line of lamps across the Park."

Miranda forgot the glove. She was touched by the deep sincerity of his voice, by the modesty of his manner. She rose from her chair and stood by his side at the balustrade. "Yes," she answered, looking at the circling lights on the outer rim of the Park. "I think that is true. It spares one the long carriage-road of ceremonial acquaintanceship. But," she said thoughtfully, "I do not know whether after all I shall soon return to Ronda."

She heard a little sound of something tearing, and there was Charnock contemplating in amazement upon his left hand a white kid glove of which the kid was ripped across the palm. He felt in his pocket with his right hand and drew out both of his own gloves, which he had taken off while he was talking in the alcove. Then he looked at Miranda and his amazement became remorse.

"It's yours!" he said. "Of course, I picked it up. I had forgotten even that I was holding it. I had no notion that I was putting it on."

"I gave you fair warning," said Miranda, with a frank laugh, "but you would not pay any attention."

Charnock looked at her with absolute incredulity. "You mean to say that you don't mind? You are wonderful!"

"It seems almost too late to mind," said she, looking at the tattered glove.

"Or to mend," said he, ruefully, drawing it off with extreme care, and as a new thought struck him. "Oh!" he exclaimed, "suppose it had belonged to anyone else, the dowager in the window, for instance." He dangled the glove in the air. "Now that's a lesson!"

"Perhaps it's a parable," said Miranda, as she took the glove from him.

Charnock saw that she had grown quite serious. "If so," said he, "I cannot expound it."

"Shall I?" The smile had faded from her lips, her eyes shone upon his, with no longer a sparkle of merriment, but very still, very grave.

"Yes."

"Well, then," she said slowly, "shall I say that no man can offer a woman his friendship or help without doing her a hurt in some other way?"

His eyes as steadily answered back to hers. "Do you believe that?" he said. He spoke quite simply without raising his voice in any way, but none the less Mrs. Warriner was certain that she had but to say "yes," and there would be an end, now and forever, of his questions, of his help, of his friendship, of everything between them beyond the merest acquaintanceship. Perhaps some day they might cross the harbour together in the same ferry from Algeciras to Gibraltar, and bow and exchange a careless word, but that would be all—and only that until his work was finished there.

"Do you believe that?"

She was half tempted to say "yes"; but she had an instinct, a premonition, that whatever answer she made would stretch out to unknown and incalculable consequences. She seemed to herself to be drawing the lots which one way or another would decide and limit all her years to come. Upon the tiny "yes" or "no" between which she had to make her choice, her whole life was destined to pivot. Accordingly, she made up her mind to say neither, but to turn the matter into a jest. "Here's the proof," said she, as lightly as she could, and she flourished the glove.

But the man steadily held her to his question, with his eyes, with his voice, with his very attitude. "Do you believe that?" he repeated.

"I don't know whether I believe it," she murmured resentfully. "I don't see why I should be asked to mean what I say, or whether I mean what I say. . . But it might be so, I think. . . I don't know. . . I don't know."

To her relief Charnock moved. If he had stood like that, demanding an answer with every line of his body, for another instant, she knew she would have been compelled to answer one way or another; and she felt certain, too, that whatever answer she gave it would have been the one she would have wished afterwards to take back. "Now if you are satisfied," she added with a touch of petulance, "we will go in."

He moved aside for her to pass, but before she had time to step forward, he moved back again and barred the way. "No, please," he said quickly, and his voice thrilled as though he had hit upon an inspiration.

"Lady Donnisthorpe told me you were rather unconventional," she remarked with a sigh, which was only half of it a jest; and she drew back as though she did not wish to hear what he had to say, as though she almost feared to hear it.

But Charnock barely even remarked her reluctance. "That glove," he said, and pointed to it. Miranda imagined that he was reaching out a hand for it.

"I have *heaps* of pairs," she exclaimed, whipping it behind her back; "there is no need to trouble about it at all."

"I do not ask for it; I had no thought of that. On the contrary, I would ask you to keep it if you will. There is something else which I was trying to say, if you remember."

"Dear, dear!" said Miranda, ruefully, "I could wish after all that you had trodden on my toes."

"I beg your pardon," said Charnock, and instantly he drew aside. He left the way clear for her. She passed him, and went towards the window, from which the lights and the music streamed out into the night. Had he followed, she would have stepped into the room, amongst the dancers; she would have been claimed by a partner, and she would have seen no more of Charnock, and the only consequences of this interview upon the balcony would have been a memory in her thoughts, a curiosity in her speculations.

But Charnock did not follow her. He remained where she left him, and her feet loitered more with every step she took. At the edge of the window she stopped. For the second time that evening she became aware that one way or other she must do the irrevocable thing. It was a mere step to make across the sill of the window, from the stone of the balcony to the parquet of the ball-room floor,—a thing insignificant in itself and in its consequences most momentous. She stood for a second undecided. The sight of her partner looking about the room decided her. She came back to where Charnock stood in a soldierly rigidity.

"You might have come half-way to meet me," she said in a whimsical complaint, and then very gently: "I will hear what you wish to say, if you will still say it."

"What I mean is this," he replied; "it is what I was trying to say. The hardest thing, if one ever wants help, is—don't you think?—the asking for it. I could not say that to you until I had hit upon a means by which the asking, should it ever be necessary, might be dispensed with. And it seemed to me that there was something providential in my tearing that glove; for that torn glove can be the means, if ever you see fit to use it. You live at Ronda; for the next year I am to be found at Algeciras; you will only have to send that torn glove to me in an envelope. I shall know without a word from you; and when I answer it by coming up to you at Ronda, it will be understood by both of us, again without a word, why I have come. I shall not need to speak at all; you will only need to say the precise particular thing which needs to be done."

Miranda stood with her eyelids closed, and her ungloved hand pressed over her heart. The blood darkened her cheeks. Charnock saw her whole face soften and sweeten. "I understand," she said in a low voice. "I might appeal and be spared the humiliation of appealing, like the face in your mirror."

"I believe," said he, "that my mirror sent me a message on that night. I have tried to deliver it."

Miranda slowly raised her eyes and they glistened with something other than the starlight. "Thank you," she said; "for the delicacy of the thought I am most grateful. What woman would not be? But I do not think that I shall ever send you the glove: not because I would not be glad to owe gratitude to you, but just for the same reason which has kept me from telling you anything of my troubles. Such as they are I must fight them through by myself."

This time she passed over the sill into the ballroom; but she was holding the glove tight against her breast, and she had a feeling that Charnock very surely knew that at some time she would send it to him.

VI

While Charnock Builds Castles in Spain, Miranda Returns There

The anxious dowager, who was preparing to depart with her daughter, had just risen from her seat by the window as Miranda stepped over the sill into the ball-room. She sat down again, however, for she had a word or two to say concerning Miranda's appearance.

"Muriel," she observed, "take a good look at that woman, and remember that if ever you sit out with one man for half-an-hour on a cool balcony you can make no greater mistake than to return with a flushed face."

"Thank you, mother," said Muriel, who was growing restive under this instructional use of an evening party. "I will take the first opportunity of practising your advice."

At this moment Charnock stepped over the sill. He stepped up to Mrs. Warriner's side and spoke to her. Mrs. Warriner stopped within a couple of yards of the dowager and gave her hand, and with her hand her eyes, to her companion.

"Muriel, look!" said the censorious one. "How vulgar!"

"Shall I listen too?" asked Muriel, innocently.

"Do, my child, do!" said the dowager, who was impervious to sarcasm.

What was said, however, did not reach the dowager's ears. It was, indeed, no more than an interchange of "good-nights," but the dowager bridled, perhaps out of disappointment that she had not heard.

"An intriguing woman I have no doubt," said she, as through her glasses she followed Miranda's retreat.

"Surely she has too much dignity," objected the daughter.

"Dignity, indeed! My child, when you know more of the world, you will understand that the one astonishing thing about such women is not their capacity for playing tricks but their incredible power of retaining their self-respect while they are playing them. Now we will go."

The dowager's voice was a high one. It carried her words clearly to Charnock, who had not as yet moved. He laughed at them then with entire incredulity, but he retained them unwittingly in his memory. The next moment the dowager swept past him. The daughter Muriel followed, and as she passed Charnock she looked at him with an inquisitive friendliness. But her eyes happened to meet his, and with a spontaneous fellow-feeling the girl and the man smiled to each other and at the dowager, before they realised that they were totally unacquainted.

Lady Donnisthorpe was lying in wait for Charnock. She asked him to take her to the buffet. Charnock secured for her a chair and an ice, and stood by her side, conversational but incommunicative. She was consequently compelled herself to broach the subject which was at that moment nearest to her heart.

"How did you get on with my cousin?" she asked.

Charnock smiled foolishly at nothing.

"Oh, say something!" cried Lady Donnisthorpe, and tapped with her spoon upon the glass plate.

"Tell me about her," said Charnock, drawing up another chair.

Lady Donnisthorpe lowered her voice and said with great pathos: "She is most unhappy."

Charnock gravely nodded his head. "Why?"

Lady Donnisthorpe settled herself comfortably with the full intention of wringing Charnock's heart if by any means she could.

"Miranda comes of an old Catholic Suffolk family. She was eighteen when she married, and that's six years ago. No, six years and a half. Ralph Warriner was a Lieutenant in the Artillery, and made her acquaintance when he was staying in the neighbourhood of the Pollards, that's Miranda's house in Suffolk. Ralph listened to Allan Bedlow's antediluvian stories. Allan was Miranda's father, her mother died long ago. Ralph captured the father; finally he captured the daughter. Ralph, you see, had many graces but no qualities; he was a bad stone in a handsome setting and Miranda was no expert. How could she be? She lived at Glenham with only her father and a discontented relation, called Jane Holt, for her companions. Consequently she married Ralph Warriner, who got his step the day after the marriage, and the pair went immediately to Gibraltar. Ralph had overestimated Miranda's fortune, and it came out that he was already handsomely dipped; so that their married life began with more than the usual disadvantages. It lasted for three years, and for that time only because of Miranda's patience and endurance. She is very silent about those three years, but we know enough," and Lady Donnisthorpe was for a moment carried away. "It must have been intolerable," she exclaimed. "Ralph Warriner never had cared a snap of his fingers for her. His tastes were despicable, his disposition utterly mean. Cards were in his blood; I verily believe that his heart was an ace of spades. Add to that that he was naturally cantankerous and jealous. To his brother officers he was civil for he owed them money, but he made up for his civility by becoming a bully once he had closed his own front door."

"Yes, yes," interrupted Charnock, hurriedly, as though he had no heart to hear more; "I understand."

"You can understand then that when the crash came we were glad. Two years after the marriage old Allan Bedlow sickened. Miranda came home to nurse him and Ralph—he bought a schooner-yacht. Allan Bedlow died; Miranda inherited, and the estate was settled upon her. Ralph could not touch a farthing of the capital, and he was aggrieved. Miranda returned to Gibraltar, and matters went from worse to worse. The crash came a year later. The nature of it is neither here nor there, but Ralph had to go, and had to go pretty sharp. His schooner-yacht was luckily lying in Gibraltar Bay; he slipped on board before gunfire, and put to sea as soon as it was dark; and he was not an instant too soon. From that moment he disappeared, and the next news we had of him was the discovery of his body upon Rosevear two years afterwards."

Charnock hunted through the jungle of Lady Donnisthorpe's words for a clue to the distress which Miranda had betrayed that evening, but he did not discover one. Another question forced itself into his mind. "Why does Mrs. Warriner live at Ronda?" he asked. "I have never been there, but there are no English residents, I should think."

"That was one of her reasons," replied Lady Donnisthorpe. "At least I think so, but upon that too she is silent, and when she will not speak no one can make her. You see what Ralph did was hushed up,—it was one of those cases which are hushed up,—particularly since he had disappeared and was out of reach. But everyone knew that disgrace attached to it. His name was removed from the Army List. Miranda perhaps shrank from the disgrace. She shrank too, I think, from the cheap pity of which she would have had so much. At all events she did not return home, she sent for Jane Holt, her former companion, and settled at Ronda." Lady Donnisthorpe looked doubtfully at Charnock. "Perhaps there were other reasons too, sacred reasons." But she had not made up her mind whether it would be wise to explain those other reasons before her guests began to take their leave of her; and so the opportunity was lost.

Charnock walked back to his hotel that night in a frame of mind entirely strange to him. He was inclined to rhapsodise; he invented and rejected various definitions of woman; he laughed at the worldly ignorance of the dowager. "A woman, madam "—he imagined himself to be lecturing her—"is the great gift to man to keep him clean and bright like a favourite sword." He composed other and no less irreproachable phrases, and in the midst of this exhilarating exercise was struck suddenly aghast at the temerity of his own conduct that night, at the remembrance of his persistency. However, he was not in a mood to be disheartened. The dawn took the sky by surprise while he was still upon his way. The birds bustled among the leaves in the gardens, and a thrush tried his throat, and finding it clear gave full voice to his song. The blackbirds called one to the other, and a rosy light struck down the streets. It was morning, and he stopped to wonder whether Miranda was yet asleep. He hoped so, intensely, for the sake of her invaluable health.

But Miranda was seated by her open window, listening to the birds calling in the Park, and drawing some quiet from the quiet of the lawns and trees; and every now and then she glanced across her shoulder to where a torn white glove lay upon the table, as though she was afraid it would vanish by some enchantment.

But the next day Miranda packed her boxes, and when Charnock called upon Lady Donnisthorpe, he was informed that she had returned in haste to Ronda. Charnock was surprised, for he remembered that Mrs. Warriner had expressed a doubt whether she would ever return to Ronda, and wondered what had occurred to change her mind. But the surprise and bewilderment were soon swallowed up in a satisfaction which sprang from the assurance that Miranda and he were after all to be neighbours.

VII

In which Major Wilbraham Describes the Steps by which he Attained his Majority, and Gives Miranda Some Particular Information

A month later at Ronda, and a little after midday. In the cool darkness of the Cathedral, under the great stone dome behind the choir, Miranda was kneeling before a lighted altar. That altar she had erected, as an inscription showed, to the memory of Ralph Warriner, and since her return from England she had passed more than an ordinary proportion of her time in front of it.

This morning, however, an unaccountable uneasiness crept over her. She tried to shake the sensation off by an increased devoutness, but though her knees were bent, there was no prayer in her mind or upon her lips. Her uneasiness increased, and after a while it defined itself. Someone was watching her from behind.

She ceased even from the pretence of prayer. Her heart fluttered up into her throat. She did not look round, she did not move, but she knelt there with a sinking expectation, in the light of the altar candles, and felt intensely helpless because their yellow warmth streamed full upon her face and person, and must disclose her to the watching eyes behind.

She knelt waiting for a familiar voice and a familiar step. She heard only the grating of a chair upon the stone flags beyond the choir, and a priest droning a litany very far away. Here all was quiet—quiet as the eyes watching her out of the gloom.

At last, resenting her cowardice, she rose to her feet and turned. At once a man stepped forward, and her heart gave a great throb of relief, as she saw the man was a stranger.

He bowed, and with an excuse for his intrusion, he handed her a card. She did not look at it, for immediately the stranger continued to speak, in a cool, polite voice, and it seemed to her that all her blood stood still.

"I knew Captain Warriner at Gibraltar," he said. "In fact I may say that I know him, for he is alive."

Miranda was dimly aware that he waited for an answer, and then excused her silence with an accent of sarcasm.

"Such good news must overwhelm you, no doubt. I have used all despatch to inform you of it, for I was only certain of the truth yesterday."

And to her amazement Miranda heard herself reply:

"Then I discovered it a month before you did."

The next thing of which she was conscious was a thick golden mist before her eyes. The golden mist was the clear sunlight in the square before the Cathedral. Miranda was leaning against the stone parapet, though how she was there she could not have told. She had expected the news. She had even thought that the man standing behind her was her husband, come to tell her it in person; but nevertheless the mere telling of it, the putting of it in words, to quote the stranger's phrase, had overwhelmed her. Memories of afternoons during which she had walked out with her misery to Europa Point, of evenings when she had sat with her misery upon the flat house-top watching the riding lights in Algeciras Bay, and listening to the jingle of tambourines from the houses on the hillside below—all the sordid unnecessary wretchedness of those three years spent at Gibraltar came crushing her. She savoured again the disgrace which attended upon Ralph's flight. Her first instinct, when she learned Ralph was alive, had urged her to hide, and at this moment she regretted that she had not obeyed it. She regretted that she had returned to Ronda, where Ralph or any emissary of his at once could find her.

But that was only for a moment. She had returned to Ronda with a full appreciation of the consequences of her return, and for reasons which she was afterwards to explain, and of which, even while she stood in that square, she resumed courage to approve.

The stranger came from the door of the Cathedral and crossed to her.

"Your matter-of-fact acceptance of my news was clever, Mrs. Warriner," he said with a noticeable sharpness. "Believe me, I do homage to cleverness. I frankly own that I expected a scene of sorts. I was quite taken aback —a compliment, I assure you, upon my puff," and he bowed with his hand on his breast. "You were out of the Cathedral door before I realised that all this time you had been the Captain's—would you mind if I said accomplice?"

That her matter-of-fact acceptance of the news was entirely due to the fact that the news dazed her, Miranda did not trouble to explain.

"The altar," continued the stranger, in a voice of genuine admiration, "was a master-stroke. To erect an altar to the memory of a husband who is still alive, to pray devoutly before it, is highly ingenious and—may I say?—brave. Religion is a trump-card, Mrs. Warriner, in most of the games where you sit with law and order for your opponents; but not many women have the bravery to play it for its value."

Miranda coloured at his words. There had been some insincerity in her daily prayers before the altar, though the self-satisfied man who spoke to her had not his finger upon the particular flaw,—enough insincerity to cause Miranda some shame, now that she probed it, and yet in the insincerity there had been also something sincere. The truth is, Miranda could bring herself to wish neither that her husband was dead if he was alive, nor that he should come to life again if he was dead; she made a compromise—she daily prayed with great fervour for his soul's salvation before the altar she had erected to his memory. But this again was not a point upon which she troubled to enlighten her companion. She was more concerned to discover who the man was, and on what business he had come.

"You knew my husband at Gibraltar," she said, "and yet—"

"It is true," replied the man, in answer to her suspicion. "You need not be afraid, Mrs. Warriner. I have not come from Scotland Yard. I have had, I admit, relations with the police, but they have always been of an involuntary kind."

"You assume," said she, with some pride, "that I have reason to fear Scotland Yard, whereas nothing was further from my thoughts. Only you say that you knew my husband at Gibraltar. You pretend to come from him—"

"By no means. We are at cross-purposes, I fancy. I do not come from him, though most certainly I did know him at Gibraltar. But I admit that he never invited me to his house."

"In that case," said Miranda, with a cold bow, "I can do no more than thank you for the news you give me and wish you a good day."

She walked by him. He turned and imperturbably fell into step by her side. "Clever," said he, "clever!" Miranda stopped. "Who are you? What is your business?" she asked.

"As to who I am, you hold my card in your hand."

Mrs. Warriner had carried it from the Cathedral, unaware that she held it. She now raised it to her eyes and read, *Major Ambrose Wilbraham*.

Wilbraham noted, though he did not understand, the rapid,

perplexed glance which she shot at him. Charnock had spoken to her of a Major Wilbraham, had described him, and undoubtedly this was the man. "As to my business," he continued, "I give you the news that your husband is alive, but I have also something to sell."

"What?"

"Obviously my silence. It might be awkward if it was known in certain quarters that Captain Warriner, who sold the mechanism of the new Daventry quick-firing gun to a foreign power; who slipped out of Gibraltar just a night before his arrest was determined on, and who was wrecked a year ago in the Scillies, is not only alive, but in the habit of paying periodical visits to England."

Mrs. Warriner again read the name upon the card. "Major Ambrose Wilbraham," she said, with an incredulous emphasis on the *Major*.

"Captains," he retorted airily, "have at times deviated from the narrow path, so that a Major may well be forgiven a peccadillo. But I will not deceive you, Mrs. Warriner. The rank was thrust upon me by a barman in Shaftesbury Avenue, and I suffered it, because the title after all gives me the entrance to the chambers of many young men who have, or most often have not, just taken their degrees. So Major I am, but my mess is any bar within a mile of Piccadilly Circus. Shall we say that I hold brevet rank, and am seconded for service in the noble regiment of the soldiers of fortune?"

"And the enemies you fight with," said Miranda, with a contemptuous droop of the lips, "are women like myself."

"Pardon me," retorted Wilbraham, with unabashed good humour. "Women like yourself, Mrs. Warriner, are the *vivandières* whom we regretfully impress to supply our needs upon the march. Our enemies are the rozzers—again I beg your pardon—the gentlemen in blue who lurk at the street corners, by whom from time to time we are worsted and interned."

They walked across the square along a narrow street down towards the Tajo, that deep chasm which bisects the town. The heat was intense, the road scorched under foot, and they walked slowly. They made a strange pair in the old, quaint streets, the woman walking with a royal carriage, delicate in her beauty and her dress; the man defiant, battered and worn, with an eye which from sheer habit scouted in front and aside for the chance which might toss his day's rations in his way.

Their talk was stranger still, for by an unexpressed consent, the subject of the bargain to be struck was deferred, and as they walked

Wilbraham illustrated to Miranda the career of a man who lives by his wits, and dwelt even with humour upon its alternations of prosperity and starvation. "I have been a manager of theatrical companies in 'the smalls,'" he said, "a billiard-marker at Trieste, a racing tipster, a vender of—photographs, and I once carried a sandwich-board down Bond Street, and saw the women I had danced with not so long before draw their delicate skirts from the defilement of my rags. However, I rose to a better position. It is funny, you know, to go right under, and then find there are social degrees in the depths. I have had good times too, mind you. Every now and then I have struck an A1 copper-bottomed gold mine, and then there were dress suits and meals running into one another, and ormolu rooms on the first floor."

Dark sayings, unintelligible shibboleths, came and went among his words and obscured their meaning; accents and phrases from many countries betrayed the vicissitudes of his life; but he spoke with the accent of a gentleman, and with something of a gentleman's good humour; so that Miranda, moved partly by his recital and perhaps partly because her own misfortunes had touched her to an universal sympathy, began to be interested in the man who had experienced so much that was strange to her, and they both slipped into a tolerance of each other and a momentary forgetfulness of their relationship as blackmailer and blackmailed.

"I could give you a modern edition of Don Guzman," he said. "I was a money-lender's tout at Gibraltar at one time. It's to that I owed my acquaintance with Warriner. It's to that I owe my present acquaintance with you." He came to a dead stop in the full swing of narration. He halted in his steps and banged the point of his stick down into the road. "But I have done with it," he cried, and drawing a great breath, he showed to Miranda a face suddenly illuminated. "The garrets and the first floors, the stale billiard rooms, the desperate scouting for food like a damned sea-gull—I beg your pardon, Mrs. Warriner. Upon my word, I do! But imagine a poor beggar of a bankrupt painter who, after fifteen years, suddenly finds himself with a meal upon the table and his bills paid! I am that man. Fifteen years of what I have described to you! It might have been less, no doubt, but I hadn't learnt my lesson. Fifteen years, and from first to last not one thing done of the few things worth doing; fifteen years of a murderous hunt for breakfast and dinner! And I've done with it, thanks to you, Mrs. Warriner." And his face hardened at once and gleamed at her, very cruel and menacing. "Yes, thanks to you! We'll not forget that." And as he resumed his walk the astounding creature began gaily to quote poetry:

> *"I resume*
> *Life after death; for 'tis no less than life*
> *After such long, unlovely labouring days.*

A great poet, Mrs. Warriner. What do you think?"

"No doubt," said Miranda, absently. That one cruel glance had chilled the sympathy in her; Major Wilbraham would not spare either Ralph or herself with the memory of those fifteen years to harden him.

They came to the Ciudad, the old intricate Moorish town of tortuous lanes in the centre of Ronda. Before a pair of heavy walnut doors curiously encrusted with bright copper nails Wilbraham came to a stop. "Your house, I think, Mrs. Warriner," and he took off his hat and wiped his forehead.

"I should prefer," said she, "to hear what you have to say in the Alameda."

"As you will. I am bound to say that I could have done with a soda and I'm so frisky, but I recognise that I have no right to trespass upon your hospitality."

They went on, crossed a small plaza, and so came down to the Tajo. A bridge spans the ravine in a single arch; in the centre of the bridge Miranda stopped, leaned over the parapet and looked downwards. Wilbraham followed her example. For three hundred feet the walls of the gorge fell sheer, at the bottom the turbulence of a torrent foamed and roared, at the top was the span of the bridge. In the brickwork of the arch a tiny window looked out on air.

"Do you see that window?" said Miranda, drily. "The prison is underfoot in the arch of the bridge."

"Indeed, how picturesque," returned Wilbraham, easily, who was quite untouched by any menace which Miranda's words might suggest. Miranda looked across the road towards a guardia. Wilbraham lazily followed the direction of her glance; for all the emotion which he showed blackmail might have been held in Spain an honourable means of livelihood. Miranda turned back. "That window," she said, "is the window of the prison."

"The view," remarked Wilbraham, "would compensate in some measure for the restriction."

"Chains might add to the restriction."

"Chains *are* unpleasant," Wilbraham heartily agreed.

Miranda realised that she had tempted defeat in this little encounter. She accepted it and walked on.

"You were wise to come off that barrow, Mrs. Warriner," Wilbraham remarked in approval.

They crossed the bridge and entered the Mercadillo, the new Spanish quarter of the town, ascended the hill, and came to the bull ring. Before that Wilbraham stopped. "Why do we go to the Alameda?"

"We can talk there on neutral ground."

"It seems a long way."

"On the other hand," replied Miranda, "the Alameda is close to the railway station. By the bye, how did you know where I lived?"

"There was no difficulty in discovering that. I learnt at Gibraltar that you lived at Ronda, and the station-master here told me where. When I saw your house I did not wonder at your choice. You were wise to take a Moorish house, I fancy—the patio with the tamarisks in the middle and the fountain and the red and green tiles—very pleasant, I should think. A door or two stood open. The rooms seemed charming, low in roof, with dark panels, of a grateful coolness, and so far as I could judge, with fine views."

"You went into the house, then?" exclaimed Miranda.

"Yes, I asked for you, and was told that Miss Holt was at home. I thought it wise to go in—one never knows. So I introduced myself, but not my business, to Miss Holt—your cousin, is she not? A profound sentimentalist, I should fancy; I noticed she was reading *Henrietta Temple*. She complained of being much alone; she nurses grievances, no doubt. Sentimentalists have that habit—what do you say?" Miranda could have laughed at the shrewdness of the man's perceptions, had she not been aware that the shrewdness was a weapon directed against her own breast.

They reached the Alameda. Miranda led the way to a bench which faced the railings. Wilbraham looked quickly and suspiciously at her, and then walked to the railings and looked over. The Alameda is laid out upon the very edge of the Ronda plateau, and Wilbraham looked straight down a sheer rock precipice of a thousand feet. He remained in that posture for some seconds. From the foot of that precipice the plain of the Vega stretched out level as a South-sea lagoon. The gardens of a few cottages were marked out upon the green like the squares of a chess-board; upon the hedges there was here and there the flutter of white linen. Orchards of apples, cherries, peaches, and pears, enriched the plain with their subdued colours, and the Guadiaro, freed from the confinement of its chasm, wound through it with the glitter and the curve of a steel spring. A few white Moorish mills upon the banks of the stream were at work, and the sound of them came droning through the still heat up to Wilbraham's ears.

Wilbraham, however, was not occupied with the scenery, for when he turned back to Miranda his face was dark and angry.

"Why did you bring me to the Alameda?" he asked sternly.

"Because I will not listen to you in my own, house," she answered with spirit.

Wilbraham did not resent the reason, but he watched her warily, as though he doubted it.

"Now," said Miranda, as she stood before him. "You tell me that my husband is living. I have your bare word for it, and out of your lips you have proved to me that your bare word has very little worth."

"The buttons are off the foils," said he; "very well. In the Cathedral you corroborated my word. You know that he lives; I know it."

"How do you know it?"

"By adding two and two and making five, as any man with any savvy always can," replied Wilbraham. "Indeed, by adding two and two, one can even at times make a decent per annum."

Mrs. Warriner sat down upon the bench, and Wilbraham, standing at her side, presented the following testimonial to his "savvy." First of all, he drew from one pocket four pounds of English gold, and from the other a handful of dollars and pesetas. "This is what is left of two hundred and thirty pounds, which I won at Monte Carlo in the beginning of May. There's a chance for philosophy, Mrs. Warriner. If I hadn't won that money I shouldn't be standing here now with my livelihood assured. For I shouldn't have been able to embark on the P. and O. mail steamer *India* at Marseilles, and so I shouldn't have fallen in with my dear young friend Charnock."

Miranda fairly started at the mention of Charnock's name in connection with Wilbraham's discovery. Instantly Wilbraham paused. Miranda made an effort to look entirely unconcerned, but Wilbraham's eye was upon her, and she felt the blood colouring her cheeks.

"Oho!" said Wilbraham, cocking his head. Then he whistled softly to himself while he looked her over from head to foot. Miranda kept silence, and he resumed his story, though every time he mentioned Charnock's name he looked to surprise her in some movement.

"Off Ushant we came up with a brigantine, and I couldn't help fancying that her lines were familiar to me. Charnock lent me his binoculars—a dear good fellow, Charnock!—and I made out her name, the *Tarifa*. I should not have given the boat another thought but for Charnock. Charnock said she had the lines of a Salcombe clipper. Did you happen to know that the *Ten Brothers* was a Salcombe clipper? I did, and the moment Charnock had spoken I understood why the look of her hull was familiar; I had seen her or her own legitimate sister swinging at Warriner's moorings in Algeciras Bay. I did not set any great store upon that small point, however, until Charnock kindly informed me that her owner could have gained no possible advantage by altering her rig from a schooner's into a brigantine's. Then my interest began to rise, for he had altered the rig. Why, if the change was to his disadvantage? I can't say that I had any answer ready; I can't say that I expected to find an answer. But since I landed at Plymouth, from which Salcombe is a bare twenty miles, I thought that I might as well run over. One never knows—such small accidents mean everything for us—and, as a matter of fact, I spent a very pleasant half-hour in the back parlour of the Commercial Inn, watching the yachts at anchor and the little sailing boats spinning about the river, and listening to an old skipper, who deplored the times when the town rang with the din of hammers in shipbuilding yards, and twelve—observe, Mrs. Warriner, twelve—schooners brought to it the prosperity of their trade. The schooners had been sold off, but the skipper had their destinies at his fingers' ends as a man follows the fortunes of his children. Two had been cast away, three were in the Newfoundland trade, one was now a steam-yacht, and the others still carried fruit from the West Indies. He accounted for eleven of them, and the twelfth, of course, was the *Ten Brothers* wrecked upon Rosevear. I eliminated the *Ten Brothers*, the two which had been cast away, and the steam-yacht. Eight were left."

"Yes?" said Mrs. Warriner.

"I went back to Plymouth and verified the skipper's information. He had given me the owners' names and the names of the vessels. I looked them up in the sailing-lists and I proved beyond a shadow of doubt, from their dates of sailing and arrival at various ports, that not one of those eight schooners could have been the brigantine we passed off Ushant. There remained, then, the four which I had eliminated, or

A.E.W. MASON

rather the three, for the steam-yacht was out of the question. Do you follow?"

Miranda made a sign of assent.

"Those three boats had been cast away. Two of them belonged to respectable firms, the third to Ralph Warriner. It would of course be very convenient for Ralph Warriner, under the circumstances, to be reputed dead and yet to be alive with a boat in hand, so to speak. On the other side, would it profit either of the two respectable firms to spread a false report that one of their boats had been cast away? Hardly; besides, it would of course be to Warriner's advantage, from the point of view of concealment, to change the rig and the name of his boat. It was all inference and guess-work, no doubt. Charnock, for instance, might have been entirely wrong; the *Tarifa* might never have been anything but the *Tarifa* and a brigantine; but the inference and the guess-work all pointed the one way, and I own that my interest was rapidly changing to excitement. My suspicions were strengthened by the behaviour of the *Tarifa* herself. No news of her approach was recorded in the papers. She didn't make any unnecessary noise about the port she was bound for, nor had she the manners to pass the time of day with any of Lloyd's signal-stations. The *Tarifa's* business began to provoke my curiosity. Here was (shall we say?) a needless lack of ceremony to begin with. It didn't seem as if the *Tarifa* had many anxious friends awaiting her arrival. Besides that, supposing that my suspicions were right, that the *Tarifa* was the *Ten Brothers* masquerading under another name, and that perhaps Ralph Warriner was on board, it stood to reason Ralph Warriner would not risk his skin in an English port, without a better reason than a cargo of trade. Comprenny, Mrs. Warriner? I was guessing, conjecturing, inferring; I had no knowledge. So I thought the cargo of the *Tarifa* was the right end of the stick to hang on to. If I could know the truth about that, I should be in a better position to guess whether it had anything to do with Ralph Warriner. Is that clear?"

It was clear enough to Miranda, who already felt herself enmeshed in the net of this man's ingenious deductions. "Yes," she said.

"Very well. From the brigantine's course, she was evidently making for one of the western harbours. I lay low in Plymouth for a couple of days, and read the shipping news. That wasn't all I did during those two days, though. I went to the Free Library besides, overhauled the file of the *Western Morning News* and assimilated information about the inquest at St. Mary's. The faceless mariner chucked up on Rosevear struck one as interesting. I noticed too that there had been a good many wrecks in the Channel during the heavy weather and the fog just about that time. But before I had come to any conclusion, I opened my newspaper on the third morning and read that the *Tarifa* had dropped her anchor at Falmouth. I took the first train out of Plymouth, and sure enough I picked the *Tarifa* up in Falmouth docks. Then I made friends with the port-officers, but I got never a glimpse of Ralph Warriner."

Miranda's hopes revived. She knew very well that Ralph Warriner was not at that time in Falmouth. For the moment, however, she let Wilbraham run on.

"I frankly admit that my hopes sank a little," he continued. "Of course Warriner might have been put ashore; but it seemed to me impossible to obtain sufficient certainty of my suspicions unless I actually clapped eyes on him."

Miranda agreed, and her prospects of escaping from this man's clutches showed brighter; for she was not in a mood of sufficient calmness to enable her to realise that Wilbraham would hardly have been so frank, if he had not by now at all events acquired absolute certainty.

"My hopes were to sink yet more," Wilbraham continued. "The brigantine passed for a tramp out from Tarifa with a cargo of fruit. I saw that cargo unloaded. There was no pretence about it; it was a full cargo of fruit. The boat was sailing back to Tarifa with a cargo of alkali, and I saw that cargo stowed away in her hold. Mrs. Warriner, my spirits began to revive. That cargo of alkali was most uncommon small; the profit on it wouldn't have paid the decky's wages. Again I inferred. I inferred that the alkali was a blind, and that the *Tarifa* meant to pick up a cargo of another sort somewhere along the coast, though what the cargo would be I could not for the life of me imagine."

"But it is all guess-work," said Miranda, with an indifference which she was far from feeling.

"I learned one piece of solid cheering information from my friends the port-officers," retorted Wilbraham. "The *Tarifa's* papers were all quite recent, and yet she was an old boat. She was supposed to be owned by her master."

"And no doubt was," added Miranda, with an assumption of weariness.

"It appeared that her saloon had caught fire; the saloon had been gutted and the *Tarifa's* papers destroyed a year before," Wilbraham

A.E.W. MASON

resumed, untroubled by Mrs. Warriner's objections. "A pretty careless captain that, eh? A most uncommon careless captain, Mrs. Warriner? For a boat to lose her papers—well, its pretty much the same as when a girl loses her marriage lines in the melodramas. A most uncommon careless captain! Or a most astute one, you say. What? Well, I'll not deny but what you may be right. For that brigantine caught fire and burned her papers just about the date when the *Ten Brothers* went ashore on Rosevear. How's that for the long arm?"

"But you did not see my husband," said Miranda, stubbornly.

"And why?" asked Wilbraham, and answered his question. "Because your husband wasn't onboard."

"Then the whole story falls to the ground," exclaimed Miranda, as she rose from her seat.

"Wait a bit, Mrs. Warriner," said Wilbraham, and he sat down on the seat and nursed his leg. "The *Tarifa* was supposed to belong to her master, who went by the name of John Wilson. Now here's a funny thing. I never saw John Wilson, though I prowled about the docks enough. The port-officers described him to me, a grizzled seafaring man of fifty; but he was always snug in his cabin, and a mate did the show business with the cargo. I grew curious about John Wilson; I wanted to see John Wilson. Accordingly I located the chart-room from the wharf, then I put on a black thumb tie and a dirty collar so as to look like a clerk, and I walked boldly down the gangway and stepped across the deck. I chose my time, you understand. I knocked at the chart-room door. 'Come in,' said a voice, and in I walked. Mrs. Warriner, you could have knocked me down with that dainty parasol of yours if you had been present when I first saw John Wilson.

"'What do you want?' says he, short and sharp.

"'Will you take a load of cotton to Valencia?' says I, and I quoted an insignificant price.

"'I am not such a fool as you look,' said he, and out I went and shook hands with myself on the quay. For John Wilson—"

"Was not my husband," exclaimed Miranda, with almost a despairing violence. "He was not! He was not!"

"You are right, Mrs. Warriner, he was not. But he was a man whom you and I knew as Thomas Discipline, first mate of the schooner-yacht the *Ten Brothers*, of which Captain Ralph Warriner was the certificated master. And observe, please, the whole crew of the *Ten Brothers* was reported lost upon Rosevear."

"Thomas Discipline might have left the *Ten Brothers* before," argued Miranda. "His presence on the *Tarifa* does not connect my husband with that boat."

"That's precisely the objection which occurred to me," said Wilbraham, coolly. "But here was at last a fact which fitted in with my guess-work, and I own to being uplifted. That evening I got the ticket that the *Tarifa* was to put to sea the next day, and sure enough in the morning she swung out into the fairway and waited for the evening ebb. I passed that day in an altogether unenviable state of anxiety, Mrs. Warriner; for if by any chance I was wrong, if she did not mean to take up another cargo of a more profitable kind by dark, if she were to sail clean away for Ushant on the evening ebb, why, the boat might be the *Ten Brothers* or it might not, and the master might be the late Captain Warriner or he might not. Any way the bottom fell clean out of my little business. But she did not; she got her anchors in about eight o'clock and reached out towards the Lizard in the dusk with a light wind from the land on her beam."

"The story so far," Miranda interrupted, "seems nautical, but hardly to the point."

"Think so?" said Wilbraham, indifferently. "Did I mention that at the mouth of the harbour the *Tarifa* passed a steam launch pottering around the St. Anthony Light? Between you and me, Mrs. Warriner, I was holding the tiller of that steam launch."

"You!" she exclaimed.

"Just poor little me," said he, smiling politely, "with a few paltry thick-uns in my pocket to speculate in the hire of a steam launch. I gave the *Tarifa* a start and followed, keeping well away on her lee with her red light just in view. That first half-hour or so was a wearing time for me, Mrs. Warriner, I assure you," and he took off his hat and wiped his forehead, as though the anxiety came back upon him now. He laboured his breath and broke up his sentences with short nervous laughter. He seemed entirely to forget his companion, and the sun, and the Andalusian sierras across the plain; he was desperately hunting the *Tarifa* along the Spit to the Lizard point.

"I was certain of one thing: that no Captain Warriner had come aboard at Falmouth. So if the *Tarifa* kept out to sea, why, there was no Captain Warriner to come aboard, and here was I spending my last pounds in running down a will-o'-the-wisp, and the world to face again to-morrow in the grim old way, without a penny to my purse. On the

A.E.W. MASON

other hand, if there was a Captain Warriner, he would come aboard with the cargo somewhere that night, and I fancied I could lay my finger on that somewhere. I had another cause for anxiety. Grant my guess-work correct, and the last thing the *Tarifa* was likely to hanker after would be a wasp of a steam launch buzzing in her wake. The evening was hazy, by a stroke of luck, but the wind was light and the sea smooth, and my propeller throbbed out over the water until I thought it must reverberate across the world, and the Esquimaux on Franz Josef Land and the Kanaka in the Pacific would hear it plain as the pulsing of a battleship. However, I slowed the launch down to less than half-speed, and the crew of the *Tarifa* made no account of me. The brigantine was doing only a leisurely five knots—she was waiting for the dark, I conjectured. Conjectured? I came near to praying it. And as if in answer to my prayer—it sounds pretty much like blasphemy now, doesn't it?—but at that moment I believed it—all at once her red light vanished and my heart went jumping in the inside of me as though it had slipped its moorings. For the *Tarifa* had changed her course; she was pointing closer to the wind and the wind came offshore; she was showing me her stern instead of her port beam; on the course she was lying now she couldn't clear the Manacles—not by any manner of means. She was heading for the anchorage I hoped she would; she was standing in towards Helford river. In a little she went about, and seeing her green light, I slowed down again. I could afford to take it easy."

He drew a breath of relief and lolled back upon his seat. Miranda no longer put questions; there was a look of discouragement upon her face; she began bitterly to feel herself helpless in this man's hands, as clay under the potter's thumb.

"Do you know the creek?" he asked, and did not wait for an answer. "I hadn't anchored there for twenty years, but I had a chart of it in my memories." His voice softened, with perhaps some recollection of a yachting trip in the days before his life had grown sour. "Steep hills on each side, and on each side woods. The trees run down and thrust their knees into the water like animals at their watering places of an evening. A mile or so up, a little rose and honeysuckle village nestles as pretty as a poem. There's a noise of birds all day, and all night and day the trees talk. Given a westerly wind, and the summer, I don't know many places which come up to Helford river," and his voice ceased, and he sat in a muse. A movement at his side recalled him. "But that's not business, you say," he resumed briskly. "I left the *Tarifa* at the mouth of the creek. The little village a mile or more up is on the southward side; opposite to it, on the Falmouth side, is the coast-guard station; nearer to the mouth, and still on the Falmouth side, a tiny dingle shelters a school-house and half-a-dozen cottages, and still nearer, the road from Falmouth comes over the brow of the hill and dips down along the hill-side. At one point the steep hill-side is broken, there's an easy incline of sand and bushes and soil between the water and the road. The incline is out of sight of the coast-guard. Besides, it is only just round the point and close to the sea. And for that reason I was in no particular hurry to follow the *Tarifa*. I edged the launch close in under the point, waded ashore, and scrambled along in the dark until I reached the break in the hill-side. Then I lay down among the bushes and waited. All lights were out on the *Tarifa*, but I could see her hull dimly, a blot of solid black against the night's unsubstantial blackness. I waited for centuries and æons. There was neither moon nor any star. At last I heard a creaking sound that came from the other end of the world. It was repeated, it grew louder, it became many sounds, the sounds or cart wheels on the dry road. I looked at my watch; the glimmer of its white face made it possible for me to tell the hour. It was five minutes to eleven. For five minutes the sounds drew infinitesimally nearer. Higher up the creek six bells were struck upon a yacht, and then over the waters from the direction of the *Tarifa* came cautiously the wooden rattle of oars in the rowlocks of a boat. A boat, I say, but it was followed by another and another. The three boats grounded on the sand as the carts reached the break in the hill-side. There were few words spoken, and no light shown. I lay in the bushes straining my ears to catch a familiar voice, my eyes on the chance that a match might be struck and light up a familiar face."

"Well?" said Miranda, breaking in upon his speech. She was strung to a high pitch or excitement, and her face and voice betrayed it.

"I was disappointed," replied Wilbraham, "but I saw something of the cargo which the waggons brought over the hill and the boats carried on board. Backwards and forwards between the *Tarifa* and the shore they were rowed with unremitting diligence and caution, carrying first longish packing-cases of some weight, as I could gather from the conduct of the men who stumbled with them down the incline. And after the packing-cases, square boxes, yet more unwieldy than the long cases, if one takes the proportion of size. The morning was breaking before the last boat was hoisted on board, and the last waggon had creaked out of hearing over the hill."

"And what was the cargo?" asked Miranda.

"That was the question which troubled me," replied Wilbraham. "I lay on the hill-side in the chill of the morning as disheartened a man as you can imagine. Through a break in the bushes I watched the *Tarifa* below me, her decks busy with the movement of her crew and from her galley the comfortable smoke coiling up into the air. Breakfast! A Gargantuan appetite suddenly pinched my stomach. Had Warriner gone on board with the cargo? And what was the cargo? And into what harbour would the *Tarifa* carry it? I had found out nothing. Then on board the brigantine men gathered at the windlass, a chain clinked musically as the anchor was hove short, the gaff of her mainsail creaked up the mast, and the festoons of her canvas were unfolded. The *Tarifa* was outward bound and I had discovered nothing. I was like a man tied hand and foot and a treasure within his reach. I had had my fingers on the treasure. Again the chain rattled on the windlass; she broke out her foresail and her jib; I saw the water sparkle under her foot and stream out a creaming pennant in her wake. I had lost. In the space of a second I lived through every minute of my last fifteen years and their dreary vicissitudes. I lived in anticipation through another fifteen similar in every detail, and fairly shuddered to think there might be another fifteen still to follow those. I stretched myself out and ground my face in the sand and cursed God with all my heart for the difference between man and man. And meanwhile the *Tarifa*, with a hint of the sun upon her topsails, slipped out over the tide to sea."

Wilbraham's face was quite convulsed by the violence of his recollections; and with so vivid a sincerity, with a voice so mutable, had he described the growth and extinction of his hopes, that Miranda almost forgot their object, almost found herself sympathising with his endeavours, almost regretted their failure—until she remembered that after all he had not failed, or he would not have been sitting beside her in the Alameda.

"Well," she said in a hard voice, "you failed. What then?"

"I crawled down to my launch, the cheapest man in the United Kingdom. My engineer was muffled up in a pilot jacket and uncommon surly and cheap too. I hadn't the pluck left in me to resent his impudence, and we crept back to Falmouth. All the way I was pestered with that question, 'What was the cargo I had seen shipped that night in Helford river?' I couldn't get it out of my head. The propeller lashed it out with a sort of vindictiveness. The little waves breaking ashore whispered about it, as though they knew very well, but wouldn't peach. When I had landed in Falmouth, I found that I was walking towards the Free Library. The doors, however, were still closed. I breakfasted in a fever of impatience and was back again at the doors before they were opened. You may take it from me, Mrs. Warriner, I was the first student inside the building that morning. I read over again every scrap of news and comment about the inquest in Scilly which I could pester the Librarian to unearth; and points which in my hurry I had overlooked before, began to take an air of importance. The old man Fournier, for instance; it seemed sort of queer that a taxidermist of Tangier should come all the way to Scilly for a month's holiday. Eh, what? What was old man Fournier doing at Scilly? Scilly's a likely place for wrecks. Was old man Fournier a hanger-on upon chance, a nautical Mr. Micawber waiting for a wreck to turn up which would suit his purpose? Or had he stage-managed by some means or other the *coup de theater* on Rosevear? It seemed funny that the short-sighted man should spot the wreck on Rosevear before the St. Agnes men, eh? Suppose M. Fournier and Ralph Warriner were partners in that pretty cargo! I walked straight out of that library, feeling quite certain that I held the right end of the skein. I had made a mistake in following up Warriner. I ought to have followed up the taxidermist. I walked about Falmouth all that day puzzling the business out; and I came to the conclusion that the sooner I crossed to the Scillies the better. I was by this time fairly excited, and I think I should have spent my last farthing in the hunt even if I had known that when I had run the mystery to earth, it would not profit me at all. I took a train that very evening, and pottered about from station to station all night. In the morning I got to Penzance, and kicked my heels on the wharf of the little dock there until nine o'clock, when the *Lyonnesse* started for St. Mary's. Three hours later I saw the islands hump themselves up from the sea, and I stared and stared at them till a genial being standing beside me said, 'I suppose you haven't been home for a good many years.'—By the way, Mrs. Warriner," he suddenly broke off, "I have heard that natural sherry is a drink in some favour hereabouts. I can't say that it's a beverage I have ever hankered after before, but what with the sun and the talk, the thought of it is at the present moment most seductive. What if we rang down the curtain for ten minutes and had an *entr'acte*, eh? Would you mind?" And Wilbraham rose from his seat.

"No," said Miranda. "Please finish what you have to say now."

Wilbraham sighed, resumed his seat and at the same time his story.

A.E.W. MASON

VIII

Explains the Mystery of the "Tarifa's" Cargo

At St. Mary's," he continued, "I called at once upon the doctor. 'Ah,' said he, 'liver, I suppose.'

"'Permanently enlarged by excessive indulgence in alcohol,' said I. 'I had once a very dear friend in the same case called Ralph Warriner.'"

Here Miranda interrupted with considerable indignation. "There is not a word of truth in that."

"There is not," Wilbraham agreed pleasantly; "but I had to introduce the subject some way, and my way was successful. 'Ralph Warriner!' exclaimed the doctor. 'And what was he dismissed the service for?' I winked very slowly, with intense cunning; 'I understand,' said the doctor, with a leer, though Heaven only knows what he did understand; I fancy he thought his reputation as a man of the world was at stake. After that the conversation went on swimmingly.

"I was more than ever convinced that the discovery on Rosevear was a put-up job. If so, old man Fournier must have been aware of that wreck before he discovered it. He must have landed on the island and shoved those papers into the dead man's pocket; and someone must have sailed him out to the island. I determined to lay myself out to discover who that someone was; but I went no farther than the determination. There was not indeed any need that I should, for I sailed myself the next day to Rosevear. I hired the *St. Agnes* lugger, and Zebedee Isaacs, as he sat at the tiller, gave me news of old man Fournier. Old man Fournier was a desperate coward on the sea, yet he had put out to the Bishop on a most unpleasing day. It was old man Fournier who insisted that they should run through the Neck and examine Rosevear, and when Zebedee Isaacs declined the risk, old man Fournier flung himself in a passion on the tiller and nearly swamped the boat. All very queer, eh? M. Fournier must have had some fairly strong motive to nerve him to that pitch of audacity. And what that motive was I should discover when I discovered the nature of the *Tarifa's* cargo. I thought perpetually about that cargo, all the way to Rosevear, and after I had landed on that melancholy island. The truth came upon me in a moment of inspiration.

The ground I remember gave way under my foot. I had trodden on a sea-bird's nest and stumbled forward on my knees, and with the shock of the stumble came the inspiration. I remained on my knees, with the gulls screaming overhead, and the grey wastes of ocean moaning about the unkindly rocks. And I knew! The taxidermist from Tangier, the longish packing-cases, the square boxes—Ralph Warriner and old man Fournier were running guns and ammunition into Morocco!"

Miranda could not repress an exclamation. She had no doubt that Wilbraham was right; the theory fitted in with Ralph's adventurous character. M. Fournier no doubt made the arrangements, and provided the capital; Ralph worked the cargo across from England to Morocco. And to make it safe for himself to venture upon English soil, he had altered the rig of the *Tarifa* in some unfrequented port, and somehow arranged the deception concerning his death.

"You think as I thought in Rosevear," said Wilbraham, looking shrewdly into her face. "I only wish you could participate in the delight I felt. I had my fingers on the secret now, and it was such a perfect, profitable secret, for, quite apart from the other affair, gun-running in Morocco is itself an offence against the law. I fairly hugged myself. 'Ambrose,' said I, 'never in all your puff have you struck anything like this. Fouché you shall trample under foot and Sherlock Holmes shall be your washpot; you are the best in the world. The faceless mariner was a fraud, a freak from Barnum's. Here at last is Eldorado, and there's no fly anywhere upon the gilding.' Thus, Mrs. Warriner, I soliloquised, and took the next boat back to Penzance; from Penzance I travelled by train to Plymouth; from Plymouth I sailed in an Orient boat to Gib, and from Gib I crossed to Tangier, where I had a few minutes' conversation with one or two officers of the custom-house.

"Morocco as a social institution has many points of convenience which it is useful for men like Warriner and myself to know. Here's a small case in point. If you wish to smuggle forbidden goods into the country, you hire the custom-house officials to unload your cargo for you at night somewhere on the beach. Thus you avoid much trouble, all chance of detection and you secure skilled workmen. I had no doubt that Warriner had followed this course. So I hired the custom-house officials to tell me the truth, and out it came. The *Tarifa* had landed its cargo in the bay a mile and a half from Tangier a couple of days before I arrived, and M. Fournier had supervised the unloading, and the captain of the *Tarifa* was no longer the grizzled sea-dog, Mr. Thomas

Discipline, but a gentleman of a slight figure, blue eyes, and fair hair. That middle-aged cherub, in a word, with whom you and I are both familiar, and who now calls himself Mr. Jeremy Bentham. When I had derived this information I walked into M. Fournier's shop and bought a stuffed jackal. There was a tourist making purchases, so I asked my question quietly as I leaned my elbows on the counter.

"'How did you work the situation on Rosevear?' said I, 'and how's my sweet friend, Ralph Warriner?'

"The little Frenchman turned white and sick. He babbled expostulations and denials. He demanded my name—"

"You gave him your card, I hope," interrupted Miranda, biting her lip. Wilbraham gazed at her with admiration. "Well, you have got some spirit. I will say that for you, Mrs. Warriner."

"I am not in need of testimonials," said Miranda. "What of M. Fournier?"

"He talked to me mysteries after that. 'You were in Tangier a month ago,' said he. 'You shouted "Look out!" through the door; you startled a friend of mine; you are a coward.' Would you believe it, the little worm turned? He flew into a violent passion; I suppose it was in just such a passion that he flung himself on Zebedee Isaacs at Scilly. A plucky little man for all his cowardice! He called me a number of ill names. However, I had got what I wanted. I crossed back to Gibraltar, and here I am."

Wilbraham crossed his legs, and with a polite "You will permit me?" lighted a cigarette.

"I see," said Miranda, with a contemptuous droop of her lips. "Having failed to blackmail M. Fournier and my husband, you fall back upon blackmailing a woman."

Wilbraham's answer to the sneer was entirely unexpected, even by Miranda, who was prepared for the unexpected in this man. He showed no shame; he did not try to laugh away the slur; but removing his cigarette from his mouth, he turned deliberately his full face to her and in a deliberate voice said: "I do not take the conventional view upon these matters. And, all other things being equal, had I to choose between a man and a woman, I should spare the man and strike the woman."

He spoke without any bitterness, but in a hard, calm voice, as though he had sounded the question to the bottom. Miranda gasped, the words for a second took her breath away, and then the blood came warmly into her cheeks, and her eyes softened and brightened and she smiled. A sudden glory seemed to illuminate her face. Wilbraham wondered why. He could not know that the brutal shock of his speech had sent her thoughts winging back to a balcony overlooking St. James's Park, where a man had held a torn glove in his hand and in a no less decided voice than Wilbraham's had spoken quite other words.

"I never intended to address either Fournier or your husband upon the subject of—shall we call it compensation? At the best I should have got a lump sum now and again from them, and as I say, I have learnt my lesson. If I had a lump sum, it would be spent, and I should again be penniless. I apply to you because I propose a regular sum per annum paid quarterly in advance."

Miranda was still uplifted by the contrast between her recollections and Wilbraham's words. She had the glove at home locked up, an evidence that succour was very near—a hundred miles only down the winding valley which faced her—and she had not even to say a word in order to command it. When she spoke again to Wilbraham she spoke emboldened by this knowledge.

"And what if I were to refuse you even a shilling for your dinner?"

"I should be compelled to lay my information before the proper authorities, that Ralph Warriner is alive and may at times be captured in England."

"Would you be surprised to hear that Mr. Warriner committed no crime for which he could be captured?"

"I should be surprised beyond words. Mr. Warriner sold the mechanism of the Daventry gun to a foreign government."

"Are you so sure of that?"

"I was his agent."

"You! Then you are also his accomplice."

"True,—and I look forward to turning Queen's evidence."

Miranda withdrew from the contest. The discussion was hardly more than academic, for she knew both that her husband was alive and that this particular crime he had committed.

"What is your price?" she asked, and she sat down upon the bench.

Wilbraham did not immediately reply. He took a pocket-book from his coat and a letter from the pocket-book.

"I should wish you fully to understand the strength of my position," he said. "This letter you will see is in your husband's handwriting. This passage," and he folded the letter to show Miranda a line or two, "enjoins me to be very careful about the plans. The gun is not mentioned by name, but the date of the letter and the context leave no possible doubt."

He fluttered the letter under Miranda's eyes and within reach of her fingers.

"It is my one piece of evidence, but a convincing piece."

He made a pretence of dropping it at her feet and snatched it up quickly. Then he replaced it in his pocket-book and shut up his pocket-book with a snap.

"Why didn't you snatch at it?" he exclaimed with irritation.

"Why did you wish me to snatch at it?" she replied.

"Because—because," he said angrily, "you have made me feel real mean, as mean as a man in the commission of his first dishonourable act towards a woman, and I wanted you to look mean at all events; it would have made my business easier to handle. Well, let's have done with it. I know Ralph Warriner is alive. I can give information which may lead to his capture; and there's always the disgrace to publish."

He blurted out the words, ashamed and indignant with her for the shame he felt. Miranda, in spite of herself, was touched by Wilbraham's manner, and she answered quite gently: "Very well. I will buy your silence."

"Coals of fire!" he replied with a sneer. Miranda understood that he was defying her to make him feel ashamed. "Is that the ticket, Mrs. Warriner? It won't lessen the amount of the per annum I can assure you. What I propose is to live for the future in some more or less quiet hole, where none of my acquaintances are likely to crop up. Tarifa occurred to me; for one thing I can reach you from Tarifa; for another I can do the royal act at Tarifa on a moderate income; for a third it is a quiet place where I can have a shot at—well, at what I want to do," and his voice suddenly became shy. She looked at him and he coloured under her glance, and he shifted in his seat and laughed awkwardly.

Miranda was familiar with those signs and what they signified. Wilbraham wanted her to ask him to confide in her. Many men at Gibraltar had brought their troubles to her in just this way, with just these marks of diffidence, this fear that the troubles would bore her. She had been called upon to play the guardian-angel at times and had not shrunk from the responsibility, though she had accepted it with a saving modesty of humour at the notion of herself playing the guardian-angel to any man.

"What is it you want to do?" she asked, and Wilbraham confided in her. The position was strange, no doubt. Here was a woman whom he had bullied, whom he meant to rob, and on whom he meant to live until he died, and he was confiding in her. But the words tumbled from his lips and he did not think of the relationship in which he stood to her. He was only aware that for fifteen years he had not shared a single one of his intimate thoughts with either man or woman, and he was surcharged with them. Here was a woman, frank, reliable, who asked for his confidence, and he gave it, with a schoolboy's mixture of eagerness and timidity.

"Do you know," said he, "the Odes of Horace have never been well translated into English verse by anyone? Some people have done an ode or two very well, perhaps as well as it could be done—Hood for instance tried his hand at it. But no one has done them all, with any approach to success. And yet they ought to be capable of translation. Perhaps they aren't—I don't know—perhaps they are too wonderfully perfect. Probably I should make an awful hash of the job; but I think I should like to have a shot. I began years and years ago when I was an attaché at Paris, and—and I have always kept the book with me; but one has had no time." As he spoke he drew from his side pocket a little copy of Horace in an old light-brown cover of leather very much frayed and scratched. "Look," said he, and half stretched it out to her, as though doubtful whether he should put it into her hands or refuse to let her take it at all. She held out her hand, and he made up his mind and gave it into her keeping.

The copy was dated 1767; the rough black type, in which all the s's looked like f's, was margined by paper brown with age and sullied with the rims of tumblers and the stains of tobacco; and this stained margin was everywhere written over with ink in a small fine hand.

"You see I have made a sort of ground-work," said Wilbraham, with a deprecating laugh, as though he feared Miranda would ridicule his efforts. The writing consisted of tags of verse, half-lines, here and there complete lines, and sometimes, though rarely, a complete stanza. "You must not judge by what you see there," he made haste to add. "All I have written on the margin is purely tentative; probably it's no good at all." Miranda turned over a page and came upon one ode completely translated. "I did that," explained Wilbraham, "one season when I

A.E.W. MASON

shipped as a hand on a Yarmouth smack. We got bad weather on the Dogger Bank, out in the North Sea at Christmas. We spent a good deal of time hove to with the wheel lashed, and on night-watches I used to make up the verses. Indeed, those night-watches seem the only time I have had free during the last fifteen years. The rest of the time—well, I have told you about it. I got through one complete ode out in the North Sea, and did parts of others."

Mrs. Warriner began to read the ode. "May I?" she asked.

"Of course," said he, with a flush of pleasure, and he watched her most earnestly for the involuntary signs of approval or censure. But her face betrayed neither the one nor the other; and he was quick to apologise for the ode's shortcomings.

"You mustn't think that I had a great deal of time on those night-watches. For one thing we did not get over-much sleep on the voyage, and so one's brains no doubt were a trifle dull. Besides, there were always seas combing up above the bows and roaring along the deck. You had to keep your eyes open for them and scuttle down the companion before they came on board. Otherwise, if the weight of the water took you, it was a case of this way to the pit. The whole hull of the smack disappears, and you just see the foresail sticking up from the hungry, lashing tumble of green water. So, you see, it stands to reason that ode is subject to revision."

But Miranda was not thinking of the ode. She had a vision of the smack labouring on a black night in the trough of a black sea flecked with white, at Christmas time, and a man on the watch, who had been an attaché at Paris, and was, even with the rude sailor-folk for his companions, engaged in translating Horace; and the vision had an exquisite pathos for her.

"What was the beginning of it all?" she asked in a low voice, and since Wilbraham was in the train of confidences, he told her that too.

He told her perhaps more than he meant to tell. It was an old story, the story of the faithless woman and the man who trusts her, and what comes of it all. The story of Helen and Menelaus, but disfigured into a caricature of its original by the paltriness of the characters and the vulgarity of the incidents. The throb of primitive passion was gone from the story, and therefore all dignity too. Subtle and intricate trivialities of sentiment took the place of passion, and made the episode infinitely mean. Menelaus was an attaché at Paris: Helen lived at Knightsbridge, and the pair of them were engaged to be married. Helen was faithless merely through a cheap vanity, and a cheaper pose of wilfulness, and even so she was faithless merely in a low and despicable way. It was an infidelity of innumerable flirtations. She passed from arm to arm without intermission, and almost allowed those who fondled her to overlap. Yet all the day she talked of her pride, and was conscious of no inconsistency between the vulgarity of her conduct and the high words upon her lips. She practised all the small necessary deceits to conceal her various meetings and appointments, and was unaware of the degradation they involved; for still she talked loudly of her pride. And when Menelaus lifted his hat and wished her good-morning, she only felt that she was deeply aggrieved.

Menelaus, however, was in no better case. He had not the strength to thrust her from his mind, but let his thoughts play sensuously with his recollections, until he declined upon a greater and a greater weakness.

"I went back to Paris," continued Wilbraham. "I had good prospects, but they came to nothing. Even now men going in for Mods. have to get up a book which I once wrote, and as for the service, if I were to tell you my real name, it is just possible that you might have heard it, for I was supposed to have done something quite decent at Zanzibar. Well, I went back to Paris. It's a hard thing, you know, to discover that the woman you have been working for, and in a way succeeding for, isn't worth the nicotine at the bottom of your pipe-bowl. At that time I reckon I would rather have been the wreck I am now, and believed it was all my fault, for, you see, I might then have imagined that if I had done all right, I should have won the desirable woman. . . Anyway, after I got back to Paris, a little while after, there was trouble." Wilbraham examined his cane and drew diagrams upon the ground. "The woman blabbed, in a moment of confidence. . . to her husband. There was a sort of a scandal. . . I had to go. I didn't blame the woman who blabbed; no, Mrs. Warriner, I blamed the first woman, the woman in Knightsbridge. Was I right? I came back to England. I was a second son, and my father slammed the door in my face. Then, Mrs. Warriner, I blamed all women, you—you—you amongst the others, even though I didn't know you." He spoke in a gust of extraordinary violence, and so brought his confidences to an end. "Now your income is—" he resumed, and fetched out his pocket-book again. "I made a note about your estate when I was doing business with Warriner," he said. "The note comes in usefully now."

He found the details of which he was in search, and made a neat little sum at the corner of the leaf, to which Miranda paid no attention whatsoever. The queer inclination towards pity which had moved her to ask for his confidence, had been entirely and finally destroyed by the confidence she had asked for. The story was so utterly sordid; the characters in it so utterly puny. Before he told it he had acquired in her eyes even a sort of dignity, the dignity of a man battered and defeated in a battle wherein his wits were unequally matched against the solid forces of order; but in the telling he had destroyed that impression. Miranda had no feeling now but one of aversion for the wreck of a man at her side. She looked at the Horace, which still lay open on her lap, and the contrast between the fine scholar's handwriting and the stains of the pothouse had no longer any power to touch her. She set the book down on the bench, and stood up.

Wilbraham stopped his calculations, and, with the stump of his pencil in his mouth, looked at her alertly and furtively. She took a step or two towards the parapet of the Alameda. Wilbraham instantly laid his pocket-book on the seat with the pencil to mark the place, and without any noise, stood up. Miranda reached the railings at the edge of the gardens and leaned her arms upon it. The next moment she felt a firm grip upon her elbow. She turned round and saw Wilbraham's face ablaze with passion. "I suspected that," he said fiercely, "when first I saw where you had brought me," and he shook her elbow.

"Suspected what?" exclaimed Miranda, and she drew away to free herself from his grasp. Wilbraham's next movement answered her question. For he slipped between her and the railings with a glance at the precipice below.

"But you shall not do it," he continued. "I was robbed that way once before; I'll take care the robbery is not repeated." He leaned his back against the railings and shook his finger at her.

"Besides, there's no sense in it," and he jerked his head backwards to signify the abysm. "You are crying out before you are hurt. You don't even know how much I want; I shan't ruin you. I made a mistake that way once; I had the best secret conceivable, and ran my man down across two continents. Then I was fool enough to put my hand too deep in his sky, and I suppose he thought—well, he blew his brains out that night, and then was I robbed."

Mrs. Warriner stared at him with a growing horror in her eyes. "You murdered him," she said slowly.

"We won't quarrel over words," said Wilbraham, callously.

Miranda walked back to the bench. She was not troubled to explain Wilbraham's misconception of her movement. She was only anxious to be rid of him. "What income do you want?" she asked.

"You have three thousand a year," he returned. "Of that I take it Warriner takes a largish slice."

Miranda flushed. "My husband has never asked for a farthing since the *Ten Brothers* slipped out of Gibraltar. He has never received a farthing," she said angrily.

"An imprudent remark," said Wilbraham. "I might feel inclined to raise my price."

"At all events you shall not slander him."

Wilbraham looked at her with his head cocked on one side. "You are very loyal," said he, with genuine admiration. "I will not raise my price."

Miranda did not, by any gesture or word, acknowledge his compliment. She stood over against him with a face just as hard and white as he had shown to her.

"I say seven hundred a year," he said briefly. "I will call for it myself every quarter."

"I will send it to you," she interrupted.

"I prefer to call for it," said he; for so he concealed his own address and kept her within his reach. "You will not leave Ronda even for a week without giving me due notice of your destination. I will take a quarter's payment to-day. You draw on a bank in Ronda, I suppose, so a cheque will serve."

"If you will wait here, I will bring you the cheque."

Twenty minutes afterwards she returned with it to the Alameda, where she found Wilbraham seated on the bench with his Horace in his hand. He put down the book awkwardly, and rose. He had the grace to feel some discomfort as he took the cheque, and that discomfort his manner expressed.

Miranda had no word, no look, for him. He stood perhaps for the space of a minute fingering the cheque. Then he said suddenly: "I can't imagine what a woman like you sees in Ralph Warriner to trouble about. In your place I should have let him go his own way, without paying to keep him out of prison."

Miranda kept her reasons to herself, as she had done with the reason of her return to Ronda. She waited for him to go, and he walked sullenly away—for ten yards. Then he returned, for he had left his copy of Horace lying upon the bench. He picked it up with a curious and almost timorous glance of appeal towards Miranda. She did not move but waited implacably for his departure. Wilbraham worked his shoulders in discomfort.

"My clothes don't fit and God hates me," he cried irritably. Then this jack-in-the-box of fortune slunk out of her sight.

IX

Shows the Use Which a Blind Man May Make of a Dark Night a Week

A week after Wilbraham's departure from Ronda, the night fell very dark at Tangier. In the Sôk outside the city gate, the solitary electric lamp from its tall mast threw a pale light over a circle of the trampled grass, but outside the circle all was black. There was no glimmer in the tents of the shoemakers at the upper corner of the Sôk; nor was there any stir or noise. For it was past midnight and the world was asleep—except at one spot on the hill-side above the Sôk, and a little distance to the right.

There a small villa, standing by itself, shone gaudily in the heart of the blackness. From its open windows a yellow flood of light streamed out, and besides the light, the music of a single violin and the rhythmical beat of feet. There were other noises too, such as the popping of corks, and much laughter.

Outside the villa, and beyond the range of its light, a man and a boy sat patient and silent. The man for his sole clothing wore a sack, but a dark cloak lay on the ground beside him. With his hands he continually tested a cord twisted from palmetto fibres, as though doubtful of its strength. At length the door of the villa opened.

"Who comes out?" asked the man.

"A man and a woman," answered the boy.

"Describe the man to me."

"Big, fat—"

"That is enough."

The man and the woman passed through the little garden of the villa, and walked down across the Sôk towards the city gate. The door opened again and again. There was a continual sound of leave-taking in different languages, mostly German and French, and between the man and the boy the same dialogue was repeated and repeated. Some wore evening dress, others did not. Some walked across the Sôk, others rode.

"They are all gone," said the boy.

"Wait," commanded the man.

"They are putting out the lights."

"Are all the lights out?"

"No, one light is burning."

"Wait!"

The door opened again, and two men in evening dress came out on to the steps.

"There are two men," said the boy, "but only one wears a hat."

"Describe him to me."

"He is not tall, he is thin, but I cannot see his face for his hat."

"Look! look well!"

"He goes back into the house. He takes off his hat. Wait! He is smoking. He strikes a match and holds it to his mouth. I can see him now."

"Well! Of what colour is his hair?"

"Very fair—yellow. His face is round, his eyes are light."

The man in the sack ceased from his questions, but he gave no sign of either approval or disappointment. He sat still in the darkness until a voice from the little garden cried out with a French accent: "I cannot think what has come to the beast. He has got loose. And he was hobbled, Jeremy. You did hobble him, *hein?* "

The boy began to laugh. "The little fat Christian is looking for the mule in the garden," said he. "Hush!" whispered the man, laying his hand upon the boy's mouth. "Listen! What does the other answer? Listen for his voice."

"He does not answer," returned the boy. "He leans against the door, and smokes and waits, while the little fat Room searches for the mule."

"Help to find the mule!"

The boy laughed again, rose from the ground, and disappeared into the darkness. In a few minutes he returned, driving the mule in front of him. He drove it through the wicket of the garden. A few words passed between the little Frenchman and the boy. Then the boy came back to the man seated patiently outside the rim of the villa's lights.

"What did he say to thee?" said the man.

"He asked me if I had stolen the hobbles."

"And thou didst answer?"

"That I knew nothing of the hobbles. I said that I had found the mule loose in the Sôk, and seeing the lights, brought it to the house."

"It is well. Now go, my son; go home and sleep, and forget the hours we have waited in the darkness outside the villa of the Room. Forget, so that in the morning they shall never have been. Go! God will reward thee!"

The boy turned upon his heel, and ran down towards the town. The man was left alone. He remained squatting on the ground. He heard the French voice exclaim: "Good-night, Jeremy."

But no answering voice returned the wish. Jeremy indeed contented himself with a careless nod of the head, mounted his mule, and passed out of the wicket gate. Jeremy passed within ten yards of the man seated upon the ground, who heard the padding of the mule's feet upon the grass and smelt the cigar.

He did not move, however. A road ran between this stretch of grass and the Sôk beyond, and he waited until the mule's hooves rang upon it. Then he picked up the dark cloak by his side and ran swiftly and noiselessly down the grass, across the road, over the trampled Sôk. Ahead of him he heard the leisurely amble of the mule.

"Stop!" he cried out in the Moghrebbin dialect. "I have the hobbles of the most noble one."

He heard the mule stop, and ran lightly forward.

"Who is it?" asked Jeremy, in the same tongue, as he bent round in his saddle.

"Hassan Akbar," cried the other, leaping at the point from which the voice came. "Bentham, it is Hassan Akbar."

The man addressed as Bentham turned quickly in his saddle with a cry and gathered up the reins; but he was too late. Even the cry was stifled upon his lips. For Hassan threw the cloak over his head, gathered it in tight round his neck, and still holding him by the neck, dragged him out of the saddle and flung him on to the ground. Bentham, half-throttled, half-stunned, lay for a moment or two upon his back, limp and unresisting. When he came to himself, it was no longer within his power to resist, for Hassan knelt straddled across his body, pinning him to the ground with the weight of his stature. One bony knee pressed upon his chest insufferably. Bentham's ribs cracked under it; he felt that his ribs were being driven into his lungs. The other knee held down his thighs, and while he lay there incapable of defence, Hassan bound his arms tightly together with the cord of palmetto fibres.

Bentham tried to shout, but the cloak was over his mouth: the knee was grinding and boring into his chest, and his shout was an exiguous wail which, when it had penetrated the cloak, was no more than a sigh. He waited for the moment when the knee would be removed, and waited motionless without a twitch of his muscles, so that Hassan might be deceived into the belief that he had swooned, and remove his knee and the cloak.

Hassan removed his knees, bent down to Bentham, twined one arm about his legs, thrust the other underneath his neck, and lifted him from the ground as though he was a child. Bentham was now less able to shout than before, for the hand of the arm which was about his neck pressed the cloak close upon his mouth.

Bentham struggled for his breath; Hassan's arms only tightened their grip and held him like a coil of wire. An utter terror seized upon Bentham. He remembered the darkness of the night, the lateness of the hour, the silence of the Sôk, and from the manner of Hassan's walk, he knew that he was being carried up the hill and away from Tangier. He was helpless in the hands of a Moor whom he had irreparably wronged. Death he knew he must expect; the question which troubled him was what kind of death.

Hassan's foot struck against a rope drawn tight across his path, and in Bentham hope for a moment revived. The rope was the stay of a tent, no doubt. What if Hassan had lost his way and stumbled among the tents of the shoemakers? But Hassan loosened the grip of the arm which held his legs, and Bentham heard him fumbling with his hand for the door-flap of the tent. Plainly Hassan had not missed his way.

Hassan dropt him on the ground, thrust him through the small opening, and crawled in after him. Then he knelt beside Bentham, turned back the cloak from his face, but tied it securely about his mouth. Bentham could now see, and the flap of the tent was open. The tent was indeed one of the low, tiny gunny-bag tents of the shoemakers, but it was set far apart from that small cluster, as Bentham recognized in despair, for through the aperture he could see a long way below him and a long way to his right the electric light in the middle of the Sôk.

Outside the tent there was a sound of something moving. Bentham sat up and tore at his gag with his bound hands.

"Why cry for help to a mule?" said Hassan, calmly. "Will a mule help thee?" He leaned forward and tightened the knot which fastened the cloak at the back of his head. Then he crawled out of the tent and Bentham heard him tethering the mule to one of the tent-pegs.

Bentham was thus left alone. He had a few seconds, and he had at once to determine what use he would make of those seconds. There was not enough time wherein to free his hands. It would have been sheer waste of time to free his mouth from the cloak. For none was within earshot of that tent who would be concerned to discover the reason of a cry, and the cry would not be repeated, since Hassan outside the tent was still within arm's reach.

Instead, he hitched and worked his white waistcoat upwards from the bottom, leaning forward the while, until his watch fell from the pocket and dangled on the end of the chain; after his watch a metal pencil-case rolled out and dropped between his knees. One of the two things he meant to do was done. Hassan had bound his hands not palm to palm, but wrist across wrist; and raising his hands he was able with the tips of his right-hand fingers to feel in the left-hand breast-pocket of his dress-coat. His fingers touched a small pocket-book, opened it, and plucked out a leaf of paper. This leaf and the pencil-case he secreted in the palm of his hand.

Hassan crawled back into the tent and closed the flap. Bentham, with his knees drawn up to his chin, crouched back against the wall of the tent. Now that the flap was closed, it was pitch-dark; that, however, made no difference to Hassan Akbar, who lived in darkness, and out of the darkness his voice spoke.

"The ways of God are very wonderful. You gave me this tent. With the dollar you dropped on my knees at the gate of the cemetery, I bought this tent and set it up here apart, to keep you safe for the little time before you start upon your journey."

Bentham took no comfort from the passionless voice, though his heart leaped at the words. He was not then to be killed. He did not answer Hassan, but remained crouched in his corner.

"Now the dog of a Christian will speak," said Hassan, quietly. Bentham made no movement. Hassan crawled towards him, felt his feet, his up-drawn knees, and reaching his face untied the cloak from his mouth. "Now the dog of a Christian will speak," he repeated softly, in a low gentle voice, "so that I may know it is indeed Bentham, who took shelter with me at Tangier, and ate of my *kouss-kouss*, and thereafter betrayed me."

Bentham did not reply. If Hassan had a doubt, then it was his part to make the most of it to prolong the solution of the doubt, to defer it, if it might be, till the morning came. This was summer—July—the morning comes early in July, not so early as in June, but still early. Would that this had happened one month back!

Hassan kneeled upon his hams by Bentham's side. "Will not the dog of a Christian speak?" he asked in a wheedling voice, which daunted and chilled the man he spoke to. "Let us see!" And again his sinuous hands lingered and stole over Bentham's face. The thumbs lingered about Bentham's eyes.

Bentham shivered; but still, though the desire to shout, to curse, to relieve by some violence, if only of speech, the tension he was suffering, was strong, he mastered himself, he held his tongue, for if once he did speak he betrayed himself. His only chance lay in Hassan's doubt, which lived upon his silence. Again Hassan's fingers returned to his face. Bentham closed his eyes; the thumbs touched and retouched them, now pressing gently upon the eyeballs, now working about the corners of the sockets. Finally Hassan snatched his hands away. "If I did that," he murmured, "they would not take him, for he would fetch no price;" and Bentham understood the fate which was in store for him—if he spoke.

Hassan left his side, and was busy in a corner of the tent, at what Bentham could not for the moment discover. He heard a cracking of twigs; what was to follow? One instant he dreaded, the next he burned to know, and all the while he shivered with terror. Hassan struck a match and lit the twigs, and breathed upon the little blue flames, until they warmed to yellow, and spirted up into a fire.

Bentham watched Hassan's gaunt, disfigured, inexpressive face, as he crouched over the twigs, and his terror increased. He saw that he held something in each hand, something that flashed bright, like a disk of iron. Hassan laid the disks upon the twigs; they were the hobbles which Bentham had placed upon his mule early that evening.

Bentham began to count the seconds; at any moment the morning might begin to break, surely, surely. As he watched the hobbles growing hot and the sparks dance upon the iron, he continued to count the seconds, not knowing what he did, and at an incredible speed.

Hassan picked up the hobbles, each with a cleft stick, and brought them over to Bentham. "Now the dog of a Christian will speak," said he.

Bentham summoned all his courage, all his strength, and was silent. Hassan reached out his hands, and drew his legs from under him, and fitted the hobbles over his slippers, and fixed them round his ankles like a pair of fetters.

Bentham uttered a cry—it was almost a scream—as the iron burnt into his flesh. He kicked, he struggled to free his legs, to free his hands; but Hassan Akbar dragged him forward, thrust him down upon his back, and pinned his shoulders to the ground. Bentham could do no more than vainly writhe in convulsive movements of his limbs. The hot iron rings clung to his ankles; the smoke from the wood fire choked him; the smell of burning flesh was acrid in his nostrils. Agony redoubled his strength, but even so, he was too crippled, and Hassan's grasp upon his shoulders did not relax.

In the end Hassan had his heart's desire, and Bentham spoke. He spoke too in the low voice which Hassan enjoined, though he used it without thought to obey,—low, voluble, earnest prayers for mercy, and then again voluble curses, and again voluble appeals for pity, and at the end of it a broken whimpering, as though his strength was gone, and the convulsive jerks which a fish makes in a basket.

All the while Hassan held him down, listening to the appeals, the prayers, the curses, with an untouched gravity of face. "It is indeed you; I have made no mistake," and he freed him from the burning fetters, and opened the flap of the tent. Bentham rolled over on his side with his face to the opening, and lay there shaking, moaning. "Now I will tell you what I have planned for you," continued Hassan. "I thought at first to kill you, but it is so small a thing. Then I remembered words you once told me, that you had trouble with your own people, and could not ask them for protection. So friends of mine from Beni Hassan, who go upon their way to-night, will take you with them, and sell you when they are far away. And for the rest of your days you will carry loads upon your back up and down the inlands of Morocco, and your masters will beat you, and if you faint and are tired, they will do strange things to make you suffer, even as I did with the hobbles. Lo, here my friends come!"

The sound of steps came to their ears. A few moments later a hand fumbled at the flap of the tent, opened it, and a head was thrust in. "Is it you, Hassan Akbar?"

"Yes," replied Hassan; "and here is the Room whom you promised to take out of my path. He will fetch a price, and besides I give to you his mule, which you will find tethered to the tent."

"And the saddle too, Hassan, is it not so?"

"It is."

Meanwhile Hassan cut Bentham's clothes from him as he lay upon the ground, and taking off his own sack, cast it for a garment over Bentham's shoulders, and wrapped himself in the dark cloak. In the place of that cloak he tied over Bentham's mouth a thick rag. Then he thrust him out of the tent, and jerked him on to his feet. Bentham made no longer any resistance; he let them do with him as they were pleased; and he stood tottering and swaying.

Five Arabs waited outside the tent. "He cannot walk, he shall ride the mule this night," said the chief of them. "To-morrow he shall learn to walk."

They hoisted Bentham on to the back of the mule, and tied him there with leathern thongs. Then they started on their long journey.

The cool night air after the stifling tent revived the man who perforce rode the mule. It did not give him strength to resist, or as yet even the impulse to cry out; but it restored to him the power to hear and to understand. What he heard was a distant clock below him in Tangier striking an hour; what he understood was that the hour it struck was only one o'clock.

X

M. Fournier Expounds the Advantages which Each Sex has Over the Other

The long interview with Wilbraham in the Alameda of Ronda had consequences for Miranda which she felt but did not trace to their source. It was not merely that she sickened at the vulgar, futile story of his ruin; that she saw in imagination the wretched victim he had run to earth across two continents, closing the door and slipping the pistol-barrel between his teeth; that she loathed the knowledge that this man was henceforward her gaoler; but she took him and the bitter years of her marriage together in her thoughts, and using them as premises began doubtfully to draw universal conclusions.

These conclusions Miranda hazarded at times in the form of questions to her companion Jane Holt, and sought answers from her as from one who had great experience of the tortuous conduct of men. Were men trustworthy at all? If so, were there any means by which a woman could test their trustworthiness? These two questions were the most constant upon Miranda's tongue, and Jane Holt answered them with assurance, and in her own way.

Wilbraham had not erred when he described her as a sentimentalist with grievances. Sentimentalism was the shallows of her nature, and she had no depths. Her conversation ran continually upon the "big things," as she termed them, such as devotion, endurance, self-sacrifice, and the rest, in which qualities men were singularly deficient. She meant, however, only devotion to her, endurance of her, self-sacrifice for her, of which it was not unnatural that men should tire, seeing who it was that demanded them. Yet she had enjoyed her share, and more than her share. For though incapable of passion herself, she had in her youth possessed the trick of inspiring it, but without the power, perhaps through her own incapacity, of keeping it alive, and no doubt too because upon a moderate acquaintance she conveyed an impression of inherent falsity. For, being a sentimentalist, she lived in a false world, on the borders of a lie, never quite telling it perhaps, and certainly never quite not telling it. She was by nature exigent, for she was in her own eyes the pivot of her little world, and for the wider world beyond, she had no eyes whatever. And her exigence took amusing or irritating shapes according to the point of view of those who suffered it. For instance, you must never praise her costumes, of which she had many, and those worthy of praise, but the high qualities of her mind, which were few and often of no taste whatever. It should be added that she had always favoured an inferior before an equal. For it pleased her above all things to condescend, since she secured thus a double flattery, in the knowledge of her own condescension, and in the grateful humility of those to whom she condescended.

It can be foreseen, then, what answers this woman,—who was tall, and still retained the elegance of her figure, and would have still retained the good looks of her face, but that it was written upon by many grievances—would give to Miranda's questions.

"You can trust no men. You must bribe them with cajoleries; you must play the coquette; you must enlist their vanity. They are all trivial, and the big things do not appeal to them."

Miranda listened. She was accustomed to Jane Holt, and had no longer a reasoned conception of her character. Habit had dulled her impressions. She remembered only that Jane Holt had had much experience of men wherein she herself was wofully deficient. Jane Holt embroidered her theme; a pretty display of petulance, the seemingly accidental disclosure of an ankle, a voluntary involuntary pressure of the arm, these things had power to persuade the male mind, such as it is, and to enmesh that worthless thing the male heart.

"One might have a man for a friend, perhaps," suggested Miranda, hopefully.

"My poor Miranda!" exclaimed Miss Holt. "No wonder your marriage was a failure. Men pretend friendship for a woman at times, but they mean something else."

The moral was always that they were not to be trusted, and Miranda, vividly recollecting Ralph Warriner and Wilbraham, listened and wondered, listened and wondered, until she would rise of a sudden and take refuge in her own parlour, of which the window looked out across the valley to the hills, where she would sit with a throbbing forehead pressed upon her palms, certain, certain, that the homily was not true, and yet half distracted lest it should be true.

On the morrow of one such conversation, and one such flight, Miss Holt came into the little parlour—a cool, dark-panelled, low-roofed room of which the door gave on to the patio—and found Miranda searching the room.

"Do you know what month this is?" Miss Holt asked severely.

"October."

"Quite so," and great emphasis was laid upon the words.

"I know," replied Miranda, penitently, as she crossed over to a table and lifted the books. "We have been here all the summer; it has been very hot. I am sorry, but I was compelled to stay. I did not know what might occur, and," she anxiously turned over the letters and papers on her writing-table in the window, "it was some comfort, I admit, to feel that one was near—" She stopped suddenly and resumed in confusion, "I mean I did not know what might happen."

Jane Holt looked at her with great displeasure, but said nothing until Miranda began hurriedly to open and shut the drawers of her writing-table. Then she said irritably: "What in the world are you looking for?"

Miranda stood up and looked round the room. "There was a glove," she said absently.

"Yes, I threw it away."

"Threw it away!" Miranda stared at Jane Holt with a look of complete dismay. "You don't mean that. Oh, you can't mean it!"

"Indeed I do; it was torn across the palm."

"I left it lying there, on my writing-desk, yesterday, after you and I had been talking—" She left the sentence unfinished.

"Yes, and I found it there. It was torn, so I had it thrown away."

Miranda rang a hand-bell, and ordered search to be made for the glove. It could not be found; it had been burnt with the answered letters.

"Very well," said Miranda, and the servant retired. Miranda sat down, and showed to Jane Holt a face of which the expression was almost scared.

"What does it matter?" exclaimed Jane. "The glove was torn; you could never have used it."

"No," answered Miranda, quickly, almost guiltily it seemed. "I should never have used it; I never meant to use it. The glove was only a symbol; it was no more than that, it represented a belief. I can retain the belief, no doubt. No doubt, though, I have lost the glove—"

"What in the world are you talking about?" interrupted Jane Holt.

"Nothing, nothing," answered Miranda, with a start. The loss of the glove had so dismayed her that she had forgotten who it was she had been speaking to, or indeed that she was speaking to anyone. She had merely uttered her thoughts, for she had come to look upon that glove, which, under no circumstances, would she use, as none the less a safeguard, and of late, in particular, she had fallen into a habit of taking it from the drawer in which it rested and setting it before her eyes; of stating it, as it were, as a refutation of Jane Holt's ready opinions.

Jane Holt shook her head. "You have changed very much towards me, Miranda. You are growing secret. I don't want to know. I would not press anyone for their confidence; but I may think it strange, I suppose?" She folded her arms across her breast and tapped with her fingers upon her elbows. "I suppose I may think it strange; and if anyone took the trouble to give me a thought, perhaps anyone might believe that I had a right to feel hurt. But I don't! Please don't run away with that idea! No, I cannot allow you, Miranda, to fancy for a moment that I should feel hurt. But I do notice that you jump whenever there is a knock at the door. There! What did I say?"

The door of the parlour stood open to the patio; in the corner of the opposite side of the patio there was the mouth of a passage which led to the outer door; and upon that outer door just at this moment someone rapped heavily, as though he came in haste. Miranda started nervously, and to cover the movement, rose from her chair and closed the door.

"And as for the glove," resumed Jane Holt, who found it difficult to leave any subject alone when it was evident that it was unwelcome, "you could never have used it."

"No," answered Miranda, thoughtfully. "Of course—of course, I could never have used it;" and a servant entered the room and handed to her a card on which was engraved M. Fournier's name and address.

Miranda held the card beneath her eyes for some little while. Then she walked out into the patio, where M. Fournier awaited her. He came towards her at once, in an extreme agitation, but she signed to him to be silent, and opening a second door on the same side of the patio as the door of her parlour, but farther to the right, she led the way into a tiny garden rich with deep colours. Jonquils, camellias, roses, wild geraniums, and pinks, tended with a care which bespoke a mistress from another country, made a gay blaze in the sun, and sweetened the air with their delicate perfumes.

The garden was an irregular nook with something or the shape of a triangle, enclosed between the back wall of the house and a wing flung out at a right angle. The base of the triangle was an old brick wall, breast-high, which began at the end of the house wall and curved outwards until it reached the wing. Over this wall the eye looked through air to the olive-planted slope of a mountain. For the house was built on the brink of the precipice, it was in a line with the Alameda, though divided from it by the great chasm, and if one leaned over the crumbling wall built long ago by the Moors, one had an impression that one ought to see the waves churning at the foot of the rock and to hear a faint moaning of the sea; so that the sight of the level carpet of the plain continually surprised the eyes.

Into this garden Miranda brought M. Fournier. No windows overlooked it, for those which gave light to Miranda's parlour were in the end and the other side of the wing, and so commanded the valley without commanding this enclosure. A little flagged causeway opened a path between the flowers to the nook between the wing of the house and the old wall, where two lounge chairs invited use.

Miranda seated herself in one of these chairs and with a gesture offered the other to M. Fournier. M. Fournier, however, took no heed of the invitation. He had eyes only for Miranda's face. He held his hat in one hand, and with a coloured handkerchief continually mopped his forehead, a dusty perspiring image of anxiety.

"You come from my husband?" said Miranda.

M. Fournier's face lightened. "Ah, then, you know—"

"That he is alive? Yes. You come from him?"

"From him, no; on his behalf, yes."

Miranda smiled at the subtle distinction. "You need money, of course," she said drily. "How much do you want? You have, no doubt, some authority from my husband."

The little Belgian's anxiety gave place to offended pride. "We do not need money, neither he nor I; but as for authority, perhaps this will serve."

He drew from his pocket a soiled scrap of paper and handed it to Miranda. The paper, as she could see from the blue lines, the shape, and the jagged border, had been torn from a small pocketbook. It was so crumpled and soiled that a few words scribbled with a pencil on the outside in Arabic were barely visible. Miranda unfolded the paper slowly, for the mere look of it was sinister. The words within were written also in pencil, and her face altered as she read them.

"What does J. B. mean?" she asked.

"J. B. are the initials of the name he took."

"You are sure this comes from my husband? I do not recognise his hand."

"Quite sure."

"Here is bad news," said she, and she conned the words over again, and could nowhere pick out the familiar characteristics of Ralph Warriner's handwriting. The words themselves were startling. *Reward the bearer well, and for God's sake do quickly what you can.* But more startling, more significant, than the words was the agitation of the writer's hand. Haste and terror had kept the hand wavering. Here the pencil had paused, yet even when pausing, its point had trembled on the paper, as the blurred dots showed. Miranda imagined that so it had paused and trembled, while someone walked by the writer's back and had but to glance over his shoulder to discover the business he was engaged upon. Then again the pencil had raced on, running the words one into the other, fevered to get the message done. A whole tragedy was indicated in the formation of the letters. Or a malady? Miranda turned eagerly to the letter. The writing wavered up and down. The small letters were clear; the capitals and the long letters, the "f's," the "q's," the "y's," weak, as though the fingers could not control the pencil. Illness might account for the message, and Miranda chose that supposition.

"He is lying very ill somewhere," she said.

M. Fournier shook his head. "No. I tried to believe that myself at first; but I never did believe it, and I thought and thought and thought—*Tenez*, look!" He drew a piece of blank paper from one pocket, a pencil from another. The paper he spread upon his knee, the pencil he took between his teeth; then he held out his wrists.

"Now fasten them together."

Miranda uttered a cry. Her face grew very white. "What with?" she asked.

"Your belt."

She unclasped her belt from her waist and strapped Fournier's wrists together.

"Tighter," said he, "tighter. Now see!"

With great difficulty and labour he copied out Warriner's message on the blank paper; and while he wrote Miranda saw the sentence wavering up and down, the small letters coming out clear and small, the long strokes and tails straggling. She seized the copy almost before he had finished, and held it side by side with the original. There was a difference, of course, the difference which stamped one man's hand as Warriner's and the other as Fournier's, the difference of fear, but that was the only difference. The method in each case was identical; the same difficulties had produced the same results.

"There can be no doubt, *hein?* " asked Fournier, as Miranda unfastened the belt.

"How did this come to you?" she returned.

"I tell you," said he, "from the beginning. Bentham—that is what M. Warriner calls himself now, Bentham—Jeremy Bentham he calls himself, because he says he's such an economist—well, he and I are partners in a little business, and we have prospered. So when Bentham came back from Bemin Sooar to Tangier a week ago, I give a dinner in my house to a few friends and we dance afterwards. Perhaps ten or eleven of us and Bentham. Bentham he came and danced and he was the last to go away. He did not stay in my house—it was better for our little business that we should not be thought more than mere friends. He had a lodging in the town, while my house was outside up the hill. He rode away alone on a mule, for he was in evening dress and one cannot walk across the Sôk in dancing shoes, and he never reached his lodging. He disappeared. I heard no word of him, until yesterday; yesterday about mid-day, an Arab brought that scrap of paper to my shop."

"But the Arab told you how and where he got it?" said Miranda.

"Yes. He belonged to a douar, a tent village, you understand. The village is three days from Tangier on the road to Mequinez. The Arab was leading down his goats to the water a week ago, in the morning, when six men passed him at a distance. They were going up into the country; they had a mule with them. He watched them pass and noticed that one of them would now and then loiter and fall a little behind, whereupon the rest beat him with sticks and drove him again in front. And he did not resist, Madame, I am afraid we know why he did not resist."

Miranda pressed her hands to her forehead.

"Well," she said with an effort, and her voice had sunk to a whisper, "finish, finish!"

"It seemed to the Arab," continued Fournier, whose anxiety seemed in some measure to diminish, and whose face grew hopeful as he watched Miranda's increasing distress, "that this victim made a sign to him, and when the party had gone by he noticed something white gleaming on the brown soil in the line of their march. He went forward and picked it up. It was this piece of paper. He read the writing on it, these marks." M. Fournier turned over the sheet, and pointed to the indecipherable Arabic. "They mean, 'Take this to Fournier at Tangier and you will get money.' He opened it, he could not read the inside, but seeing that it was written in one of the languages of the Nazarenes, he thought there might be some truth in the promise. So he brought the paper to Tangier yesterday and I have brought it to you."

M. Fournier settled his glasses upon his nose and leaned forward for his answer. Miranda sat with knitted brows, gazing out to the dark mountains. Fournier would not interrupt her; he fancied she was searching her wits for a device to bring help to Warriner; but, indeed, she was not thinking at all.

Miranda had a trick of seeing pictures. She was not given to arguments and inferences; but a word, a sentence, would strike upon her hearing, and at once a curtain was rolled up somewhere in her mind, and she saw men moving to and fro and things happening as upon a lighted stage. Such pictures made up her arguments, her conclusions, even her motives; and it was because of their instant vividness that she was so rapidly moved to sympathy and dislike. So now there was set before her eyes the picture of a man riding down the hill of Tangier at night in the civilisation of evening dress, and, as she looked, it melted into another in which the same man, clad in vile rags, with his hands bound, was flogged forwards under a burning sun into the barbaric inlands of Morocco. She saw that brutal party, the five gaolers, the one captive, straggle past the tent village. She guessed at Ralph's despairing glance as though it was directed towards herself, she saw the scrap of paper flutter white upon the dark soil. And as she contemplated this vision, she heard M. Fournier speaking again to her; but the sound of his voice had changed. He was no longer telling his story; he was pleading with a tenderness which had something grotesquely pathetic, when she considered who it was for whom he pleaded. His foreign accent became more pronounced, and the voluble words tumbled one over the other.

"So M. Warriner does not ask you for money; that sees itself, is it not? Nor even does he ask you for help. Be sure of that, Madame; read the note again. He would not come to you for help; he is not so mean; he has too much pride;" and as Mrs. Warriner smiled, with perhaps a little bitterness, M. Fournier, noticing her smile, became yet more astonishing and intricate in his apologies. "He take your money, oh yes, I know very well, while he is with you; but then you get his company in exchange. That make you both quits, eh? But once he has gone away, he would not come back to you for money or help at all. He has so much pride. Oh no! He just take it from the first person he meet, me or anyone else. He has so much pride; besides, it would be simpler. No! It is I who come to you. He often speak to me of you—oh, but in the highest terms! And I say to myself: That dear Ralph, he is difficult to live with. He is not a comfortable friend. We know that, Mrs. Warriner and I, but we both love him very much—"

"No!"

The emphatic interruption fairly startled M. Fournier. Miranda had risen from her seat and stood over him. He would not have believed that so gentle a face could have taken on so vigorous an expression. He stammered a protest. Miranda repeated her denial: "No, no, no!" she cried. "Let us be frank!"

She turned aside from him, and leaning her elbows upon the crumbling parapet of the wall, looked across the valley and down the cliff's side where one road was cut in steep zigzags, and winding down to the plain as to the water's edge, helped to complete the illusion that the sea should fitly be breaking at the base.

M. Fournier's hopes dwindled in the face of this uncompromising denial. He had come to enlist her help; he had counted upon her affections, and had boldly counted, because Warriner had so surely attracted his own. M. Fournier would have been at a loss to explain his friendship for Warriner, to account for the causes or the qualities which evoked it, but he felt its strength, and he now knew that Mrs. Warriner had no lot or share in it.

He was therefore the more surprised when she turned back to him with eyes which were shining and moist, and said very gently: "But of course I will help." Her conduct was not at all inconsistent, however much it might appear so to M. Fournier. She was acting upon the same motive which had induced her, the moment she was aware of Ralph Warriner's existence, to return to Ronda, the one spot where Warriner would be sure to look for her if he needed her, and which had subsequently persuaded her to submit to the blackmail of Major Wilbraham. "Of course I will help. What can I do?"

M. Fournier's eyes narrowed, his manner became wary and cunning. "I hoped that you might perhaps hit upon some plan," he suggested.

"I?" Miranda thought for a moment, then she said: "We must appeal to the English Minister at Tangier."

M. Fournier sprang out of his chair. "No, that is the very last thing we must do. For what should we say? That Mr. Ralph Warriner, who was thought to be dead, has just been kidnapped in Morocco?"

"No, but that Mr. Bentham has," she returned quickly.

M. Fournier shrugged his shoulders. "Why am I here?" he exclaimed, stamping his foot. "I ask you, why am I here? *Saperlipopette!* Would I have come to you if any so simple remedy had been possible? Suppose we go politely to the English Minister and ask him to find Mr. Jeremy Bentham! The Minister goes to the Sultan of Morocco, and after many months, perhaps Mr. Bentham is found, perhaps he is not. Suppose that he is found and brought down to Tangier,—what next, I beg you? There will be talk about Mr. Bentham, there will be gentlemen everywhere, behind bushes, under tables, everywhere, so that the great British public may know the colours of the ties he wears, and at last be happy. His name will be in the papers, and more, Mrs. Warriner, his portrait too. His portrait; have you thought of that?"

"But he might escape the photographers."

"Suppose he do, by a miracle. Do you think there will be no inquiry as to what is Mr. Bentham's business in Morocco? Do you think the English Minister will not ask the inconvenient question? Do you think that you can hide his business, once an inquiry is set on foot, in that country? He might pass as a tourist, you think perhaps, *hein?* And any one man has only got to give a few dollars to some officer in the custom-house, and he will know that Mr. Bentham is smuggling guns into Morocco, and selling them to the Berbers of Bemin Sooar. What then? He would be taken for trial to Gibraltar, where only two years ago he was Captain Warriner."

Miranda had already heard enough from Wilbraham to confirm M. Fournier's statement about the custom-house.

"No," continued Fournier, "the risk is too great. And I call it risk!" He hunched his shoulders and spread out his hand. "It is a red-hot cert, as he would say. His identity would be established, and he had better, after all, be a captive in Morocco than a convict in England. There is some chance of an escape in Morocco."

"There is also in Morocco some chance of a—" Miranda's lips refused to speak the word. M. Fournier supplied it.

"Murder? I do not fear that. Had they intended murder, they would have killed that night, then and there, in the Sôk of Tangier. There would have been no letter dropped three days inland."

Miranda eagerly welcomed the argument. "Yes, yes," she exclaimed, and the colour came back to her lips. "He is held for ransom then, surely?"

M. Fournier shook his head. "Hardly. Had they captured him for ransom, they would have got from him the names of his friends. They would have used measures," said he, with some emphasis upon the word, at which Miranda shivered; "sure measures to get the names, and Warriner would have given mine. They would have come to me for the ransom, and I should have given it—if it was everything I had—and Warriner would be safe by now."

Fournier was aware that Miranda looked curiously and even with a sort of compunction towards him, though he did not understand the reason of her look. To him it was the most natural, simple thing in the world that he should care for Warriner.

"No, it is not ransom," and he threw a cautious glance this way and that, and then, even in that secret spot, continued in a whisper: "Warriner has enemies, enemies of his own race. I do not wonder at it," he explained impartially. "He treats me, yes, even me, who am his one friend, as though—well, his own phrase is the best. He wipes the floor with me. He has promised to do it many times, and many times he has done it too. No doubt he has enemies, and they have arranged his capture."

"Why?"

"Suppose they sell him for a slave, a long way off and a long way inland. It would not be pleasant at all, and most of all unpleasant to him, for he is particular. Of course you know that, Mrs. Warriner. He likes his linen very clean and fine. He would not enjoy being a slave, yet he could not appeal to his Government, even if he got the chance."

"Oh, don't, please!" cried Miranda. That intimate detail about Ralph's habits brought home to her most convincingly his present plight. "But what enemies?" she asked in a moment or two. "Is it a guess of yours, or do you know of any?"

M. Fournier hitched his chair nearer. His voice became yet more confidential.

"Three months ago an Englishman came to my shop."

"Three months ago?" interrupted Miranda. "He leaned over your counter and he said, 'How did you work that little affair on Rosevear, and how's my dear friend, Ralph Warriner?'"

"Ah, you know him!" cried Fournier, springing up in excitement.

"Yes, and he has nothing to do with Ralph's capture," replied Miranda. "He only went that one time to Tangier." M. Fournier resumed his seat, and she briefly explained to the Belgian the reason and the consequence of Wilbraham's visit. Fournier's face fell as he listened. He had hoped that the necessary clue had been discovered, and when Miranda finished he sat silent in a glum despair. After a little his face lightened.

"Only once you say he came to Tangier, this man you speak of—only once?" he asked eagerly, stretching out his hand.

"Only the once."

"He was not there earlier in the year? He was not there in May? Think carefully. Be very sure!"

Mrs. Warriner reflected for a second. "I am sure he was not," she replied. "He travelled by train from Monte Carlo to Marseilles in May. From Marseilles he came directly by boat to England."

"Good," said M. Fournier. He sat forward in his chair and rubbed the palms of his hands together. "Now listen! There was another Englishman who came in May. He came to my shop, though the shutter was on the window and the shop closed."

"Who was he?" asked Mrs. Warriner.

"I cannot guess."

"Tell me what he was like."

"Ah! there's the trouble. Neither of us saw him. Warriner heard his voice, that is all. And a voice? There is no clue more deceptive. The one thing Warriner is sure of is that he had never heard the voice before."

"But what was it that he heard?"

"I tell you. Warriner came down to Tangier that very morning from the country. He travelled as always in the dress of a Moor, for he speaks their tongues, no Moor better, and our little business, you understand, needs secrecy. I closed my shop, shuttered the window, locked the door. Warriner told me he had arranged with the sheikhs of the Berber tribes to deliver so many Winchesters, so much ammunition, within a certain period. The period was short; Warriner's boat, the *Ten Brothers*, was waiting at Tarifa. I leave him to change his dress and shave his beard, while I go down to the harbour and hire a felucca to put him over to Tarifa. But Warriner forgot to lock the door behind me. In a minute or two he hear a hand scrape softly, oh so softly, up the door towards the latch. For a second he stood, with the razor in his hand like this," and the Belgian, in the absorption of his narrative began to act the scene, "looking at the latch, waiting for it to rise, and listening. Then he remembered that he had not locked the door. He crept on tip-toe towards it; just as he reached it he heard a loud English voice shout to him violently, 'Look out!' That phrase is a menace, eh?" he stopped to ask.

"It might be. It would more naturally be a warning," said Mrs. Warriner.

"In either case it means an enemy. As he shouted Warriner's hand was already on the key. Warriner turn the lock, and immediately the Englishman batter and knock at the door, but he could not get in, and after a little he went away. Ah! how often we have wondered who that man was, and why he shouted out his threat and tried to force the door. To know that you have one enemy at your heels, but you cannot pick him out because you have not seen his face! That frightens me, Madame Warriner. I am a coward, and it is no wonder that it frightens me." The perspiration broke out on Fournier's forehead as he made his frank confession. "But it frightens Warriner too, who is no coward. Often and often have I seen him lift up a finger, so," he suited the action to the word, "when a new voice speak within his hearing, and listen, listen, listen, to make sure whether that was the voice which shouted through the door or no. But a voice! You cannot be certain you recognise it, unless you can recognise also the face of the man to whom it belongs. A singer's voice, yes! Perhaps you might know that again though you heard it for the first time blindfold. But a voice that merely speaks or shouts, no!"

M. Fournier picked up his hat and rose from his chair. Miranda rose too, and they stood face to face with one another under the awning.

"So I ask you this. Will you help to recover your husband?" he asked, with a simplicity of appeal which went home to Miranda all the more, because it did not presume to claim her help. "Either a search must be made privately through Morocco until he is found and bought, and such a search seems hopeless; or the unknown man who shouted through the door must be discovered. That is the simplest way. For this I do believe"—and he expressed his belief with a great solemnity and conviction which sank very memorably into Miranda's mind—"I believe that if we lay our hands upon that man we shall lay our hands also upon the means to rescue Warriner from his servitude."

"But how can I help? I do not know the man who shouted through the door." The words were flung at Fournier in a passion of impotence. "You say you need no money. I cannot scour Morocco. How can a woman help?"

M. Fournier hesitated. He took off his glasses. He found it easier to speak the matter of his thoughts when he saw her face dimly, and could not take note of its expressions.

"A woman very often has friends," he hinted.

He saw her face grow rosy and then pale.

"Yes, but I have lost the glove," she cried impulsively, and as she turned towards the perplexed M. Fournier, the blood rushed back into her cheeks. "I mean," she stammered, and broke off suddenly into a question which was at once an accusation and a challenge.

"And men, have they no friends?"

Fournier did not affect to misunderstand her.

"Here and there, perhaps a man has one friend who will deliberately risk much, even life, for him, but in those cases he has only one such friend. Warriner has one, but alas! that one friend is myself. Already, it is true, I have risked my life for him at the Scillies, and I would gladly lose it for him now, if I could only lose it without foreknowledge. But what can I do? A little fat Belgian bourgeois, of middle age, who speaks no language correctly but his own, and has only a few poor words of Arabic, a man of no strength, and, Madame, a coward,—what could I do inland in Morocco?" He made no parade of humility as he described himself; he used the simple, straightforward tone of one who advances cogent arguments. Miranda was moved by an impulse to hold out her hand to him.

"I beg your pardon," she said.

M. Fournier was encouraged to continue his plea.

"But to possess sufficient friends so that one may choose the adequate instrument,—ah, that is the privilege of women!" He added timidly, "Of women who have youth and beauty," but in a voice so low that the words hardly reached Miranda's ears, and their significance was not understood by her at all.

"I have not many friends," she returned frankly, "but I have one who would be adequate. I cannot tell whether I can bring myself to—I mean I cannot tell whether he could go; he has duties. It is asking much to ask any man to set out into Morocco on such an errand. However, I must think of it; I could at all events send for him and tell him of my husband—"

M. Fournier interposed quickly: "He knows nothing of Ralph Warriner?"

"He believes my husband dead."

"Then why should he not continue to believe your husband dead?" asked Fournier, with a sly cunning. "It is Mr. Jeremy Bentham he goes out to find,—a friend of yours—a relation perhaps—is it not so? We can keep Ralph Warriner dead for a while longer."

The little man's intention was becoming obvious.

"Why?" asked Miranda, sharply.

"It would be more prudent."

"I don't understand."

Her voice was cold and dangerous.

"A man has one friend, a woman many," explained M. Fournier; "but there are compensations for the man in that his friend will serve him for friendship's sake. But a man will not serve a woman for friendship's sake. Not if he serve her well."

M. Fournier was prepared for an outburst of indignation; he was not prepared for the expression which came over Miranda's face, and he could not understand it. She looked at him fixedly and, as it seemed, in consternation. "That is not true," she said; "it is not true. Surely, surely it cannot be true."

M. Fournier made no answer. She turned away from him and walked along the flagged pathway, turned at the end and came slowly back. "A man will only serve a woman if he cares for her?"

M. Fournier bowed.

"And men can be made to care?"

M. Fournier smiled.

"But it needs time?"

M. Fournier shrugged his shoulders and spread out his hands.

"And it needs tricks?"

M. Fournier made a pun.

"Nature, Madame, has put the tricks in your hand."

Miranda nodded her head once or twice, and made a remark which M. Fournier was at a loss to apply. "The old question," said she, "and the old answer;" and at once an irrational anger flamed up within her, anger with M. Fournier for posing the question again, anger with herself for her perplexity, anger even against Charnock, because he did not magically appear in the garden and answer the question and dissolve her perplexity. But M. Fournier alone was in the garden with her, and the full force of her anger broke upon him. "I am to throw out my net," she cried, "and catch my friend! I am to trick him, to lie to him, and to earn with the lie the use of his life and his brains and his time and his manhood. How dare you come to me with such a thought? A coward's thought indeed!"

"The thought of a man who loves his friend," said M. Fournier, stubbornly; and he continued without any sarcasm: "Your sentiments, Madame Warriner, are most correct; they do you honour, but I love my friend."

To his surprise Miranda suddenly smiled at him, and then laughed. "I was never treated with such absolute disregard in all my life," she said. "No, don't apologise, I like you for it."

"Then you will do as I propose?" he exclaimed.

Miranda grew serious. "I cannot. If I ask my friend to go upon this errand, he must know before he goes who it is I ask him to bring back. I must think what can be done. You will go back to Tangier; perhaps you may find Ralph there when you return. I will write to you at Tangier."

M. Fournier had plainly no opinion of her plan; but he saw that he could not dissuade her. He took the hand which she held out to him, and returned sorrowfully through the patio to the street.

XI

In Which Miranda Adopts a New Line of Conduct and the Major Expresses Some Discontent

Miranda was left with two convictions, of which she was very certain. Somehow, somewhither, help must be sent to Ralph; and if Charnock carried the help, he must know why and for whom before he went.

She stood in the patio until the outer door closed behind M. Fournier. A local newspaper lying upon a wicker chair caught her eye, and harassed and unresolved as she was, she turned eagerly for rest to its commonplaces. She read an anecdote about an unknown politician, and a summary of Don Carlos's prospects, with extreme care and concentration; for she knew that her perplexities lay in wait for her behind the screen of the news sheet, and she was very tired.

She turned over the sheet, and in spite of herself, began to feel at a third idea. She applied herself consequently to the first paragraph which met her eye, and read it over with great speed, perhaps ten times. But the words she read were not the printed words. They were these:—

"Send me the glove, and when I come up to Ronda, it will be understood without a word why I have come. There will be no need for me to speak at all, and you will only have to tell me the particular thing that wants doing."

And the idea became distinct. She could choose her own time for telling Charnock the particular thing which wanted doing. He would ask no questions; he had indeed hit upon that device of the glove to spare her; she could send the glove, and she could tell him after he had come in answer, but at her own discretion, why she had sent it. Therefore she had time—she had time.

She turned to her paragraph again, read it with comprehension, and from the paragraph her trouble sprang at her and caught her by the heart. For what she read was the account of the opening of the branch line to Algeciras. Charnock's work was done, then; he would be leaving Algeciras. Even at that moment her first feeling was one of approaching loneliness, so closely had the man crept into her thoughts. She took a step towards her parlour, stopped, stood for a moment irresolute, ran up the winding iron staircase to the landing half-way up the patio, and fetched a new long white kid glove from her dressing-room. She moulded it upon her hand, soiled it by a ten minutes' wearing, ripped it across the palm, and sealed it up in an envelope.

Jane Holt came into the patio while Miranda was still writing the address.

"What's that?" she asked.

"A sham, Jane, a sham," said Miranda, in a queer, unsteady voice; "a trick, the first of them."

Jane Holt shook her head. "You are very strange, Miranda," but Miranda picked up the envelope, and putting on her hat hurried to the post-office. As she crossed the bridge over the Tajo a man barred her way. She tried to pass him; he moved again in front of her, and she saw that the man was Wilbraham.

"I wish to speak to you."

"In ten minutes," said she, "in the Alameda. I have a letter to post."

"The letter can wait," said he.

"If it did, it would never be posted," said she, and she hurried past him.

The Major followed her with inquisitive eyes; he felt a certain admiration for her buoyant walk, her tall slight figure, which a white muslin dress with a touch of colour at the waist so well set off, and for the pose of her head under the wide straw hat. But business instincts prevailed over his admiration. He lit a cigarette.

"What is the large sealed letter which must be posted at once, or it will never be posted at all?" he asked himself. "Why must it be posted at once?"

He strolled to the Alameda unable to find an answer. In the Alameda, at the bench before the railings, Miranda was waiting for him. She rose at once to meet him.

"Why have you come?" she asked. "It is not quarter-day. We made our bargain. I have kept my part of it."

"Yes," said he. "But it was not a good bargain for me. I underrated my necessities. I overrated my taste for a quiet life."

"And the Horace?" she asked scornfully. "One of the few things worth doing, was it not?"

Wilbraham flushed angrily.

"So it is," he said. "But I find it difficult to settle down. I need, in fact,—do we not all need them?—intervals of relaxation." He spoke uneasily; he looked even more worn and tired than when he first came to Ronda. Miranda understood that here indeed was the real tragedy of the man's life.

"All these years, fifteen years," she said, "you have dreamed of doing sooner or later this one thing. You have played with the dream. You have kept your self-respect by means of it. It has set you apart from your companions. And now, when the opportunity comes, you find that you were only after all on the level of your companions, lower, perhaps a trifle lower, by this trifle of delusion. For you cannot do the work."

Wilbraham did not resent the speech, which was uttered without reproach or accusation, but in the tone of one who notes a fact which should have been foreseen.

"A topping fellow Horace, of course," Wilbraham began.

"And I trusted you to do it," she said suddenly, and looked at him for a moment full in the face, not angrily, but with a queer sort of interest in the mistake she had made. Then she turned from him and walked away.

The Major followed quickly, but before he could come up with her she turned round on him.

"Follow me for one other step," she said, "and I call that guardia twenty yards away."

She meant to do it, too; this was unmistakable. She resumed her walk, and the Major thought it prudent to remain where he was. He remained in fact for some time on that spot, whistling softly to himself. Wilbraham's menaces had sunk to a complete insignificance in Miranda's mind, since she had been confronted with the actual positive disaster which had befallen Ralph Warriner. Wilbraham, however, was not in a position to trace Miranda's sudden audacity to its true source. He fell therefore, and not unnaturally, into the error of imagining that she drew her courage to refuse his demands from some new and external support. His thoughts went back to the letter which must be posted at once. Had that letter anything to do with that support? Had it anything to do with her refusal?

Wilbraham asked himself these questions with considerable uneasiness, for after all the seven hundred per annum was not so absolutely assured. He came to the conclusion that it would be wise to transfer his quarters from Tarifa to Ronda.

XII

The Hero, Like All Heroes, Finds Himself in a Fog

At eight o'clock the next morning Charnock was crushing the remainder of his clothes into a portmanteau. A couple of corded trunks stood ready for the porters, while the manager of the line sat in the window overlooking Algeciras Bay, and gave him gratuitous advice as to totally different and very superior methods of packing.

The manager suddenly rose to his feet.

"Here's the P. and O. coming into the bay," he said. "Man, but you have very little time. I'm thinking you'll miss it."

Charnock raised a flushed face from his portmanteau, and so wasted a few seconds. He made no effort to catch them up.

"I'm thinking, too, you would not be very sorry to miss it," continued the manager, sagely. "Though what charms you can discover in Algeciras, it's beyond my powers to comprehend."

Charnock did not controvert or explain the manager's supposition. He continued to pack, but perhaps a trifle more slowly than before.

"You have got my address, Macdonald?" he said. "You won't lose it, will you?"

He shut up the portmanteau and knelt upon it.

"You will forward everything that comes—everything without fail?" he insisted.

"In all human probability," returned Macdonald, "I will forward nothing at all. For I am thinking you will lose the boat."

There was a knock on the door; Charnock's servant brought in a letter. The letter lay upon its face, and the sealed back of the envelope had an official look.

"Open it, will you, Macdonald?" said Charnock, as he fastened the straps. "Well, what's it about?"

"I cannot tell. It's written in a dialect I do not understand," said the manager, gravely, and Charnock, turning about, saw that he dangled and deliberated upon a long white kid glove.

Charnock jumped up and snatched it away.

"It's a female's," said the manager, sagely.

"It's a woman's," returned Charnock, with indignation.

"You are very young," observed Macdonald. "And I'll point out to you that you have torn your letter."

Charnock was turning the glove over, and showed the palm at that moment. He smiled, but made no answer. He folded the glove, wrapped it in its envelope, took it out again, and smoothed its creases. Then he folded it once more, held it for a little balanced on his hand, and finally replaced it in the envelope and hid the envelope in his pocket.

"Man, but you are *very* young," remarked Macdonald, "and I'm thinking that you'll lose—"

"There's a train to Ronda pretty soon?" interrupted Charnock.

"There is," replied Macdonald, drily, "and I'll be particular to mind your address, and forward everything that comes. Eh, but you have paid your passage on the P. and O."

Charnock, in spite of that argument, took his seat in the train for Ronda, and travelled up through the forest of cork trees whose foliage split the sunshine, making here a shade, there an alley of light. The foresters were at work stripping the trunks of their bark, and Charnock was in a mood to make parables of the world, so long as they fitted in with and exemplified his own particular purposes and plans. He himself was a forester, and the rough bark he was stripping was Miranda's distress, so it is to be supposed that the bare tree-trunk was Miranda herself; and, to be sure, what simile could be more elegant?

Charnock's dominant feeling, indeed, was one of elation. The message of his mirror was being fulfilled. He had the glove in his pocket to assure him of that, and the feel of the glove, of its delicate kid between his strong fingers, pleased him beyond measure. For it seemed appropriate and expressive of her, and he hoped that the strength of his fingers was expressive of himself. But beyond that, it was a call, a challenge to his chivalry, which up till now, through all his years, had never once been called upon and challenged; and therein lay the true cause of his elation.

The train swept out of the cork forest, and the great grass slopes stretched upwards at the side of the track, dotted with white villages, seamed with rocks. Charnock fell to marvelling at the apt moment of the summons. Just when his work was done, when his mind and his body were free, the glove had come to him. If it had come by a later post on that same day, he would have been on his way to England. But it had not; it had come confederate with the hour of its coming.

A.E.W. MASON

The train passed into the gorge of tunnels, climbing towards Ronda. He was not forgetful that he was summoned to help Miranda out of a danger perhaps, certainly out of a great misfortune. But he had never had a doubt that the misfortune from some quarter, and at some time, would fall. She had allowed him on the balcony in St. James's Park to understand that she herself expected it. He knew, too, that it must be some quite unusual misfortune. For had she not herself said, with a complete comprehension of what she said, "If I have troubles I must fight them through myself"? He had been prepared then for the troubles, and he was rejoiced that after all they were of a kind wherein his service could be of use.

At the head of the gorge he caught his first view of Ronda, balanced aloft upon its dark pinnacle of rock. It was mid-day, and the sun tinged with gold the white Spanish houses and the old brown mansions of the Moors; and over all was a blue arch of sky, brilliant and cloudless. At that distance and in that clear light, Ronda seemed one piece of ivory, exquisitely carved and tinted, and then exquisitely mounted on a black pedestal. Charnock was not troubled with any of Lady Donnisthorpe's perplexities as to why Miranda persisted in making that town her home. To him it seemed the only place where she could live, since it alone could fitly enshrine her.

The train wound up the incline at the back of the town and steamed into the station. Charnock drove thence to the hotel in the square near the bull-ring, lunched, and asked his way to Mrs. Warriner's house. He stood for a while looking at the blank yellow wall which gave on to the street, and the heavy door of walnut wood.

For the first time he began to ponder what was the nature of the peril in which Miranda stood. His speculations were of no particular value, but the fact that he speculated at this spot, opposite the house, opposite the door, was. For, quite unconsciously, his eyes took an impression of the geometrical arrangement of the copper nails with which it was encrusted, or rather sought to take such an impression. For the geometrical figures were so intricate in their involutions that the eyes were continually baffled and continually provoked. Charnock was thus absently searching for the key to their inter-twistings when he walked across the road and knocked. He was conducted through the patio. He was shown into the small dark-panelled parlour which overlooked the valley. The door was closed upon him; the room was empty. A book lay open upon the table before the window. Charnock stood in front of this table looking out of the window across to the sierras; so that the book was just beneath his nose. He had but to drop his eyes and he would have read the title, and known the subject-matter, of the book, and perhaps taken note or some pencil lines scored in the margin against a passage here and there, for the book had been much in Miranda's hands these last few days. But he did not, for he heard a light step cross the patio outside and pause on the threshold of the door.

Charnock turned expectantly away from the table. The door, however, did not open, nor on the other hand were the footsteps heard to retreat. A woman then was standing, quite silent and quite motionless, on the other side of that shut door; and that woman, no doubt, was Miranda. Charnock was puzzled; he, too, stood silent and motionless, looking towards the door and wondering why she paused there and in what attitude she stood. For the seconds passed, and there must have been a lapse of quite two minutes between the moment when the footsteps ceased and the moment when the door was flung open.

For the door was flung open, noisily, violently, and with a great bustle of petticoats an unknown woman danced into the room humming a tune. She stopped with all the signs of amazement when she saw Charnock. "Oh!" she exclaimed, "why didn't they tell me?" She cast backwards over her shoulder that glance of the startled fawn which befits a solitary maid in the presence of a devouring man. Then she advanced timidly, lowered her eyes, and said: "So you have come to Ronda, then?"

This unknown woman had paused outside the door, yet she had swung into the room as though in a great hurry, and had been much surprised to see her visitor. Charnock was perplexed. Moreover, the unknown woman wore the semblance of Miranda. She was dressed in a white frock very elaborate with lace, he noticed; there was a shimmer of satin at her throat and waist, and to him who had not seen her for these months past, and who had thought of her as of one draped in black,—since thus only he had seen her,—she gleamed against the dark panels of the room, silvered and wonderful.

"So you have come to Ronda?" said she.

"Of course."

She held out her hand with a gingerly manner of timidity, and pressed his fingers when they touched hers, as though she could not help herself, and then hastily drew her hand away, as if she was ashamed and alarmed at her forwardness. Charnock could not but remember a

A.E.W. MASON

frank, honest hand-clasp, with which she had bidden him goodbye in London.

"Is this your first visit to Ronda?" she asked.

"Yes."

"Sure?" She looked at him with her eyebrows raised and an arch glance of provocation. "Sure you have not come up once or twice just to see in what corner of the world I lived?"

"No; I have been busy."

Miranda shrugged her shoulders.

"I had no right to expect you would." She pushed out a foot in a polished shoe beyond the hem of her dress, contemplated it with great interest, and suddenly withdrew it with much circumstance of modesty. Then with an involuntary gesture of repugnance which Charnock did not understand, she went over to the window and stood looking out from it. From that position too she spoke.

"You promised that night, if you have not forgotten, at Lady Donnisthorpe's, on the balcony, to tell me about yourself, about those years you spent in Westminster." And Charnock broke in upon her speech in a voice of relief.

"I understand," said he.

"What?"

"You," he replied simply.

"Oh, I hope not," she returned; "for when a woman becomes intelligible to a man, he loses all—liking for her," and she spoke the word "liking" with extreme shyness as though there were a bolder word with which he might replace it if he chose. "Is not that the creed?"

"A false creed," said he, and her eyes fell upon the open book. She uttered a startled exclamation, threw a quick glance at Charnock, closed the book and covered it with a newspaper.

"Let us go into the garden," said she; "and you shall talk to me of those years in which I am most interested."

"That I can understand," said he, and she glanced at him sharply, suspiciously, but there was no sarcasm in his accent. He had hit upon an explanation of the change in her. She stood in peril, she needed help, and very likely help of a kind which implied resource, which involved danger. She knew nothing of him, nothing of his capacity. It was no more than natural that he should require to know and that she should sound his years for the knowledge, before she laid him under the obligation of doing her a service.

He sat down on the chair in which M. Fournier had sat only yesterday.

"It will sound very unfamiliar to you," he said with a laugh. "My father was vicar of a moorland parish on the hills above Brighouse in Yorkshire. There I lived until I was twelve, until my father died. He had nothing but the living, which was poor—the village schoolmaster, what with capitation grants, was a good deal better off—so that when he died, he died penniless. I was adopted by a maiden aunt who took me to her home, a little villa in the south suburbs of London of which the shutters had never been taken down from the front windows since she had come to live there three years before."

"Why?" asked Miranda, in surprise.

"She was eccentric," explained Charnock, with a smile, and he resumed. "Nor had the front door ever been opened. My aunt was afraid that visitors might call, and, as she truly said, the house was not yet in order. The furniture, partly unpacked, with wisps of straw about the legs of the chairs, was piled up in the uncarpeted rooms. For there was only a carpet down in one room, the room in which we lived, and since the room was in the front and the shutters were up, we lived in a perpetual twilight."

"But did the servants do nothing?" exclaimed Miranda.

"There were no servants," returned Charnock. "My aunt said that they hampered her independence. Consequently of course we made our meals of tinned meat and bottled stout, which we ate standing up by the kitchen table in the garden if it was fine. But wet or fine the kitchen table always stood in the garden."

Here Miranda began to laugh and Charnock joined with her.

"It was a quaint sort of life," said he, "but rather ghostly to a boy of twelve."

"But you went to school?"

"No, my schooldays were over. I just lived in the twilight of that house, and through the chinks of the shutters watched people passing in the street, and lay awake at night listening to the creak of the bare boards. The house was in a terrace, and since we went to bed as soon as it grew dark to save the gas, I could hear through the wall the sounds of people laughing and talking, sometimes too the voices of boys of my own age playing while I lay in bed. I used to like the noise at times; it was companionable and told me fairy stories of blazing firesides. At times, however, I hated it beyond words, and hated the boys who laughed and shouted while I lay in the dark amongst the ghostly piles of furniture."

Miranda was now quite serious, and Charnock, as he watched her, recognised in the woman who was listening, the woman he had talked with on the balcony over St. James's Park, and not the woman he had talked with five minutes since.

"Only to think of it," she exclaimed. "I was living then amongst the Suffolk meadows, and the great whispering elms of the Park, and I never knew." She spoke almost in a tone of self-reproach as she clasped her hands together on her knees. "I never knew!"

"Oh, but we had our dissipations," returned Charnock. "We dug potatoes in the garden, and sometimes we paid a visit to Marshall and Snelgrove."

"Marshall and Snelgrove!"

"Yes, those were gala days. My aunt would buy the best ready-made bodice in the shop, which she carried away with her. From Marshall and Snelgrove's we used to go to Verrey's restaurant, where we dined amongst mirrors and much gilding, and about nine o'clock we would travel back to our suburb, creep into the dark house by the back door, and go to bed without a light. Imagine that if you can, Mrs. Warriner. The clatter, the noise, the flowers, the lights, of the restaurant, men and women in evening dress, and just about the time when they were driving up to their theatres, these people, in whose company we had dined, we were creeping into the dark, close-shuttered villa of the bare boards, and groping our way through the passage without a light. I used to imagine that every room had a man hiding behind the door, and all night long I heard men in my room breathing stealthily. It was after one such night that I ran away."

"You ran away?"

"Yes, and hid myself in London. I picked up a living one way and another. It doesn't cost much to live when you are put to it. I sold newspapers. I ran errands—"

"You didn't carry a sandwich-board?" exclaimed Miranda, eagerly. "Say you didn't do that!"

"I didn't," replied Charnock, with some surprise at her eagerness. "They wouldn't have given a nipper like me a sandwich-board," and Miranda drew an unaccountable breath of relief. "Finally I became an office boy, and I was allowed by my employer to sleep in an empty house in one of the small streets at the back of Westminster Abbey. There weren't any carpets either in that house, but I was independent, you see, and I saved my lodging. I wasn't unhappy during those three years. I understood that very well, when I heard the big clock strike twelve again on Lady Donnisthorpe's balcony. It was the first time I had heard it since I lived in the empty house, and heard it every night, and the sound of it was very pleasant and friendly."

"Then you left London," said Miranda.

"After three years. I was a clerk then; I was seventeen, and I had ambitions which clerking didn't satisfy. I always had a hankering after machinery, and I used to teach myself drawing. The lessons, however, did not turn out very successful, when I put them to the test."

"What did you do?" asked Miranda.

"I went up North to Leeds. There's a firm of railway contractors and manufacturers of locomotives. Sir John Martin is the head partner, and I had seen him once or twice at my father's house, for he took and takes a great interest in the Yorkshire clergy."

"I see. You went to him and told him who you were," said Miranda, who inclined towards Charnock more and more from the interest which she took in a youth so entirely strange, and apart from her own up-bringing, just as he on his part had been from the first attracted to her by the secure traditional life of which she was the flower, of which he traced associations in her simplicity, and up to this day, at all events, her lack of affectations.

"No," replied Charnock, "it would have been wiser if I had done that; but I didn't. I changed my name, and applied for a vacancy as draughtsman. I obtained it, and held the post for three weeks. Why they suffered me for three weeks is still a mystery, for of course I couldn't draw at all. At the end of three weeks I was discharged. I asked to be taken on as anything at thirteen shillings a week. I saw Sir John Martin himself. He said I couldn't live on thirteen shillings; I said I could, and he asked me how." Charnock began to laugh at his own story. "I told him how," he said. "I lived practically for nothing."

"How?" said Miranda. "Quick, tell me!" Charnock laughed again. "I had been three weeks at the works, you see, where hands were continually changing. I lived in a sort of mechanics' boarding-house, and I lived practically for nothing, on condition that I kept the house full, which I was able to do, for I got on very well with the men at the works. Sir John laughed when I told him, and took me into the office. So there I was a clerk again, which I didn't want to be; however, I was not a clerk for long. One Sunday Sir John Martin came down to the boarding-house and asked for me. It was dinner time, and he was shown straight into the dining-room, where I was sitting, if you please, at the head of the table, in my shirtsleeves, carving for all I was worth. He leaned against the door and shook with laughter. 'You are certain to get on,' he said; 'but I would like a few minutes with you alone.' I put on my coat, and went out with him into the street. 'Is your name Charnock?' he asked, and I answered that it was. 'I thought I knew your face,' said he, 'and that's why I took you into my office, though I couldn't put a name to you. So if you are proud enough to think that I took you on your own merits, you are wrong. You might as well have told me your real name, and saved yourself some time. Look at that!' and he gave me a newspaper, and pointed out an advertisement. A firm of solicitors in London was advertising for me, and the firm, I happened to know, looked after my aunt's affairs. I went to London that night. My aunt had died sixteen months before, and had left me six hundred a year. The rest was easy. I took Sir John's advice. 'Railways,' he said, 'railways; they are the white man's tentacles;' and Sir John gave me my first employment as an engineer."

Miranda was silent for a long while after Charnock had ended his story. Charnock himself had nothing further to say. It was for her to speak, not for him to question. She had sent the glove. She knew why he had come. Miranda, however, took a turn along the flagged pathway, and leaned over the breast-high wall and pointed out a vulture above the valley, and talked in inattentive, undecided tones upon any impersonal topic. It was natural, Charnock thought, that she should wish to con over what he had told her. So he rose from his chair.

"Shall I come back to-morrow?" he asked, and she rallied herself to answer him.

"Will you?" she exclaimed. "I should be so glad," and checking the ardour of her words, she explained, "I mean of course if you have nothing better to do," and she examined a flower with intense absorption, and then looked at him pathetically over her shoulder, as he moved away. So again he lost sight of the Miranda of the balcony, and carried away his first impression, that he had met that afternoon with a stranger.

His fervour of the morning changed to a chilling perplexity. He wondered at the change in her. Something else, too, seized upon his thoughts, and exercised his fancies. Why had she stood so long outside the door before she hurried in with her simulated surprise? How had she looked as she paused there, silent and motionless? That question in particular haunted him, for he thought that if only he could have seen her through the closed door he would have found a clue which would lead him to comprehend and to justify her.

Absorbed by these thoughts he sat through dinner unobservant of his few neighbours at the long table. He was therefore surprised when, as he stood in the stone hall, lighting his cigar, a friendly hand was clapped down upon his shoulder, and an affable voice remarked:—

"Aha, dear friend! Finished the little job at Algeciras, I saw. What are you doing at Ronda?"

"What are you?" asked Charnock, as he faced the irrepressible Major Wilbraham.

"Trying to make seven hundred per annum into a thousand. You see I have no secrets. Now confidence for confidence, eh, dear friend?" and his eyes drew cunningly together behind the glowing end of his cigar.

"I am afraid that I must leave you to guess."

"Guessing's not very sociable work."

"Perhaps that's why I am given to it," said Charnock, and he walked between the stone columns and up the broad staircase.

The Major looked after him without the slightest resentment.

"Slipped up that time, Ambrose, my lad," he said to himself, and sauntered cheerfully out of the hotel.

Five minutes later Charnock passed through the square at a quick walk. Wilbraham was meditating a translation of the Carmen Sæculare, but business habits prevailed with him. He thrust the worn little Horace into his breast-pocket and followed Charnock at a safe distance. By means of a skill acquired by much practice, he walked very swiftly and yet retained the indifferent air of a loiterer. There was another picture of the tracker and the tracked to be seen that evening, but in Ronda instead of Tangier, and Charnock was unable to compare it with its companion picture, since, in this case, he was the tracked. The two men passed down the hill to the bridge. Charnock stopped for a little and stood looking over the parapet to the water two hundred and fifty feet below, which was just visible through the gathering darkness like a ridge of snow on black soil. Wilbraham halted at the end of the bridge. It seemed that Charnock was merely taking a stroll. He had himself, however, nothing better to do at the moment. He waited and repeated a stanza of his translation to the rhythm of the torrent, and was not displeased. Charnock moved on across the bridge, across the Plaza on the farther side of the bridge, up a street until he came to an old Moorish house that showed a blank yellow wall to the street and a heavy walnut door encrusted with copper nails.

Then he stopped again and looked steadily at the house and for a long while. Wilbraham began pensively to whistle a slow tune under his breath. Charnock walked on, stopped again, looked back to the house, as though he searched for a glimpse of the lights. But there was no chink or cranny in that blank wall. The house faced the street, blind, dark, and repellent.

Charnock suddenly retraced his steps. Wilbraham had just time to mount the doorsteps of a house as though he was about to knock, before Charnock passed him. Charnock had not noticed him. Wilbraham descended the steps and followed Charnock back into the Plaza.

Charnock was looking for a road which he had seen that afternoon from Miranda's garden, a road which wound in zigzags down the cliff. The road descended from the Plaza, Charnock discovered it, walked down it; behind him at a little distance walked Wilbraham. It was now falling dark, but the night was still, so that Wilbraham was compelled to drop yet farther and farther behind, lest the sound of his footsteps upon the hard, dry ground should betray his pursuit. He fell so far behind, in fact, that he ceased to hear Charnock's footsteps at all. He accordingly hurried; he did more than hurry, he ran; he turned an angle of the road and immediately a man seated upon the bank by the road-side said:—

"*Buenas noches.*"

The man was Charnock.

Wilbraham had the presence of mind not to stop.

"*Felices suenos,*" he returned in a gruff voice and continued to run. He ran on until another angle of the road hid him. Then he climbed on to the top of the bank, which was high, and with great caution doubled back along the ridge until Charnock was just beneath him.

Charnock was gazing upwards; Wilbraham followed his example, and saw that right above his head, on the rim of the precipice, an open window glowed upon the night, a square of warm yellow light empanelled in the purple gloom.

The ceiling of the room was visible, and just below the ceiling a gleam as of polished panels. At that height above them the window seemed very small; its brightness exaggerated the darkness which surrounded it; and both men looked into it as into a tiny theatre of marionettes and expected the performance of a miniature play.

All that they saw, however, was a shadow-pantomime thrown upon the ceiling, and that merely of a tantalising kind—the shadow of a woman's head and hair, growing and diminishing as the unseen woman moved away or to the candles. A second shadow, and this too the shadow of a woman, joined the first. But no woman showed herself at the window, and Charnock, tiring of the entertainment, returned to his hotel.

Wilbraham remained to count the houses between that lighted window and the chasm of the Tajo. He counted six. Then he returned, but not immediately to the hotel. On reaching the Plaza he walked, indeed, precisely in the opposite direction, away from the Tajo, and he counted the houses which he passed and stopped before the seventh.

The seventh was noticeable for its great doors of walnut-wood and the geometrical figures which were traced upon it with copper nails.

The Major cocked his hat on one side, and stepped out for the hotel most jauntily. "These little accidents," said he, "a brigantine sighted off Ushant; a man going out for a walk! If only one has patience! Patience, there's the secret. A little more, and how much—a great poet!" And he entered the hotel.

Charnock rose from a bench in the hall, "Pleasant night for a stroll," said he.

"Business with me, dear old boy," replied the Major. "I fancy that after all I have made that seven hundred per annum into a thou. I am not sure, but I think so. Good-night, sleep well, be good!" With a flourish of his hand over the balustrade of the stairs, the Major disappeared.

Charnock sat down again on the bench and reflected.

"Wilbraham's at Ronda. I find him at Ronda when I am sent for to Ronda. Wilbraham said good-night to me on the road. Wilbraham was following me; Wilbraham's clothes were dusty: it was Wilbraham who kicked his toes into the grass on the top of the bank while I sat at the bottom. Have I to meet Wilbraham? What has his seven hundred per annum to do with Mrs. Warriner? Well, I shall learn to-morrow," he concluded, and so went to bed.

A.E.W. MASON

XIII

Wherein the Hero's Perplexities Increase

Charnock, however, learned nothing the next morning, except perhaps a lesson in patience. For the greater part of his visit was occupied in extracting a thorn from one of Mrs. Warriner's fingers. They chanced to be alone in the garden when the accident occurred, and Miranda naturally came to him for assistance. She said no word about the glove, nor did he; it was part of the compact that he should be silent. He came the next day, and it seemed that there was something amiss with Miranda's hairpins, for the coils of her hair were continually threatening to tumble about her shoulders; at least, so she said, complaining of the weight of her hair. But again there was no mention of the glove. That afternoon Charnock was introduced to Miss Holt, whom Miranda kept continually at her side, until Charnock took his leave, when she accompanied him across the patio.

"We never seem to get an opportunity of talking to each other," said she, with the utmost innocence. "Will you ride with me to-morrow? Say at two. We might ride as far as Ronda La Viega."

Charnock, who within the last half-hour had begun to consider whether it would not be wise for him to return to Algeciras, eagerly accepted the invitation. To-morrow everything would be explained. They would ride out together, alone, and she would tell him of the dragon he was required to slay, and no doubt explain why, for these last two days, she had been marketing her charms. That certainly needed explanation—for even at this moment in the patio, she was engaged in kissing a kitten with too elaborate a preparation of her lips to avoid a suspicion that the pantomime was intended for a spectator.

Charnock was punctual to the minute of his appointment, and in Miranda's company rode through the town. As they passed the hotel, Major Wilbraham came out of the doorway. He took off his hat. Charnock nodded in reply and turned towards Miranda, remembering his suspicions as to whether Wilbraham was concerned in the mysterious peril which he was to combat. To his surprise Miranda instantly smiled at the Major with extreme friendliness, and markedly returned his bow.

"Clever, clever!" muttered the Major, as he bit his moustache and commended her man(oe)uvre. "A little overdone, perhaps; the bow a trifle too marked; still, it's clever! Ambrose, you will have that thousand."

Charnock was perplexed. "How long have you known Wilbraham?" he asked.

Miranda stammered, bent her head, and smiled as it were in spite of herself.

"A long while," she answered, and then she sighed. "A long while," she repeated softly. Charnock was exasperated to a pitch beyond his control.

"If you want to make me believe that you are in love with him," he returned sharply, almost roughly, "you will fail, Mrs. Warriner. I should find it hard to believe that he is even one of your friends."

The words were hardly out of his lips before he regretted them. They insulted her. She was hardly the woman to sit still under an insult; but her manner again surprised him. He was almost prepared to be sent curtly to the right about, whereas she made no answer whatever. She coloured hotly, and rode forward ahead of him until they were well out of the town and descending the hill into the bottom of the valley. Then she fell back again by his side, and said: "Why is your face always so—illegible?"

"Is it?" he asked.

"It's a lid—a shut lid," she said. "One never knows what you think, how you are disposed." She spoke with some irritation perhaps, but sincerely, and without any effort at provocation.

"I was not aware," returned Charnock. "You must set it down to habit, Mrs. Warriner. I was brought up in a hard school, and learned, no doubt, intuitively the wisdom of reticence."

"Is it always wisdom?" she asked doubtfully, and it seemed a strange question to come from her whose business it was to speak, just as it was his to listen. But very likely her doubt was in this instance preferable to his wisdom. Some word of surprise at the change in her, perhaps one simple gesture of impatience, would have broken down the barrier between them. But he had taken the buffets of her provocations and her advances with, as she truly said, an illegible face.

"Is it always wisdom?" she asked, and she added: "You were not so reticent when I first met you;" and just that inconsistency between his bearing at Lady Donnisthorpe's ball, and his inexpressive composure of these few last days, might have revealed to her at this moment what he thought, and how he was disposed, had she brought a cooler mind to consider it. For the man was not chary of expression when the world went well with him; it was only in the presence of disappointments, rebuffs, and aversions that his face became a lid.

They left their horses at a farm-house, and climbed up the rough, steep slope to the windy ridge on which the old Roman town was built. They sat for a while upon the stones of the old wall, looking across the great level plain of olive trees, and poplars, and white villages gleaming in the sunlight. Here was a fitting moment for the story to be told, Charnock thought, and expected its telling. But he only saw that Miranda scrutinised his looks, and he only heard her gabbling of this triviality and that with a feverish vivacity. And no doubt his face betrayed less than ever what he thought and felt.

"Shall I see you to-morrow?" she asked as they parted that afternoon outside her door.

"I will come round in the morning after lunch," he replied, and she uttered a quick little sigh of pleasure, which made Charnock turn his horse with a sharp, angry tug at the rein, and ride quickly away across the bridge.

That first impulse to leave Ronda had gone from him. He was engaged, through his own wish and action, to serve Mrs. Warriner, and he was resolved to keep the engagement to the letter. But he was beginning to realise that he should be serving a woman whom in the bottom of his heart he despised. The message of his mirror became a fable; he recalled what Miranda herself had suggested, that the look of distress which he had seen upon the face was due to his chance visit to *Macbeth*; and certain words which a woman had spoken at Lady Donnisthorpe's dance as she sat by the window recurred to him. "There's a coquette" was one phrase which on this particular evening recurred and recurred to his thoughts.

However, he returned to the house upon the rim of the precipice the next morning, and being led by a servant through the patio into the garden, came upon Miranda unawares. She was busy amongst her flowers, cutting the choicest and arranging them in a basket, and she did not notice Charnock's appearance. Charnock was well content with her inattention. For in the quiet grace of her movements, as she walked amongst her flowers, he caught a glimpse of the Miranda whom he knew, the Miranda of the balcony. The October sunlight was golden about them, a light wind tempered its heat, and on the wind were borne upwards to his ears the distant cries of peasants in the plain below. He had a view now and then of her face, as she rose and stooped, and he remarked a gentleness and a simplicity in its expression which had been foreign to it since he had come to Ronda.

But the expression changed when she saw Charnock standing in the garden.

"Who do you think I am cutting these flowers for?" she asked with an intolerable playfulness. "You will never guess."

Charnock stepped over to her side.

"Mrs. Warriner," said he, "will you give me one?"

She looked at him with a whimsical hesitation.

"They are intended for Gibraltar," she said, as she caressed the bunch which she held—but she spoke with a great repugnance, and the playfulness had gone from her voice before she had ended the sentence.

"For Gibraltar?" he exclaimed, remembering the gentle look upon her face as she had culled them. "For whom in Gibraltar? For whom?" He confronted her squarely; his voice commanded her to answer.

She drew back from him; the colour went from her cheeks; her fingers were interclasped convulsively; it seemed as though the words she tried to speak were choking her. But her emotion lasted for no more than a moment, though for that moment Charnock could not doubt that it was real. He took a step forwards, and she was again mistress of herself.

"Yes, I will give you one," she said hurriedly. "I will even fix it in your button-hole. Will you be grateful if I do? Will you be very grateful?" Charnock neither answered nor moved. He stood in front of her with a face singularly stolid. But Miranda's hands touched his breast, and at the shock of her fingers he drew in his breath, and his whole body vibrated.

And how it came about neither of them knew, but in an instant the flowers were on the ground between them, and her hands gripped his shoulders as they stood face to face and tightened upon them in a passionate appeal. He read the same passionate appeal in her eyes, which now frankly looked up to his.

"You don't know," she cried incoherently, "you don't know."

"But I wish to know," he exclaimed, "tell me;" and his arms went about her waist. She uttered a cry and violently tore and plucked his arms from her.

"No," she cried, "no, not now," and she heard the latch of the door click. Charnock heard it too.

A.E.W. MASON

"When?" said he, as he stood away, and the door opened and Major Wilbraham with his hat upon his heart bowed, with great elegance, upon the threshold. Miranda started. She looked from Charnock to Wilbraham, from Wilbraham to Charnock.

"So he is one of your friends," said Charnock.

"Have you the right to choose my friends?" she asked, and she greeted Wilbraham warmly.

The Major seemed very much at his ease. It was the first occasion on which he had had the effrontery to push his way into the house, but from his manner one would have judged him a family friend. He waved a hand to Charnock.

"So you are there, dear old darling boy!" he cried. His endearments increased with every meeting. "I saw you come in and thought I might as well call at the same time, eh, Mrs. Warriner? So pleasant, I meet Charnock everywhere. Destiny will have us friends. That dear Destiny!" And as Charnock with an ill-concealed air of distaste turned from them towards the valley, Wilbraham whispered to Miranda, "You need have no fear. I shall not say a word—unless you force me to."

Miranda drew back. She stood for a moment with her hands clenched, and her eyelids closed, her face utterly weary and ashamed. Then with a gesture of revolt she turned towards Charnock.

Instantly the Major stepped in front of her.

"May I beg one?" said he, pointing to the basket of flowers. It was all very well for him to threaten Miranda that he would tell Charnock of her husband; but it would not suit his purpose at all for her actually to tell him on an impulse of revolt against the deception and the hold he himself had upon her. So he fixed his eyes steadily upon her face.

"May I beg one?" and he bent towards the stool on which the basket was set.

"Not of those!" she cried, "not of those!" and she snatched up the basket and held it close.

"But you shall have one," she continued with a forced laugh, as over Wilbraham's shoulder she saw Charnock watching them, and she snapped off some flowers from their stems with her fingers until she held a bunch. "There! Make your choice, Major. A flower sets off a man."

"Just as a wife sets off a husband, eh, Mrs. Warriner?" returned the Major, with a sly gallantry, as he fixed the flower in his button-hole. "Eh, Charnock, did you hear?"

He joined Charnock as he spoke, and Miss Holt coming from the house, the talk became general. But Charnock noticed that at one moment Miranda moved carelessly away from the group, and leaning carelessly over the wall, carelessly dropped down the face of the cliff the whole bunch of flowers from which Wilbraham had chosen one. As she lifted her eyes, however, she saw Charnock watching her, and at once and for the rest of the time during which her guests remained, she made her court to Wilbraham with a feverish assiduity. She laughed immoderately at his jokes, she was extremely confused by his compliments, she displayed the completest deference to his opinions; so that even the unobservant Miss Holt was surprised.

Charnock was the first to break up the gathering.

"I must be going," he said curtly to Miranda.

"It would almost seem that you were displeased with us," she answered defiantly.

"I beg your pardon," said he, coldly. "I do not claim the privilege to be displeased."

"Jolly afternoon," murmured the Major, in a cheery desire to make the peace, "good company, dear old friends"—and he saw that Miranda was unmistakably bowing good-bye to himself. He took the hint at once. The Major was in a very good humour that afternoon, and as the party walked back to the house, he fell behind to Miranda, who had already fallen behind.

"Clever, clever," he remarked encouragingly, "to play me off against the real man. A little overdone perhaps, but clever. I trust I did my part. We'll make it a thousand per annum."

Miranda quickened her pace and took her leave of her visitors at the door of the garden. Wilbraham was in no particular hurry to settle his business; he was quite satisfied for that afternoon, and he entered genially into conversation with Miss Holt upon the subject of her grievances.

Thus Miss Holt and Wilbraham crossed the patio and entered the passage to the outer door. Charnock followed a few steps behind them; and just after Miss Holt with her companion had entered the passage, while he yet stood in the patio, he heard a door slam behind him.

He turned, and walked round the tiny group of tamarisks in the centre of the patio. It was not the door into the garden which had slammed, because that now stood wide open, whereas he remembered he had closed it behind him; and the only other door in that side of the house was the door of Miranda's parlour. He had left Miranda in the garden; it was plainly she who had slammed the door, and had slammed it upon herself.

Charnock was alone in the empty patio. It was very quiet; the sunshine was a steady golden glow upon the tiled floor, upon the tiled walls; above in the square of blue there was no scarf of cloud. He stood in the quiet empty patio, and the touch of her fingers tingled again upon his breast. Again he saw her drop the flowers she had culled for Wilbraham down the cliff. Amongst his doubts and perplexities those two recollections shone. They were accurate, indisputable. Her feverish vivacity, her coquetries, her friendliness to Wilbraham, her silence towards himself, the basket of flowers for Gibraltar—these things were puzzles. But twice that afternoon she had been true to herself, and each time she had betrayed the reality of her trouble and the reality of her need.

It was very still in the patio. A bee droned amongst the tamarisks. It seemed to Charnock that, after much sojourning in outlandish corners of the earth, he who had foreseen his life as a struggle with the brutality of inanimate things was, after all, here in the still noonday, within these four walls, to undergo the crisis of his destiny. He gently turned the handle of the door and entered the room.

XIV

Miranda Professes Regret for a Practical Joke

He closed the door behind him. Miranda had neither seen nor heard him enter. She sat opposite to the door, on the other side of the round oak table, her arms stretched out upon the table, her face buried in her arms. She was not weeping, and Charnock might have believed from the abandonment of her attitude that she lay in a swoon, but for one movement that she made. Her outstretched hands were clasped together and her fingers perpetually worked, twisting and intertwisting. There was no sound whatever in the room beyond the ticking of a clock, and Charnock leaned against the door and found the silence horrible. He would have preferred it to have been broken if only by the sound of her tears. All his doubts, all his accusations, were swept clean out of his brain by the sight of her distress, and, tortured himself, he stood witness of her torture. He advanced to the table, and leaning over it took the woman's clasped hands into his.

"Miranda!" he whispered, and again, "Miranda!" and there was just the same tenderness in his voice, as when he had first pronounced the name in the balcony over St. James's Park.

Miranda did not lift her head, but her hands answered the clasp of his. She did not in truth know at that moment who was speaking to her. She was only sensible of the sympathy of his touch and the great comfort of his voice.

Charnock bent lower towards her.

"I love you," he said, "you—Miranda."

Then she raised her face and stared at him with uncomprehending eyes.

"I love you," he repeated.

She looked down towards her hands which he still held and suddenly she shivered.

"I love you," he said a third time.

And she understood. She wrenched her hands away, she stretched out her arms, she thrust him away from her, in her violence she struck him.

"No, it's not true," she cried, "it's not true!" and so fell to pleading volubly. "Say that it's not true, now, at once. Say there's no truth in your words. Say that pity prompted them and only pity," and her voice rose again in a great horror. Horror glittered too in her eyes. "Say that you spoke more than you meant to speak!"

"I can say that," he answered. "When I came into this room I had no thought of speaking—as I did. But I saw you—I watched your hands," and he caught his breath, "and they plucked the truth out from me. For what I said is true."

"No!" she cried.

"Very true," he repeated quietly.

Her protesting arms fell limply to her sides. She nodded her head, submitted to his words, acknowledged their justice.

"Yes," she said, "yes. I knew this afternoon. You told me in the garden, and though I would not know, still I could not but know."

Then she rose from her chair and walked to the window. Charnock did not speak. He hung upon her answer, and yet dreaded to hear it, so that when her lips moved, he would have had them still, and when they ceased to move, he was conscious of a great relief. After a long while she spoke, very slowly and without turning to face him, words which he did not understand.

"Love," she said, in a wondering murmur, "is it so easily got? And by such poor means? Surely, then it's a slight thing itself, of no account, surely not durable," and at once her calmness forsook her; she was caught up in a whirl of passion. She raised a quivering face, and cried aloud in despair: "It's the friend I wanted; I want no lover!"

"But you have both," returned Charnock. With a hand upon the table he leaned over it towards her. "You have both."

"Ah!" exclaimed Miranda. With extraordinary swiftness she swung round and copied his movement. She leaned her hand upon the table, and bent forward to him. "But to win the one I have had to create the other. To possess the friend I have had to make the lover," and she suddenly threw herself back and stood erect. "Well, then," and she spoke with a thrill in her voice, as though she had this instant become aware of a new and a true conviction, "I must use neither—I will use neither—I want neither."

She faced Charnock resolute, and in her own fancy inflexible to any appeal. Only he made no appeal; he drew his hand across his forehead and looked at her with an expression of simple worry and bewilderment.

"My ways have lain amongst men, and men, and men," he said regretfully. "I wish I understood more about women."

The simplicity of his manner and words touched her as no protestations would have done, and broke down her self-control.

"My dear, my dear!" she cried, with a laugh which had more of tears in it than amusement, "I am not so sure that we understand so very much about ourselves;" and she dropped again into the chair and covered her face with her hands. But she heard Charnock move round the table towards her, and she dared not risk the touch of his hand, or so much as the brushing of his coat against her dress. She drew her hands from her face, held out her arms straight in front of her like bars, and shrank back in the chair behind the protection of those bars.

"I do not want you," she said deliberately, with a quiet harshness. "That, at all events, I understand and know. Go! Go away! I do not want you!" and the words, spoken this time without violence or haste, struck Charnock like a blow.

He stood dazed. He shook his head, as though it sang from the blow. Miranda drew in a breath. "Go!" she repeated.

"You do not want me?" he asked, and somehow, whether it was owing to his tone or his look, Miranda understood from the few words of his question how much he had built upon the belief that she needed him; and consequently the reply she made now cost her more than all the rest to make. "I do not," she managed to say firmly, and dared not hazard another syllable.

Charnock felt in his breast-pocket, took out an envelope, and from the envelope a glove. "Yet this was sent to me." He laid the glove upon the table. "It was sent by you." Miranda took it up. "It contradicts your words."

Miranda turned the glove over, and stretched it out upon her knees. "Does it?" she asked, with a slow smile, "does it contradict my words?"

"You sent it to me?"

"No doubt."

"You summoned me by sending it."

"Surely."

"For some purpose, then?"

"Ah, but for what purpose?" said she, leaning forwards in her chair. The cold smile was still upon her face, and seemed to Charnock unfriendly as even her violence had not been. It had some cruelty too, and perhaps, too, some cunning.

A.E.W. MASON

"For what purpose? You should know. It is for you to say," he answered in a dull, tired voice. He had built more upon this unneeded service than he himself had been aware.

"I will tell you," continued Miranda. "You have talked to my companion Miss Holt?"

"Yes."

"She has no very strong faith in men. Perhaps you noticed as much."

"No."

"I did not agree with her. I had the glove. It would be—amusing to know whether she was right or whether I was. I sent it to you."

"Just to prove whether I should keep my word or not?"

"Yes," said Miranda.

"Just for your amusement, in a word?"

"Amusement was the word I chose."

"I see, I see." His voice was lifeless, his face dull and stony. Miranda moved uneasily as she watched him; but he did not notice her movement or regard her with any suspicion. His thoughts and feelings were muffled. He seemed to be standing somewhere a long way outside himself and contemplating the two people here in the room with a deal of curiosity, and with perhaps a little pity; of which pity the woman had her share with the man. "I see," he continued. "It was all a sham?"

Miranda glanced at him, and from him to the glove. "Even the glove was a sham," she said quickly. "Look at it."

He bent down and lifted it from her knees. Then he drew up a chair to the table, sat down, and examined the glove. Miranda hitched her chair closer to the table, too, and propping her elbows there, supported her chin upon her hands.

"You see that the glove is fresh," she said.

"It has been worn," answered Charnock. "The fingers have been shaped by wearing."

"It was worn by me for ten minutes in this room the day I posted it to you."

"But the tear?" he asked with a momentary quickening of speech.

"I tore it."

"I see." He laid the glove upon the table. "And the other glove— the one you wore that night—the one I tore upon the balcony over St. James's Park? It was you I met that night in London? Or wasn't it?"

The question was put without any sarcasm, but with the same dull curiosity which had marked his other questions, and on her side she answered it simply as she had answered the others. "Yes, it was I whom you met, and the glove you speak of was thrown away."

It seemed that he had come to the end of his questions, for he sat for a little, drumming with his fingers on the table. Once he looked up and towards the window, as though his very eyes needed the relief of the wide expanse of valley.

"Now will you go? Please," said Miranda, gently, and the next moment regretted that she had spoken.

"Oh, yes, I will go," he answered. "I will go back to Algeciras, and from Algeciras to England." He was not looking at her, and so noticed nothing of the spasm of pain which for a second convulsed her face at his literal acceptation of her prayer. "But before I go, tell me;" and the questions began again.

"You say you need no one?"

"No one."

"Then why did you cry out a minute ago, 'It's the friend I want, not the lover'? You were not amusing yourself then. Why, too, did you—this afternoon in the garden, perhaps you remember—when the flowers fell on to the ground between us? Neither were you amusing yourself then."

Miranda drew the glove away from where it lay in front of him; absently she began to slip it over her hand, and then becoming aware of what she did, and of certain associations with that action at this moment, she hurriedly stripped it off.

"Perhaps I have no right to press you," he said; "but I should like to know."

Miranda spread the glove out on the table, and carefully divided and spread out the fingers. "I will tell you," she said at length, with something of a spirt in the quickness of her speech. "I am still capable of remorse, though very likely you can hardly believe that. Do you remember," she began to speak with greater ease, "when we rode out to Ronda La Viega, I asked you why you never expressed what you felt? I was then beginning to be afraid that you would take my—my trick too much to heart—that you would really think I needed you. My fear became certain this afternoon, when I—I was putting the flower in your coat. I was sorry then, as you saw when you came into the room. I was yet more sorry when you spoke to me as you did, for I thought that if you hadn't cared, if you had never intended to be more than my friend, the trick would not have mattered so much. And that was just what I meant, when I said it was the friend I wanted, not the lover."

Charnock listened to the explanation, accepted it and put it away in his mind.

"I see," he remarked, and her bosom rose and fell quickly. "All this time you have been just playing with me as you played with Wilbraham this afternoon."

"Just in the same way," she returned without flinching.

"Ah, but you dropped his flower down the cliff," he exclaimed suddenly.

"You forget that yours had already fallen on to the ground."

"Yes, that's true," and the suspicion died out of his face. "And that basket of flowers?" he asked.

This time, and for the first time since the questions had begun, Miranda did flinch. She had a great difficulty in answering, "It has already been sent off."

"To Gibraltar?" Miranda's difficulty increased. "To whom at Gibraltar? A friend, a man?"

Miranda's face grew very white; she tried to speak and failed; her throat, her lips, refused the answer. "At all events," she managed to whisper hoarsely, "not to a woman," and thereupon she laughed most mirthlessly, till the strange, harsh, strangled noise of it penetrated as something unfamiliar to Charnock's dazed mind.

"I beg your pardon," he said; "I was forgetful. I had no right to ask you," and he rose from his chair. She rose too. "I am glad," he continued with a formal politeness, "that you do not after all stand in need of anyone's help."

"Oh, no," she replied carelessly, "no one's;" and almost before she was aware, he was holding her wrists, one in each of his hands, and with his eyes he was searching her face, silently interrogating her for the truth. Once before, upon the balcony, he had bidden her in just this way answer him, and now, as then, she found herself under a growing compulsion to obey.

"You hurt me," she had the wit to say, and instantly Charnock released her wrists.

"I beg your pardon," said he, and he walked to the door. At the door he turned. "Tell me," he said abruptly, "you dropped your glove—not that one on the table, but the other—just as you stepped out on to the balcony?"

"Yes," she answered, and wondered what was coming.

"Was that an accident?"

Miranda stepped back and lowered her head.

"You remember everything," she murmured.

"Was it an accident?"

"You are unsparing."

"Was it an accident?"

"No."

"It was a trick, a sham like all the rest?"

"Just like all the rest," said Miranda, wearily.

"I see," said Charnock. "Good-bye."

He went out of the room and closed the door behind him.

It was very quiet and still in the patio. In the square of blue sky there was no cloud; the sunshine poured into the court, only in one corner there was a shadow climbing the wall, where there had been no shadow when he entered the room. He vaguely wondered what the time was, and then someone laughed. Someone above him. He looked up. Jane Holt was leaning over the railing of the balcony.

He made some sort of remark; and he gathered from her reply that he had been asking why she laughed.

"Why did I laugh?" she said. "Do you believe in affinities?"

"No," he rejoined. "Why?"

She descended the stairs as she answered him.

"I saw you standing in the doorway there with your hand on your throat, breathing hard and quick, and altogether a very tragical picture."

Charnock was not aware whether the details were true or not. "Well?" he asked.

"Well," she replied. "Do you remember the afternoon you came here? I was in that lounge chair. You were shown into the parlour. You did not notice me. Neither did Miranda when she followed you. But she stopped on the threshold."

"Yes, I remarked it. She stopped for some while. Well?"

"Well, she stood just as you were standing a minute ago, in that precise attitude, with her hand to her throat, breathing hard and quick, and with a face not less tragical."

Charnock's face now at all events ceased to look tragical. Jane Holt saw it brighten extraordinarily. Miranda, had she been there, would not at this moment have complained of its lack of expression.

"That's true?" he asked eagerly. "What you tell me is true? She stood here, and in that attitude?"

"Yes."

"That's the one point unexplained. I forgot to ask. She did not refer to it. She stood here breathing hard and quick, you say, before she entered the room—with all that appearance of surprise—she stood here! Mere remorse does not account for that, does not account for her manner. On her own showing it cannot account, since the remorse was only felt this afternoon. There *is* something more." He was talking enigmas to Miss Holt, who went into the parlour and left him in the patio to talk to himself if he would. She was not greatly interested in his relationship towards Miranda. However, Charnock was not the only person to talk enigmas to her that afternoon. She found Miranda standing just as Charnock had left her. Miranda remained standing, with any absent answer to Jane Holt's remarks, until the big outer-doors clanged to, and made the house tremble.

Then she started violently. The sound of those doors shook her as no word or look of Charnock's had done. Her ears magnified it. It seemed to her that the doors swung to from the east and from the west, clean across the world, shutting Charnock upon the one side, and herself upon the other. It seemed to her too that as they clanged together, her heart was caught and broken between them.

"You were wrong, Jane," she said. "There are men who would be friends if we would only let them. Possibly we always find it out too late; I only found it out this afternoon." The clock struck the hour as she was speaking. "Four o'clock; the train for Algeciras leaves at six-fifteen," she said.

XV

In Which the Major Loses his Temper and Recovers It

All that evening Miranda's imagination followed the 6.15 train from Ronda to Algeciras. She looked at the clock at half-past ten. The ferry would be crossing from Algeciras to Gibraltar, and no doubt Charnock was crossing upon it. She felt a loneliness of which she had never had experience. And when she woke up in the morning from a troubled sleep, it was only to picture some stately mail steamer marching out from Algeciras Bay. She was conscious to the full of the irony of the situation. If she had only met this man years ago, seven years ago—that regret was a continual cry at her heart, and not the least part of her loneliness was made up from her clear remembrance of the picture of herself which she had given him to carry away.

She ordered her horse to be brought round early that morning, and rode out past the hotel a few minutes before nine. Major Wilbraham saw her pass. He was down betimes as a rule when he stayed in a hotel, since it was his habit, as often as possible, to look over the letters which came for the different visitors. The mere postmark he had known upon occasion to give him quite valuable hints. There was only, however, a telegram for Charnock, which he genially offered to deliver himself and did deliver, running into Charnock's bedroom for that purpose. Charnock thanked him and read the telegram. It seemed to raise his spirits.

"Good news, old friend?" asked the Major.

"Well—interesting news," replied Charnock, as he lathered his face.

"Well, you shall give me it another time," said the Major, as he saw Charnock put the telegram in his pocket. "So long!"

The Major went downstairs and kept an eye upon the road. At ten o'clock he noticed Miranda returning slowly. He put on his hat and followed her. When he reached the house the horse was still at the door, but Miranda had gone in. He observed that Charnock was hesitating upon the other side of the road. Charnock was in fact debating his plan of action; the Major's was already prepared. The door stood open. Wilbraham put ceremony upon one side, the more readily since ceremony would very likely have barred the door in his face. He walked straight into the patio where Miranda stood before a little wicker table drawing off her gloves.

"Had a pleasant ride?" said the Major. "Nice horse; I am partial to roans myself—"

"What do you want?" asked Miranda.

"To so uncompromising a question, I must needs give an uncompromising reply. I want one thousand jimmies per annum," and the Major bowed gracefully.

"No," said Miranda.

"But excuse me, yes, very much yes. You see, there is my excellent young friend, the locomotive-man."

"Can't you keep his name out of the conversation?" she suggested, but with a dangerous quietude of voice.

"Indeed no," replied the Major, who was entirely at his ease. He looked sympathetically at her face. "You look pale; you have not slept well; you are tired, and so you do not follow me. Charnock is my God of the machine, a blind unconscious God—shall we say a Cupid, but a Cupid in the machine? Let me explain! May I be seated? No? So sorry! On the first night of Charnock's stay at Ronda, I had the honour to follow him while he took a stroll."

"You followed him unseen, of course?" said Miranda, contemptuously, as she tossed her gloves on to the wicker table.

"You take me, you take me perfectly," returned the Major. "I followed him unseen, a habit of mine, and at times a very profitable habit. Charnock walked—whither? Can you guess? Can't you tell?" He hummed with unabashed impertinence. "He walked down a certain road which winds down the precipice under your windows. Ah!"—he uttered the exclamation in a playful raillery, for Miranda's hand had gone to her heart; "he walked down that road until he came to an angle from which he could see your lighted window."

"Show me," said Miranda, suddenly. She walked round the patio, threw open the door of her parlour, and crossed to the window. The window was open, and the Major looked out. The window was in the outer wall of the wing, and was built on the very rim of the precipice. Wilbraham looked straight down on to the road.

"That was the angle, Mrs. Warriner," said he, pointing with his finger. "By that heap of stones he sat him down." Mrs. Warriner leaned out of the window with something of a smile parting her lips. "At the bottom of the bank he sat and aspired. Little Ambrose reclined on the top."

Miranda turned from the window abruptly. "Let us go back." She returned to the patio and took her former position by the wicker table. Wilbraham, upon the other side of it, faced her.

"We could only see the ceiling of the room," he continued, "and the shadow of your head. But so little contents an amorous engineer. He sighed, and what a sigh, and yet how typical! So hoarse it seemed the whistle of an engine; so deep, it surely came from a cutting. He went home singing beneath the stars. He did not tread the ground. How should he? Love was his permanent way."

Miranda had listened so far without interruption, though the Major, had he been less pleased with his flowery description, might have noticed something ominous in the still depths of her dark eyes. "Mr. Wilbraham," she said, "there is a little wicker table between us."

"I see it."

"And on the table?"

"A pair of gloves."

"Not only a pair of gloves."

"Ah true! A riding-whip."

"I was sure that you had not noticed it before."

The Major picked it up and examined the mounting of the handle. "It is very pretty," he remarked with emphasis, and laid it down again. "As I was about to say,"—he proceeded with his argument,—"I thus obtained on the night of Charnock's arrival a very clear knowledge of his sentiments towards you, while you, on the other hand, have been obliging enough to favour me with some hint of your own towards him, not merely this morning, when you asked me to point out the precise point of the road from which he worshipped your window, but yesterday when, in order to give an impetus to his bashfulness, you ingeniously courted myself. If I were, then, at all disposed to make unpleasantness, you see that all I have to do is to walk out of your house and inform the trustful Charnock that Mrs. Warriner is carefully concealing the existence of her husband from the man with whom she is in love."

Miranda took up the riding-whip. The Major did not give ground. If anything, he leaned a little towards her. His eyebrows drew together until they joined; his bird-like eyes narrowed.

A.E.W. MASON

"Drop it! Drop that whip," he commanded sharply. "I warn you, Mrs. Warriner. I have dealt with you gently, though you are a woman; be prudent. What if I took the gloves off? Eh?"

"You would place me in a better position," replied Miranda, who still held the whip, "to point out to you that your hands are not clean."

Wilbraham stepped back, stared at her, and burst into a laugh. "I will never deny that you are possessed or an admirable spirit," said he.

"I would rather have your threats than your compliments," said she. "For your threats I can answer with threats; I cannot do the same with your compliments."

"Threat for threat, then," said the Major; "but there's a difference in the threats. You cannot put yours into practice since I have my eyes upon the whip, whereas I can mine."

"Can you?" said Miranda, with a suspicion of triumph.

"I can," returned the Major. "I can walk straight out of your house and tell Luke Charnock," and he banged his hand upon the table and leaned over it. "Now what do you say?"

"I say that you cannot, for Mr. Charnock is at Gibraltar, if he is not already on the sea."

"Mr. Charnock is at Ronda, and contemplating the ornaments of your door at this very moment," said the Major, triumphantly.

But never did a man get less visible proofs of his triumph. Miranda, it is true, was evidently startled; her bosom rose and fell quickly; but she was pleasurably startled, as her face showed. For it cleared of its weariness with a magical swiftness, the blood pulsed warmly in her cheeks, her eyes sparkled and laughed, her contemptuous lips parted in the happiest of smiles.

Wilbraham construed her reception of his news in his own fashion.

"You may smile, my lady," said he, brutally. "It's gratifying no doubt to have your lover hanging about your doors, a wistful Lazarus for the crumbs of your favour. It's pleasant no doubt to transform a man into a tame whipped puppy-dog. There's not one of you, from Eve to a modern factory-girl, but envies Circe her enchantments, and imitates them to the best of her ability. Circes—Circes in laced petticoats and open-worked stockings—to help you in the dainty work of making a man a beast." The Major's vindictiveness had fairly got hold of him. "But in the original story, if you remember, the men resumed their shape; now what if I play Ulysses in our version of the story!—" There was a knock upon the outer door. The Major paused, and continued hurriedly: "Do you understand? That knock may have been Charnock's. Do you understand? He may be entering the house at this moment."

"He is," said Miranda, quietly.

The Major listened. He distinctly heard Charnock's voice speaking to the servant; he dropped his own to a whisper. "Then what if I told him, your lover, now and here, the truth about Ralph Warriner?"

"You shall," said Miranda.

Major Wilbraham was completely taken aback. She had spoken in no gust of passion, but slowly and calmly. Her face, equally calm, equally resolute, showed him that she intended and understood what she had said. The Major was in a predicament. The drawback to blackmailing as a profession is that the blackmailer's secret is only of value so long as he never tells it, his threats only of use so long as they are never enforced; and here he was in imminent danger of being compelled to tell his secret and execute his threat. If Charnock knew the truth, he would certainly lose his extra three hundred per annum. Moreover, since Charnock was a man, and not a woman, he would very likely lose his original seven hundred into the bargain. These reflections flashed simultaneously into the Major's mind; but already he heard Charnock's step sounding in the passage. "I don't wish to push you too far," he whispered. "Tomorrow, to-morrow."

"No, to-day," said Miranda, quietly. "You shall tell my lover the truth about Ralph Warriner, and to help you to tell it him convincingly you shall tell it with this mark across your face."

Charnock did not see the blow struck, but he heard Wilbraham's cry, and as he entered the patio, he saw the wheal redden and ridge upon his face. He stood still for a second in amazement. Wilbraham had reeled back from the table against the wall, with his coat-sleeve pressed upon his smarting cheeks. Miranda alone seemed composed. There was indeed even an air of relief about her; for she was at last to be lightened of the deception.

"Major Wilbraham," she said as she dropped the whip upon the table and walked away to a lounge chair, "Major Wilbraham,"—she seated herself in the chair as though she was to be henceforward a spectator,—"Major Wilbraham has a confidence to make to you," she said.

"And by God I have!" snarled the Major as he started forward. It would be told for a certain thing, either by Mrs. Warriner or himself, and since the slash of the whip burned intolerably upon his face, he meant to do the telling himself.

"That woman's husband is alive."

Charnock's face was a mask. He did not start; he did not even look at Miranda; only he was silent for some seconds. Then he said, "Well?" and said it in a quite commonplace, ordinary voice, as though he wondered what there was to make any pother about.

Miranda was startled, the Major utterly dumbfounded. His blow had seemingly failed to hurt, and his anger was thereby redoubled.

"A small thing, eh?" he sneered. "A husband more or less don't matter in these days of the sacred laws of passion? Well, very likely. But this husband is a peculiar sort of a husband. He slipped out of Gibraltar one fine night. Why? Because he had sold the plans of the new Daventry gun to a foreign government, being stony."

"Well?" said Charnock, again.

"Well, I know where he is."

"Well?" asked Charnock, for the third time, and with an unchanged imperturbability.

Wilbraham suddenly ceased from his accusations. He looked at Miranda, who was herself looking on the ground, and gently beating it with her foot. From Miranda he looked to Charnock. Then he uttered a long whistle, as if some new idea had occurred to him. "So you are both in the pretty secret, are you?" he said, and stopped to consider how that supposition affected himself. His hopes immediately revived. "Why, then, you are both equally interested in keeping it dark! I can't say but what I am glad, for I can point out to you precisely what I have pointed out to Mrs. Warriner. I have merely to present myself at Scotland Yard, observe that Ralph Warriner is alive, and mention a port in England where he may from time to time be found, and—do you follow me?—there is Ralph Warriner laid by the heels in a place which not even a triple-expansion locomotive, with the engineer from Algeciras for the driver, will get him out of."

"And how does that concern me?" asked Charnock.

"The consequences concern you. It will be known, for instance, that Mrs. Warriner has a real live husband."

"I see," said Charnock. He looked at Wilbraham with a curious interest. Then he spoke to Miranda, but without looking towards her at all. "It is blackmail, I suppose?"

"Yes," said she.

"It is a claim for common gratitude," Wilbraham corrected.

"What's the price of the claim?" asked Charnock, pleasantly.

"One thousand jimmies per annum is the minimum figure," replied the Major, whose jauntiness was quite restored. Since his affairs progressed so swimmingly towards prosperity, he was prepared to forgive, and, as soon as his looking-glass allowed, to forget that hasty slash of the riding-whip.

"And up till now how much have you received?" continued Charnock, in the same pleasant business-like voice.

"A beggarly two hundred and fifty."

"Then if for form's sake you will give Mrs. Warriner an I O U for that amount she can wish you good-day."

Wilbraham smiled gaily, and with some condescension. "Is it bluff?" said he. "Where's the use? My dear Charnock, I have a full hand, and—"

"My dear Major," replied Charnock, "I hold a royal straight flush."

He produced a telegram from his pocket. The Major eyed it with suspicion. "Is that the telegram I brought into your room this morning?"

"It is. To keep up your metaphor, you dealt me my hand. Do you call it?"

The Major cocked his head. Charnock's ease was so very natural; his good temper so complete. Still, he might be merely playing the game; besides, one never knew what there might be in a telegram. "I do," he said.

"Very well," said Charnock. He sat down upon a chair, and spread out the telegram on his knee. "You talk very airily, Major, of dropping in upon Scotland Yard. Would it surprise you to hear that Scotland Yard would welcome you with open arms, for other reasons than a mere gratitude for your information?"

The Major was more than disappointed; he confessed to being grieved. "I expected something more subtle, I did indeed. Really, my dear Charnock, you are a novice! Sir, a novice."

"But a novice with a royal straight flush. Major, why have you been living for four months at an out-of-the-way and unentertaining place like Tarifa?"

"I will answer you with frankness. I wished to keep my fingers upon Mrs. Warriner. An occasional tweak of the fingers, dear friend, is very useful if only to show that you are awake."

"Was that the only reason?"

"No," interposed Miranda. "He wanted quiet; he is translating Horace."

The Major actually blushed, for the first and last time that morning.

A.E.W. MASON

Accusations, even proofs of infamy, he could accept without a stir of the muscles; but to be charged, perhaps to be ridiculed, with his one honourable project—the Major was hurt.

"A little mean!" he said gently to Miranda. "You will agree with me when you think it over. A little mean!"

"But there was a third reason beyond those two," resumed Charnock. "When I saw you dining at the hotel on the night of my arrival, when I remembered that you had been living for four months at Tarifa, where from time to time I had the pleasure to come across you, I began, for reasons which there's no need to explain, to wonder whether you were causing any trouble to Mrs. Warriner. That night, too, if you remember, when I went for a stroll"—here Charnock faltered for a second, and Miranda looked quickly up—"you followed me, Major. When I sat down at the foot of the bank, you crouched upon the top. You made a mistake there, Major, for I at once thought it wise to learn what I could of your history and character. I accordingly wrote a letter that night to a friend of mine, who also happens to be an official at Scotland Yard. His answer, you see, comes by telegraph, and you will see that a reply is prepaid."

He handed the telegram to the Major. The Major read it through and glanced anxiously towards the door, taking up his hat from the table at the same time.

"I think so, too," said Charnock.

"What does the telegram say?" asked Miranda.

"Nothing definite, but every word of it is suggestive," answered Charnock. "I asked my friend if he knew anything of Major Ambrose Wilbraham. He wires me: 'Yes. Is he at Ronda?' and prepays the reply. If there's a warrant already issued, Major, I don't think I should waste time, but you of course are the best judge."

"Did you answer it?" asked the Major.

"I have not answered it yet. Do you think Scotland Yard will wait for an answer? It does not interest me very much. The one point which does interest me is this. You are hardly in a position to enter into communication with Scotland Yard in order to revenge yourself on Mrs. Warriner for not paying you blackmail."

Major Wilbraham tugged at his moustache. His jauntiness had vanished, and his face had grown very sombre and tired during the last few minutes.

"I get nothing, then?"

"Not one depreciated Spanish dollar."

There was a knock at the door. The Major started; he looked from Charnock to Miranda, his mouth opened, his eyes widened, he became at once a creature scared and hunted. The door was opened; the three people in the patio held their breath; but it was merely the postman with a letter for Miranda.

"I must get out of here," said Wilbraham. "I must get out of Ronda. My God, I have to begin it again, have I—the hunt for breakfast and dinner?"

He showed a dangerous face at that moment. His lips were drawn back from his teeth, his eyes furtive and murderous. Miranda felt very glad of Charnock's presence.

However, the Major mastered himself. He might have taken some sort of revenge by insulting Miranda, on account of her disposition towards Charnock; but he did not, and it was not fear of Charnock which restrained him.

"I go back to the regiment, Mrs. Warriner," he said, "the regiment of the soldiers of fortune. I have had my furlough—four months' furlough. I cannot complain." He endeavoured to speak gaily and to bow with grace.

"Good-bye," said Charnock.

Miranda was implacably silent.

"And they call women the softer sex," said the Major.

"One moment," exclaimed Miranda, taking no notice of his remark. "Mr. Wilbraham has a letter from my husband about the Daventry gun."

"It is mine," answered the Major; "it was written to me."

"I will buy it," said Charnock.

"For a thousand—?"

"No; for permission to answer this prepaid telegram to Scotland Yard."

"In your name?"

"In my name."

"You're not a bad fellow, Charnock," said the Major as he drew out his pocket-book. He handed the letter to Charnock, looked at him curiously, and then laughed softly, without malice.

"O lover of my life! O soldier-saint!"

he quoted. "A great poet, what? Do you know Ralph Warriner? Will you play Caponsacchi to his Guido? You might; very likely you will." The Major took the reply form and turned away.

A.E.W. MASON

"It is not always a profitable habit, it seems," said Miranda, "that habit of following."

"A little mean!" said the Major, gently. "Perhaps, too, a little overdone," and as he went out of the patio Miranda flushed and felt ashamed. Then the flush faded from her cheeks and left her white, for she was alone with Charnock and had to make her account with him.

XVI

Explains why Charnock Saw Miranda's Face in his Mirror

Miranda rose nervously from her chair. She made an effort to speak, which failed, and then yielding to a peremptory impulse she ran away. It was only, however, into her parlour that she ran, and thither Charnock followed her. She stood up rather quickly in the farthest corner of the room as soon as he entered, drew a pattern with her foot upon the floor, and tried to appear entirely at her ease. She did not look at Charnock, however; on the contrary she kept her eyes upon the ground, and felt very much like a school-girl who is going to be punished.

"Your husband is alive." Charnock's voice was cold and stern. Miranda resented it all the more because she knew she deserved nothing less than sternness. "Did you," he continued, "learn that from Wilbraham for the first time this morning?"

"No," she answered, and since she had found her voice, she added rebelliously, "No, teacher," and was at once aware that levity was not in the best of taste. Charnock perhaps was not at that moment in a mood for jocularities.

"How long have you known that your husband was alive?" he asked.

"Five months," she answered.

"Who told you?"

"You."

There was a moment's pause. Miranda's foot described more figures on the floor, and with great assiduity.

"I beg your pardon," said Charnock. "It is very humorous, no doubt, but—"

"It is true," interrupted Miranda. "If I had wished to evade you, to deceive you, I should have answered that Mr. Wilbraham brought me the news this morning."

"I should have disbelieved it."

"You could not at all events have disproved it. You would have had not a single word to say." She raised her eyes now and confronted him defiantly.

"Yes," said Charnock, "I admit that," and a great change came over Miranda. She stepped out of her corner. She raised her arms above her head like one waking from sleep. "But I have had my fill of deceptions. I am surfeited. Ask what you will, I'll answer you, and answer you the truth. And for one thing, this is true: you told me Ralph Warriner was alive, that night, at Lady Donnisthorpe's."

"I told you? On the balcony?"

"No, before. In the ball-room. You described him to me. You quoted his phrases. You had seen him that very morning. He was the stranger you quarrelled with in the streets of Plymouth."

"And you knew him from my description!" cried Charnock. All the anger had gone from his face, all the coldness from his voice. "I remember. Your face grew so white in the shadow of the alcove I should have believed you had swooned but for the living trouble in your eyes. Your face became through its pallor and distress the face which I had seen in my mirror. Oh, that mirror and its message!" He broke into a harsh bitter laugh, and seating himself at the table, beat upon his forehead with his clenched fists. "A message of appeal! A call for help! Was there ever such a fool in all the world? Here's one woman out of all the millions who needs my help, I was vain enough to think, and the first thing, the only thing that I did, was to tell her that her outcast bully of a husband was still alive to bully her. A fine way to help! But I guessed correctly even that night. Yes, even on that night I was afraid that I had revealed to you some misfortune of which you were unaware. Oh, why wasn't I struck dumb before I spoke? But you could not have been sure from my description," he cried eagerly, grasping in his remorse at so poor a straw as that subterfuge. "For men are not all unlike, and they use the same phrases. You could not have been certain. You must have had some other proof before you were convinced."

"Yes, that is true."

"And that other proof you got from someone else?" he said, and his voice implored her to assent.

Miranda only shook her head. "I promised to speak nothing but the truth. I got that other proof from you."

"No, no," he exclaimed. "Let me think! No, I told you nothing else but just my meeting with the man, my quarrel with him."

"Yes," said Miranda. "You told me how you woke up from dreaming of Ralph, and saw my face in your mirror. Don't you see? There is the convincing proof that the man you described to me, the man you quarrelled with, the man you dreamed of, was Ralph, for when you woke with that dream vivid in your mind, you saw my face vivid in your mirror. You yourself were at a loss to account for it, you had never so much as thought of me during the seven years since—since our eyes met at Monte Carlo. You could not imagine why on that particular night, after you had dreamed of someone else, unassociated with me, my face should have come back to you. But it was no mystery to me. The man you dreamed of was not unassociated with me; it was my husband, and the husband recalled to you the wife, by an unconscious trick of memory."

"But I did not know he was your husband," cried Charnock. "I had never seen him with you; I had never seen him at all before that day I quarrelled with him in the streets of Plymouth."

"You had," answered Miranda, gently. "He was with me that night at Monte Carlo seven years ago. We were on our honeymoon," she added, with a queer melancholy smile.

Charnock remembered the look of happiness upon her young face, and compared it with the tired woman's face which he saw now. "He was with you!" he exclaimed.

"Yes. You forgot us both. You met him again; you did not remember that you had ever seen him, but none the less, the memory was latent in you, and recalled me to you too. You could not trace the association, but it was very clear to me."

"Wait, wait!" said Charnock. He sat with his elbows on the table and the palms of his hands tightly pressed upon his eyes. "I can see you, as clearly as I saw you then at Monte Carlo, as though you were standing there, now, in the room and I in the room was watching you. You were a little apart from the table, you were standing a few feet behind the croupier at one end of the table. But Ralph Warriner! Was he amongst the players? Wait! Let me think!"

Charnock remained silent. Miranda did not interrupt him, and in a little he began again, piecing together his memories, revivifying that scene in the gambling-room seven years ago. "I can see the lamps with their green shades, I can see the glow of light upon the green table beneath the lamps. I can see the red diamond, the yellow lines upon the cloth, the three columns of numbers in the middle, the crowd about the table, some seated, others leaning over their chairs. But their faces! Their faces!" and then he suddenly cried out, "Ah! He was seated, in front of you, next to the croupier. You were behind him," and in

A.E.W. MASON

his excitement he reached out his arm towards her, and with shaking fingers bade her speak.

"Yes," said she, "I was behind him."

"You moved to him. I understand now. His back was towards me at the first—when I first saw you, when our eyes met. It was that vision of you, the first, which I carried away, it was that only which I remembered—you standing alone there. It was that which came back to me when I saw your face in my mirror, just the picture of you as you stood alone, distinct from the flowers in your hat to the tip of your shoe, before you moved to the table, before you laid your hand on Ralph Warriner's shoulder, before he turned to answer you and so showed me his face. I remember, indeed. I saw his hand first of all. It was reached out holding his stake. I can even remember that he laid his stake on *impare* and then he turned to you. Yes, yes, it's true," and Charnock rose from the table in his agitation, and walked once or twice across the room. "It was Ralph Warriner I met at Plymouth, and because of that trivial, ridiculous quarrel, I told you that he lived!"

He stopped suddenly in front of the writing-table, and stood staring out through the window, while his fingers idly played with a newspaper which lay upon the desk.

"But Major Wilbraham," said Miranda, thinking to lessen his remorse, "Major Wilbraham told me too, and only a month later; he came to me in the Cathedral at Ronda here, and told me. He would have told me in any case."

"Wilbraham!" said Charnock. "Yes, that's true. How did he find out? Who told Wilbraham?" and he turned eagerly towards Miranda.

Miranda stammered and faltered. She had not foreseen the question, and she tried to evade it. "He found out. He used his wits. He saw there was profit in the discovery if he could—"

"If he could make the discovery. I understand that; but how did he make the discovery?"

"Why, what does it matter?" cried Miranda. "He followed up a clue."

Charnock noticed her hesitation, her effort to evade his question. "But who gave him the clue?"

Miranda moved restlessly about the room. "He set his wits to work—he found out," she repeated. She sat down in the same chair in which Charnock had sat. "What does it matter?" she said, and even as Charnock had done, she pressed her hands upon her face.

"You promised me to answer truly whatever question I put to you," said he, who, the more she hesitated, was the more resolved to know. "I ask you this question. Who gave him the clue?"

"Since you will have it then,"—Miranda drew her hands from her face,—"my poor friend, you did," she answered gently.

Charnock was more than startled. His face changed. There was something even of horror in his eyes as he leaned across the table towards her. "I?" he gasped. "I did?"

"I would have spared you the knowledge of that," she said with a smile, "if only you would have allowed me to; but you would not. You pointed out to him a brigantine, which you passed off Ushant."

"Yes, the *Tarifa*."

"The *Tarifa* was once the *Ten Brothers*, Ralph's yacht which was supposed to have been wrecked on Rosevear."

"But the *Ten Brothers* was a schooner," urged Charnock. "I was told only a few weeks ago at Gibraltar—one of the Salcombe—oh yes, that's true too. I suggested to Wilbraham—to Wilbraham who said he was familiar with the look of the boat—I suggested to him that the *Tarifa* was one of the Salcombe clippers."

"Yes. Wilbraham had known Ralph at Gibraltar, had seen the *Ten Brothers*, very likely had been aboard of her. That was why the look of the *Tarifa* was familiar to him. When you told him the *Tarifa* was a Salcombe boat he understood why it was familiar. It was the merest clue; but he followed it up and found out."

"And blackmailed you!" continued Charnock.

He turned back to the writing-table and the window. Again his fingers played idly with the newspaper. For a while he was silent; then he said slowly, "Do you remember what you said to me on the balcony? That no man could offer a woman help without doing her a hurt in some other way."

"I spoke idly," interrupted Miranda.

"You spoke very truly, for here's the proof."

"I spoke to elude you," said Miranda, stubbornly. "It was a mere idle fancy which came into my head, and the next moment was forgotten."

"But I remembered it," cried Charnock. "It was more true than you thought."

"It was no more true than"—she hesitated. However, Charnock was not looking at her; she found it possible to proceed—"than another belief which led me astray, as this one is leading you."

A.E.W. MASON

"What other belief?"

Miranda nerved herself to answer him. "That no man would serve a woman well, except for—for the one reason."

The nature of that reason was apparent to Charnock from the very tone in which she spoke the word. "And you believed that?" he asked. In a movement of surprise he had knocked the newspaper off the writing-table. Underneath the newspaper was a book.

"I did believe it," she replied, her face rosy with confusion, "for a few mad miserable days," and she checked herself suddenly, for she saw that Charnock had absently opened and was absently turning over the leaves of the book.

"Was the message of your mirror after all so false?" she whispered. He turned towards her, with a face quite illumined. He did not, however, leave the table, and he kept the pages of the book open with his fingers.

"Then after all you do need help?" he cried.

"Need it?" she returned with a loud cry, and she stretched out hands across the table towards him. "Indeed, indeed I need it, I desperately need it! I sent the glove because I needed it."

"Then the glove was no sham?"

"It was not the glove that you tore; that was thrown away, but not by me. I searched for it, it was not to be found. So I tore the other and sent it as a substitute."

"And when I came, waited to discover," he added, "whether the one reason held me to your service. I understand."

"You see," she agreed, "really, in my heart, all the time I trusted you, for I knew you would keep your word. I knew you would say nothing, but would just wait and wait until I told you what it was I needed done."

Charnock turned abruptly towards her, and as he turned the book slipped off the table and fell to the ground. "But yesterday," he exclaimed in perplexity, "yesterday, here in this room, I gave you the assurance which you looked for. You believed a man would only help you for the one reason. Well, I told you that the one reason held with me; yet, at that moment, you rejected all help and service. You cried out, 'It's the friend I want, not the lover.'"

"Because just at that moment I understood that my belief was wrong. I understood the shame, the horror, of the tricks I had played on you."

"Tricks?" said Charnock. "Oh!" and as he stooped down to pick up the book he added in a voice of comprehension, "At last! You puzzled me yesterday when you said, 'To possess the friend you had had to *make* the lover.'"

"Yes," she said eagerly, "you understand? I want you to. I want you to understand to the last letter, so that you may decide whether you will help me or not, knowing what the woman is who asks your help. I sat down to trick you into caring for me if by any means I could. I did it deliberately, how deliberately you will see if you only open the book you hold. And it wasn't until I had won that I realised that I had cheated to win and could not profit by the gains. I won yesterday and yesterday I sent you away. Perhaps God kept you here."

Charnock made no answer. He sat down at the table opposite to Miranda and turned over the leaves of the book, whilst Miranda watched him, holding her breath. He was not angry yet, but she dreaded the moment when he should understand the subject-matter of the book.

The book was a collection of letters written by a great French lady at the Court of Louis XV to a young girl-relative in Provence, and the letters were intended to serve as a guide to the girl's provincial inexperience. There was much sage instruction as to the best methods of handling men, "ces animaux effroyables, dont nous ne pouvons ni ne voudrons nous débarrasser," as the great lady politely termed them. In the margin of the book Miranda's pencil had scored lines against passages here and there. Charnock read out one:—

"Et prends bien garde de tellement diriger la conversation qu'il parle beaucoup de lui-même."

"That accounts for the history of my life which I gave you in your garden," said Charnock. He was not angry yet; he was even smiling.

"Yes," said Miranda, seriously; "but there's worse! Go on!"

"Soyez sage, ma mie," he read, turning over a page. "On ne possede jamais un de ces animaux sans qu'on peut bien disposer d'un autre. Celui que tu aimes, t'aimera aussi si tu fais la cour a un deuxième. Ils ont bien tort qui disent qu'il ne faut que deux pour faire l'amour. Il faut au moins trois."

"That accounts for Wilbraham, and the basket of flowers for Gibraltar."

"For Wilbraham, yes," said Miranda.

Charnock did not notice that she excluded the basket of flowers from her assent. He read out other items, still without any appearance of anger. A foot carelessly exhibited and carefully withdrawn, the young lady in the country was informed, might kick a hole in any male heart, so long as the foot was slim, and the shoe all that it should be. Charnock closed the book and sat opposite to Miranda with a laughing face, enjoying her intense earnestness.

"So you won by cheating?" he said, "and this book taught you how to cheat?"

"Yes, but I don't think you have grasped it," she replied seriously, "and I want you to. I want you to understand the horrible, hateful way in which I made you care for me. I now know that I ought to have relied upon your friendship when you first came to Ronda. But I chose the worse part, and if you say that you will not help me, why, I must abide by it, and Ralph must abide by it too. But there shall be nothing but truth now between you and me. I was not content with friendship, I had the time I knew to try to make you care for me in the other way, and I did try hatefully, and hatefully I succeeded—" and to Miranda's surprise Charnock leaned back in his chair, and laughed loudly and heartily for a long while. The more perplexed Miranda looked, the more he laughed.

"Believe me, Mrs. Warriner," he said, and stopped to laugh again, "if I had met you for the first time at Ronda, I should have taken the first train back to Algeciras. Your tricks! I noticed them all, and they drove me wild with indignation."

"Do you mean that?" exclaimed Miranda, and her downcast face brightened.

"I do indeed," answered Charnock. "Oh, your tricks! I almost hated you for them." He began to laugh again as he recollected them.

"I am so glad," replied Miranda, in the prettiest confusion, and as Charnock laughed, in a little her eyes began to dance and she laughed too.

"Shall I tell you what kept me at Ronda?" he said. "Because, in spite of yourself, every now and then yourself broke through the tricks. Because, however much you tried, you could not but reveal to me, now and then, some fleeting glimpse of the woman who once stood beside me in a balcony and looked out over the flashing carriage-lights to the quiet of St. James's Park. It was in memory of that woman that I stayed."

He was speaking with all seriousness now, and Miranda uttered a long trembling sigh of gratitude. "Thank you," she said, "thank you."

"Now what can I do for you?" he asked, and Miranda made haste to reply.

XVII

Shows how a Tombstone May Convince when Arguments Fail

She showed him the scribbled note which M. Fournier had brought; she told him M. Fournier's story; how that Ralph had run guns and ammunition from England into Morocco on board the *Tarifa*; how that he had been kidnapped between M. Fournier's villa and the town-gate; how that he was not held to ransom, since no demand for ransom had come to the little Belgian; and finally how that it was impossible to apply for help to the Legation, since Ralph was already guilty of a crime, and would only be rescued that way in order to suffer penal servitude in England.

"What a coil to unravel!" said Charnock. "I know some Arabic. I could go to Morocco. I went there once, but only to Tangier. But Morocco? How shall one search Morocco without a clue?"

He rested his chin upon his hand, and stared gloomily at the wall. Miranda was careful not to interrupt his reflections. If there was a way out, she confidently relied upon this man to find it. Once she shivered, and Charnock looked inquiringly towards her. She was gazing at the soiled note which lay beneath her eyes upon the table, and saw again the picture of Ralph being beaten inland under the sun. She began to recall his acts and words, that she might make the best of them; she fell to considering whether she had not herself been in a measure to blame for the shipwreck of their marriage. And so, thinking of such matters, she absently hummed over a tune, a soft plaintive little melody from an *opéra-bouffe*. She ended it and hummed it over again; until it came upon her that Charnock had been silent for a long time, and she looked up from the note into his face.

He was not thinking out any plan. He was watching her with a singular intentness, his head thrust forward from his shoulders, his face very strained. It seemed that every fibre of his body listened and was still, so that it might hear the better.

"Who taught you that tune?" he asked in a voice of suspense.

"Ralph," said she, in some surprise at the question; "at least I picked it up from him."

And Charnock fell back in his chair; he huddled himself in it, he let his chin drop upon his breast. He sat staring at her with eyes which seemed suddenly deep-sunk in a face suddenly grown white. And slowly, gradually, it broke in upon Miranda that he held the clue after all, that that tune was the clue, that in a word Charnock knew how Ralph had disappeared.

"You know!" she cried in her elation. "You know! Oh, and I sent you away yesterday! What if you had gone! Only to think of it! You know! That tune has given you the clue? It was Ralph's favourite! You heard it—when? Where? Tell me!"

To her eager, joyous questions Charnock was silent. He did not move. He still sat huddled in his chair, with his chin fallen on his breast, and his eyes fixedly staring at her. Miranda's enthusiasm was chilled by his silence; it was succeeded by fear. She became frightened; she picked up the note and held it out to him and bade it speak for her.

Charnock did not take the note or change his position. But he said:—

"Even on your honeymoon, you see, he left you to stand alone, while he gambled at the tables."

"But you mustn't think of that," she cried. "It's so small a thing."

"But so typical," added Charnock, quietly.

Miranda gave a moan and held her head between her hands. That Charnock might refuse to help her, because with tears in her eyes she had played the sedulous coquette, she had been prepared to acknowledge. But that he would refuse to help, out of a mistaken belief that, by refusing to help, he was helping best—that supposition had not so much as occurred to her.

"Read the note again," she implored him. "*Do quickly what you can!* And see, it is a week and more since M. Fournier was here. It is a fortnight and more since Ralph was kidnapped in the Sôk. Quickly! And nothing is done, and nothing will be done, unless you do it. Oh, think of him—driven, his hands tied, beaten with sticks, sold for a slave to trudge with loads upon his back, barefooted, through Morocco! You will go," and her voice broke and was very tender as she appealed to him. "Please! You will have pity on me, and on him." And she watched Charnock's face for a sign of assent, her heart throbbing, her foot beating the ground, and every now and then a queer tremulous moan breaking from her dry lips.

Charnock, however, did not soften at the imagined picture of Ralph's misfortunes, and he hardened his heart against the visible picture of her distress.

"When I was at Algeciras, I asked many questions about Ralph Warriner. I listened to many answers," he said curtly.

"Exaggerated answers," she returned, and as Charnock opened his mouth to reply, she hastened to continue: "Listen! Listen! Here's the strange thing! Not that I should need help, not that you should help me, not that I should come to you for help. Those three things—they are most natural. But that coming to you, I should come to the one man who can help, who already knows the way to help. Don't you understand? It is very clear to me. You were *meant* to help, to help me in this one trouble, so you were shown the means whereby to help." And seeing Charnock still impenetrable, she burst out: "Oh, he will not help! He will not understand!" and she took to considering how it was that he knew, how it was that he recognised the tune.

"You were in Tangier once," she argued. "Yes. You told me that not only to-day, but at Lady Donnisthorpe's. You crossed from Gibraltar?"

"Yes, just before I came to England and met you."

"Just before! Still you won't understand? You find out somehow—somehow in Tangier you come across a tune, an incident, something. Immediately after you meet a woman, at the first sight of whom you offer her your succour, and the time comes when she needs it, and that one incident you witnessed just before you met her gives you, and you alone in all the world, the opportunity to help her. Don't you remember, when you first were introduced at Lady Donnisthorpe's, what was your first feeling—one of disappointment, because I did not seem to stand in any need? Well, I do stand in need now—and now you turn away. And for my sake too! Was there ever such a tangle! Such a needless irony and tangle, and all because a man cannot put a woman from his thoughts!" And then she laughed bitterly and harshly, and so fell back again upon her guesses.

"You were in Tangier—how long?"

"For a day."

"When? Never mind! I know. I met you in June. You were in Tangier for a day in May. In May!" she repeated, and stopped. Then she uttered a cry. "May, that was the month. M. Fournier said May. You were the man," and leaning forward she laid a clutching hand upon Charnock's arm, which lay quiet on the table. "You were the unknown man who cried 'Look out!' through the closed door of M. Fournier's shop."

Charnock started. He was prepared to deny the challenge, if assent threatened to disclose his clue. But it did not. M. Fournier knew nothing of the blind beggar at the cemetery gate where Charnock had first heard the comic opera tune and registered it in his memory. That was evident, since in all M. Fournier's story, there was no mention anywhere of Hassan Akbar.

"Yes," he admitted. "It was I."

"And you shouted it not as a menace—so M. Fournier thought and was wrong—but as a warning to Ralph, my husband, whom you will not speak a word to save. You spoke a word then, very likely you saved him then. Well, do just as much now. I ask no more of you. Only speak the word! Tell me the clue, I myself will follow it up. Oh, he will not speak!" and in her agitation she rose up and paced the room.

Charnock rose too. Miranda flew to the door and leaned her back against it.

"Just for a moment! Listen to what M. Fournier said! He said that if once we could lay our hands upon the man who shouted through the door, we should lay our hands upon the means to rescue Ralph. Think how truly he spoke, in a truer sense than he intended. You know why he disappeared. You know who captured him. And if you don't speak, I shall have no peace until I die," and she sat herself again at the table.

"Do you still care for him?" asked Charnock, with some gentleness.

Miranda, who was wrought almost to frenzy, drummed upon the table with her clenched fists.

"Must we debate that question while Ralph—" Then she mastered herself. "I know you," she said. "If I were to tell you that I loved him heart and soul, you would go upon this errand, straight as an arrow, for my sake. But I promised there should be nothing but truth between you and me. I do not love him. Now, will you go to Morocco? Or, if you will not go, will you speak?"

"No. Let him stay there! Where he cannot harm you. What if I was *meant* to keep you from rescuing him?"

"You do not know," she replied. "You can do me no greater service than by rescuing Ralph, by bringing him back to me. Will you believe that?"

"No," said he, calmly, and she rose from her chair.

"But if I proved it to you?"

"You cannot."

"I will."

She looked at the clock.

"It is four o'clock," she said. "Two hours and a quarter before the train leaves for Algeciras. Will you meet me on the platform? I had thought to spare myself—this. But you shall have the proof. I will not tell you of it, but I will show it to you to-morrow at Gibraltar."

She spoke now with great calmness. She had hit upon the means to persuade. She was convinced that she had, and he was afraid that she had.

"Very well," said he. "The 6.15 for Algeciras."

They travelled to Gibraltar that night. Miranda stayed at the Bristol, Charnock at the Albion; they met the next morning, and walked through the long main street. Here and there an officer looked at her with a start of surprise and respectfully raised his hat, and perhaps took a step or two towards her. But she did not stop to speak with anyone. It was two years since she had set foot within the gates of Gibraltar, and no doubt the stones upon which she walked had many memories wherewith to bruise her. Charnock respected her silence, and kept pace with her unobtrusively. They passed into the square with Government House upon the one side and the mess-rooms upon the other. Charnock sketched a picture of her in his fancies, the picture of a young girl newly-come from the brown solitudes of Suffolk into this crowded and picturesque fortress with the wonder of a new world in her eyes, and contrasted it with the woman who walked beside him, and inferred the increasing misery of her years. He was touched to greater depths of sympathy than he had ever felt before even when she had lain with her head upon her arms in an abandonment of distress; so that now the uncomplaining uprightness of her figure made his heart ache, and the sound of her footsteps was a pain. But of the most intolerable of all her memories he had still to learn. She led him into the little cemetery, guided him between the graves, and stopped before a headstone on which Charnock read:—

RUPERT WARRINER,
Aged 2 Years.

and the date of his birth and death.

The headstone was of marble, and had been sculptured with a poetic fancy; a boy, in whose face Charnock could trace a likeness to Miranda, looked out and laughed between the open lattices of a window.

They both watched the grave silently for a while. Then Miranda said gently, "Now do you understand? When Rupert was born, it seemed to me that here was a blossom on the thorn bush of the world. But you see the blossom never flowered. He died of diphtheria. It was hard when he died;" and Charnock suddenly started at her side.

"Those flowers!" he said hoarsely.

Upon the grave were scattered jonquils, geraniums, roses, pinks, camellias—all the rich reds and yellows of Miranda's garden.

"You were cutting them, packing them, that afternoon when Wilbraham came?"

Mrs. Warriner shrank from looking at Charnock.

"Yes," she confessed in a whisper.

"My God!" he exclaimed. Miranda glanced at him in fear. So it was coming; he was remembering the use to which she had put those flowers. Would he loathe her sufficiently to withdraw his help?

"Do you know what I thought?" he continued. "No, you can't guess. You could not imagine it. I actually believed that you were cutting those flowers so that you might send them to—" and he broke off the sentence. "But it's too odious to tell you."

"But I meant you should believe just that," she cried. "I meant you to believe it. Oh, how utterly hateful! How could I have done it? I wanted to hide that from you, but it was right you should know. I must have been mad," and she convulsively clasped and unclasped her hands.

"I understand why you dropped that bunch from the cliff," said Charnock, "after Wilbraham had picked a flower from it."

"I wanted to bring you here," said Miranda, "so that you might know why I ask this service of you. As I told you, I have no love left for Ralph, but he was that boy's father, and the boy is dead. I cannot leave Ralph in Morocco a slave. He was Rupert's father. Perhaps you remember that after I met you at Lady Donnisthorpe's I came back at once to Ronda. I had half determined not to return at all, and when you first told me Ralph was alive, my first absorbing thought was, where should I hide myself? But it occurred to me that he might be in need, and he was Rupert's father. So I came back, and when Wilbraham blackmailed me, I submitted to the blackmail again because he was Rupert's father; and because he was Rupert's father, when I learned in what sore need he stood, I sent that glove to you."

"I understand," said Charnock, and they turned and walked from the cemetery.

"Now will you speak?" she asked.

"No," he returned, "but I will go myself to Morocco."

"It is your life I am asking you to risk," said Miranda, who now that she had gained her end, began at once to realise the consequences it would entail upon her friend.

"I know that and take the risk," replied Charnock.

They walked out towards Europa Point, and turned into the Alameda.

"There is something else," said Miranda. "Your search will cost money. Every farthing of that I must pay. You will promise me that?"

"Yes."

"I wrote to M. Fournier yesterday. He will supply you. There is one thing more. This search will interrupt your career."

"It will, no doubt," he assented readily, and sitting down upon a seat he spoke to her words which she never forgot. "The quaint thing is that I have always been afraid lest a woman should break my career. I lived as a boy high up on the Yorkshire hills, two miles above a busy town. All day that town whirred in the hollow below. I could see it from my bedroom window, and all night the lights blazed in the factories; and when I went down into its streets there were always grimed men speeding upon their business. There was a certain grandeur about it which impressed me,—the perpetual shuffle of the looms, the loud, clear song of the wheels. That seemed to me the life to live. And I made up my mind that no woman should interfere. A brake on the wheel going up hill, a whip in the driver's hand going down,—that was what I thought of woman until I met you."

"And proved it true," cried Miranda.

"And learned that there are better things than getting on," said Charnock.

Miranda turned to him with shining eyes, and in a voice which left him in no doubt as to the significance of her words, she cried:—

"My dear, we are Love's derelicts, you and I," and so stopped and said no more.

They went back to the hotel and lunched together and came out again to the geraniums and bellas sombras of the Alameda. But they talked no more in this strain. They were just a man and a woman, and the flaming sword kept their lips apart. But they knew it and were not aggrieved, for being a man and a woman they knew not grievances.

The evening came down upon Gibraltar, the riding lanterns glimmered upon the masts in the bay; away to the left the lighthouse on Europa Point shot out its yellow column of light; above, the Spanish sky grew purple and rich with innumerable stars.

"The boat leaves early," said Charnock. "I will say good-bye now."

Miranda caught the hand which he held out to her and held it against her breast.

"But I shall see you again—once—please, once," she said, "when you bring Ralph back to me;" and so they separated in the Alameda.

Charnock walked away and left her standing there, nor looked back. Stray lines and verses of ballads which he had heard sung by women in drawing-rooms here and there about the world came back to him—ballads of knights and cavaliers who had ridden away at their ladies' behests. He had laughed at them then, but they came back to him now, and he felt himself linked through them in a community of feeling with the generations which had gone before. Men had gone out upon such errands as he was now privileged to do, and would do so again when he was dust, with just the same pride which he felt as he walked homewards on this night through the streets of Gibraltar. He realised as he had never realised before, through the fellowship of service, that in bone and muscle and blood he was of the family of men, son of the men who had gone before, father of the men who were to follow. The next morning he crossed the straits to Tangier.

XVIII

In Which the Taxidermist and a Basha Prevail Over a Blind Man

He went at once to the taxidermist's shop. M. Fournier expected him, but not the story which he had to tell.

"You wish to discover the man who shouted through your door six months ago," said Charnock. "It was I."

M. Fournier got together his account-books and laid them on the counter of the shop. "I have much money. Where is my friend Mr. Jeremy Bentham?"

"It is Hassan Akbar whom we must ask," said Charnock, and he told Fournier of what he had seen on the day of his previous visit to Tangier.

The two men walked up to the cemetery gate, where Hassan still sat in the dust, and swung his body to and fro and reiterated his cry "Allah Ben!" as on that day when, clothed as a Moor, Ralph Warriner had come down the hill. It was the tune which that Moor had hummed, and which Miranda had repeated, that had led Charnock to identify the victim and the enemy.

Charnock hummed over that tune again as he stood beside the Moor, and the Moor stopped at once from his prayer.

"Hassan Akbar, what hast them done with the Christian who hummed that tune and dropped a silver dollar in thy lap at this gate?"

Hassan made no answer, and as though his sole anxiety had been lest Warriner should have escaped and returned, he recommenced his cry.

"Hassan," continued Charnock, "was it that Christian who betrayed thy wealth? Give him back to us and thou shalt be rich again."

"Allah Beh!" cried Hassan. "Allah Beh!"

"It is of no use for us to question him," said M. Fournier. "But the Basha will ask him, and in time he will answer. To-morrow I will go to the Basha."

Charnock hardly gathered the purport of Fournier's proposal. He went back into the town, and that evening M. Fournier related to him much about Ralph Warriner which he did not know.

The idea of running guns in Morocco had appealed to Warriner some time before he put it into practice, and whilst he was still at Gibraltar.

"I did not know him then," said Fournier. "He had relations with others, very likely with Hassan Akbar, but nothing came of those relations. When he ran from Gibraltar in the *Ten Brothers*, he landed at Tangier, and lay hid somewhere in the town, while he sent the *Ten Brothers* over to South America and ordered the mate to sell her for as much as she would fetch. But in a little while Ralph Warriner met me and asked me to be his partner in his scheme. He had a little money then, and indeed it was just about the time when Hassan's fortune was discovered. It is very likely that our friend told the Basha of Hassan's wealth. If he knew, he would certainly have told," said M. Fournier, with a lenient smile, "for there was money in it. Anyway, he had some money then, I had some, I could get more, and I like him very much. I say yes. He tells me of his ship. We want a ship to carry over the guns. I telegraph to the Argentine and stop the sale. Warriner sent orders to change her rig, as he call it, and her name, and she comes back to us as the *Tarifa*. The only trouble left was this. The most profitable guns to introduce are the Winchester rifles. But for that purpose one of us must go between England and Tangier, must sail the *Tarifa* between England and Tangier. I could not sail a toy-boat in a pond without falling into the water. How then could I sail the *Tarifa*? So Warriner must do it. But Warriner, my poor dear friend, he has made little errors. He must not go to England, not even as Bentham. To make it safe for Jeremy Bentham to go to England, Ralph Warriner must be dead. You see?"

"Yes, I see. But why in the world did he call himself Jeremy Bentham?" asked Charnock.

"Because he was such an economist. Oh, but he was very witty and clever, my poor friend, when he was not swearing at you. At all events he decided that Ralph Warriner must die, and that there must be proofs that he was dead. So he packed up a few letters—one from his wife before he was married to her—that was clever, *hein*? A love-letter from his *fiancée* which he has carried about next to his heart for six years! So sweet! So convincing to the great British public, eh? He found that letter by chance among his charts. He gives it to me and some others in an oilskin case, and sends me with one of his sailors to the Scilly Islands. And then Providence helped us.

"All that we hoped to do was to hear of a wreck, in which many lives were lost, to go out amongst the rocks, where the ship was wrecked, and to pick up that little oilskin case. You understand? Oh, but we were helped. There was a heavy storm for many days at Scilly, and after the storm for many days a fog. On one day the sailor and I—we go out in the fog to the Western Islands, to see if any ship had come ashore. But it was dangerous! I can tell you it was very dangerous and very wet. However, we come to Rosevear, and there was the remnant of a ship, and no sailor anywhere. We landed on Rosevear, and just as I was about to place the oilskin case among the rocks where it would be naturally found, we came upon one dead sailor, lying near to the sea just as if asleep. I slipped the oilskin case into his pocket, and then with stones we broke in his face. Ah, but that was horrible! It made me sick then and there. But we did it, until there was no face left. Then for fear the waves might come up and wash him away, we dragged him up the rocks and laid him amongst the grass, again as though he was asleep. We made a little mistake there. We dragged him too far from the sea. But the mistake did not matter."

"I see," said Charnock. "And that day I shouted through the door Warriner sailed for England?"

"Yes," replied Fournier. "I hired that morning a felucca to sail himself across to Tarifa."

"I remember."

"The boat lay at Tarifa. He set sail that night."

"Yes," said Charnock. "I spent the night here. I waited two days for the P. and O. at Gibraltar, we passed the *Tarifa* off Ushant, and three days later I met Warriner in Plymouth. Yes, the times fit."

"It is very likely Ralph who told about Hassan," mused M. Fournier, with a lenient smile. "If he knew, he would have been sure to have told; for there was money in it. To-morrow I will see the Basha."

M. Fournier went down to the Kasbah and found the Basha delivering justice at the gates. The suitors were dismissed, and M. Fournier opened his business.

"We do not wish to trouble the Legation," said he. "The Legation would make much noise, and his Shereefian Majesty, whom God preserve, would never hear the end of it. Besides, we do not wish it." And upon that money changed hands. "But if the Englishman told your nobility that Hassan Akbar was hoarding his money in utter selfishness, then your nobility will talk privately with Hassan and find out from him where the Englishman is."

The Basha stroked his white beard.

"The Nazarene speaks wisely. We will not disturb the dignity of his

Majesty, whom Allah preserve, for such small things. I will talk to Hassan Akbar and send for you again."

That impenetrable man was fetched from the cemetery gates, and the Basha addressed him.

"Hassan, thou didst hide and conceal thy treasure, and truly the Room told me of it; and since thy treasure was of no profit to thee, I took it."

"When I was blind and helpless," said Hassan.

"So thou wast chastened the more thoroughly for thy profit in the next world, and thy master and my master, the Sultan, was served in this," said the Basha, with great dignity, and he reverently bowed his head to the dust. "Now what hast thou done with the Room?"

But Hassan answered never a word.

"Thou stubborn man! May Allah burn thy great-great-grandfather!" said the Basha, and chained his hands and his feet, and had him conveyed to an inner room, where he talked to him with rods of various length and thickness. At the end of the third day the Basha sent a message to M. Fournier that Hassan's heart was softened by the goodness of God, and that now he would speak.

The Basha received Charnock and M. Fournier in a great cool domed room of lattice-work and tiles. He sat upon cushions on a dais at the end of the room; stools were brought forward for his visitors; and M. Fournier and the Basha exchanged lofty compliments, and drank much weak sweet tea. Then the Basha raised his hand; a door was thrown open; and a blind, wavering, broken man crawled, dragging his fetters, across the floor.

"Good God!" whispered Charnock; "what have they done to him?"

"They have made him speak, that is all," returned M. Fournier, imperturbably. He kept all his pity for Ralph Warriner.

M. Fournier translated afterwards to Charnock the story which Hassan told as he grovelled on the ground, and it ran as follows:—

"When the son of the English first came into Morocco I showed him great kindness and hospitality, and how he returned it you know. So after I was blind I waited. More than once I heard his voice in the Sôk, and in the streets of Tangier, and I knew that he had quarrelled with his own people the Nazarenes, and dared not turn to them for help. I sit by the gate of the cemetery, and many Arabs, and Moors, and Negroes, and Jews come down the road from the country to the market-place, and at last one morning I heard the steps of one whose feet shuffled in his *babouches*; he could not walk in the loose slippers as we who are born to the use of them. And it was not an old man, whose feet are clogged by age, for his stride was long; that my ears told me which are my eyes. It was an infidel in the dress of the faithful. It may be that if I had seen with my eyes, I should never have known; but my ears are sharpened, and I heard. When he passed me he gave me greeting, and then I knew it was the Room. He dropped a dollar into my hands and whistled a tune which he had often whistled after he had eaten of my *kouss-kouss*, and so went on his way. I rose up and followed him, thinking that my time had come. Across the Sôk I followed him, hearing always the shuffle of the slippers amidst the din of voices and the hurrying of many feet. He did not see me, for he never turned or stopped, but went straight on under the gate of the town, and then turned through the horse-market, and came to a house which he entered. I heard the door barred behind him, and a shutter fixed across the window, and I sat down beneath the shutter and waited. I heard voices talking quickly and earnestly within the room, and then someone rose and came out of the door and walked down the street towards the port. But it was not the man for whom I waited. This one walked with little jaunty, tripping steps, and I was glad that he went away; for the bolt of the door was not shut behind him, and the dog of a Nazarene was alone. I rose and walked to the door. A son of the English stood in the way: I asked him for alms with the one hand and felt for the latch with the other; but the son of the English saw what I was doing and shouted through the door."

"It was I," said Charnock.

Hassan turned his sightless face towards Charnock and reflected. Then he answered: "It was indeed you. And after you had spoken the bolt was shot. Thereupon I went back to the Sôk, and asking here and there at last fell in with some Arabs from Beni Hassan with whom in other days I had traded. And for a long while I talked to them, showing that there was no danger, for the Room was without friends amongst his own people, and moreover that he would fetch a price, every okesa of which was theirs. And at the last they agreed with me that I should deliver him to them at night outside the walls of Tangier and they would take him away and treat him ill, and sell him for a slave in their own country. But the Room had gone from Tangier and the Arabs moved to Tetuan and Omara and Sôk-et-Trun, but after a while they returned to Tangier and the Room also returned; and the time I had waited for had come."

A.E.W. MASON

"What have you done with him?" said the Basha. "Speak."

"I besought a lad who had been my servant to watch the Room Bentham, and his goings and comings. With the dollar which he had given me I bought a little old tent of palmetto and set it up in the corner of the Sôk apart from the tents of the cobblers."

"Well?" interrupted M. Fournier, "speak quickly."

"One evening the lad came to me and said the Room had gone up to a house on the hill above the Sôk, where there were many lights and much noise of feasting. So I went down the Sôk to where the Arabs slept by their camels and said to them, 'It will be to-night.' And as God willed it the night was dark. The lad led me to the house and I sat outside it till the noise grew less and many went away. At last the Nazarene Bentham came to the door and his mule was brought for him and he mounted. I asked the boy who guided me, 'Is it he?' and the boy answered 'Yes.' So I dismissed him and followed the mule down the hill to the Sôk, which was very quiet. Then I ran after him and called, and he stopped his mule till I came up with him. 'What is it?' he asked, and I threw a cloth over his head and dragged him from the mule. We both fell to the ground, but I had one arm about his neck pressing the cloth to his mouth so that he could not cry out. I pressed him into the mud of the Sôk and put my knee upon his chest and bound his arms together. Then I carried him to my tent and took the cloth from his head, for I wished to hear him speak and be sure that it was Bentham. But he understood my wish and would not speak. So I took his mule-hobbles which I had stolen while he feasted, and made them hot in a fire and tied them about his ankles and in a little while I made him cry out and I was sure. Then I stripped him of his clothes and put upon him my own rags. The Arabs came to the tent an hour later. I gagged Bentham and gave him up to them bound, and in the dark they took him away, with the mule. His clothes I buried in the ground under my tent, and in the morning stamped the ground down and took the tent away."

"And the chief of these Arabs? Give me his name," said the Basha.

"Mallam Juzeed," replied Hassan.

The Basha waved his hand to the soldiers and Hassan was dragged away.

"I will send a soldier with you, give you a letter to the Sheikh of Beni Hassan, and he will discover the Room, if he is to be found in those parts," said the Basha to M. Fournier.

Charnock spent the greater part of a month in formalities. He took the letter from the Basha and many other letters to Jews of importance in the towns with which M. Fournier was able to provide him; he hired the boy Hamet who had acted as his guide on his first visit, and getting together an equipment as for a long journey in Morocco, rode out over the Hill of the Two Seas into the inlands of that mysterious and enchanted country.

XIX

Tells of Charnock's Wanderings in Morocco and of a Walnut-Wood Door

In the course of time Charnock came to a village of huts enclosed within an impenetrable rampart of cactus upon the flank of the hills southward of Mequinez and there met the Sheikh. The Sheikh laid his hands upon Mallam Juzeed and bade him speak, which he did with a wise promptitude. It was true; they had taken the Christian from Tangier, but they had sold him on the way. They had chanced to arrive at the great houseless and treeless plain of Seguedla, a day's march from Alkasar, on a Wednesday; and since every Wednesday an open market is held upon two or three low hills which jut out from the plain, they had sold Ralph Warriner there to a travelling merchant of the Mtoga. Mallam supplied the merchant's name and the direction of his journey. Charnock packed his tents upon his mules and disappeared into the south.

For two years he disappeared, or almost disappeared; almost, since through the freemasonry of the Jews, that great telephone across Barbary by which the Jew at Tangier shall hear the words which the Jew speaks at Tafilet, M. Fournier was able to obtain now and again rare news of Charnock, and, as it were, a rare glimpse of him at Saforo, at Marakesch, at Tarudant, and to supply him with money. Then came a long interval, until a Jew of the Waddoon stopped Fournier in the Sôk of Tangier, handed him a letter, and told him that many months ago, as he rode at nightfall down a desolate pass of the Upper Atlas mountains, he came to an inhospitable wilderness of stones, where one in Moorish dress and speaking the Moorish tongue was watching the antics of a snake-charmer by the light of a scanty fire of brushwood. The Moor had two servants with him but no escort, and no tent, and for safety's sake the Jew stayed with him that night. In the morning the Moor had given him the letter to M. Fournier and had bidden him say that he was well.

In that letter Charnock told in detail the history of his search. How he had held to his clue, how he had missed it and retraced his steps, how he had followed the merchant to Figuig on the borders of Algeria, and back; how he had gone south into the country of Sus and was now returning northwards to Mequinez. He had discarded the escort, because if a protection to himself, it was a warning to the Arabs with whom he fell in. They grew wary and shut their lips, distrusting him, distrusting his business; and since he could speak Arabic before, he had picked up sufficient of the Moghrebbin dialect, what with his dark face and Hamet to come to his aid, to pass muster as a native. M. Fournier sent the letter on to Mrs. Warriner at Ronda, who read it and re-read it and blamed her selfishness in sending any man upon such an errand, and wondered why she of all women in the world should have found a man ready to do her this service. Many a time as she looked from her window over the valley she speculated what his thoughts were as he camped in the night-air on the plains and among the passes. Did his thoughts turn to Ronda? Did she see her there obtruding a figure of a monstrous impertinence and vanity? For she had asked of him what no woman had a right to ask.

His frank confession of how he had defined women came back to her with a pitiless conviction; "A brake on the wheel going up hill, a whip in the driver's hand going down." It was true! It was true! She was the instance which proved it true. There were unhappy months for Miranda of the balcony.

At times Jane Holt would be wakened from her sleep by a great cry, and getting from her bed she would walk round the landing half-way up the patio, to Miranda's bedroom, only to find it empty. She would descend the staircase, and coming into the little parlour, would discover Miranda leaning out of the open window and looking down to a certain angle of the winding road.

She had dreamed, she had seen in her dream Charnock with his two servants encamped upon a hill-side or on a plain, and hooded figures in long robes crawling, creeping, towards them, crouching behind boulders, or writhing their bodies across fields of flowers. She saw him too in the narrow, dim alleys of ruined towns, lured through a doorway behind impenetrable walls, and then robbed for his money and tortured for his creed.

At such times the sight of that road whence he had looked upwards to her window was a consolation, almost a confutation of her dreams. There at that visible corner of the road, underneath these same stars and the same purple sky, Charnock had sat and gazed at this window from which she leaned. He could not be dead! And carried away by a feverish revulsion, she would at times come to fancy that he had returned, that he was even now seated on the bank by the roadside, that but for the gloom she would surely distinguish him, that in spite of the gloom she could faintly distinguish him. And so her cousin would speak to her, and with some commonplace excuse that the night was hot, Miranda would get her back to her room.

These were terrible months for Miranda of the balcony. And the months lengthened, and again no news came. Miranda began to wonder whether she had only sent Charnock out to meet Ralph's disaster, to become a slave beaten and whipped and shackled, and driven this way and that through the barbarous inlands.

The months were piled one upon the other. The weight of their burden could be measured by the changes in Miranda's bearing. Her cheeks grew thin, her manner feverish. The mere slamming of a door would fling the blood into her face like scarlet; an unexpected entrance set her heart racing till it stifled her.

MEANWHILE CHARNOCK HAD LONG CEASED to be troubled by the interruption of his career. He moved now across wide prairies of iris and asphodel under a blazing African sun, with perhaps a single palm tree standing naked somewhere within view, or a cluster of dwarf olives; he halted now for the night under a sinister sky on a dark plain, which stretched to the horizon level as the sea; he would skirt a hill and come unawares upon some white town of vast, gaunt, crumbling walls, that ran out for no reason into the surrounding country, and for no reason stopped. He passed beneath their ruined crenellations, under the great gateways into the tortuous and dark streets where men noiseless and sombre went their shrouded way. There were nights too when he sat with a Mouser pistol in his hand, searching the darkness until the dawn.

The continent he had left behind seemed very far away; the echo of its clamours diminished; the hurry of its conflicts became unreasonable and strange. He was in a country where the moss upon the palace roofs was itself of an immemorial antiquity; where neither the face of the country nor the ways of those who lived on it had changed. He had waited as he turned his back upon a town in the violet sunset, to see the white flags break out upon the tops of the minarets, and the Mueddins appear. He had waited for their cry, "Allah Akbar!" and for the great plaintive moan of prayer which rose to answer it from the terraces, the bazaars, from every corner of the town, and which trembled away with infinite melancholy over infinite plains, "Allah Akbar! Allah Akbar!"

From those very minarets, during long successive centuries, a Mueddin at just that hour had uttered just that cry; so that the Mueddin became nothing, but the cry echoed down the years. And just that same answer had risen and trembled out in just the same plaintive mournfulness, so that those who prayed became of no account, and the prayer repeated by the generations, the one thing which lived.

Charnock used to halt upon his road, turn his face backwards to the town, and picture to himself that from East to West the whole continent of Africa was murmurous with that one prayer, that the Atlantic carried away the sound of it upon its receding waves, and that the Nile floated it down from village to village through the Soudan. He ceased to wonder at the indifference, the passivity, the fatalism, of these mysterious men amongst whom he lived; for he felt something of that fatalism invading himself.

He continued his search, northwards from the Atlas, escaping here a band of robbers, there struggling in the whirl of a swollen stream, listening at night to the cries of the jackals, and yielding to the witchery of a monotonous Arab flute into which one servant blew a few yards away, while Hamet, in a high strident voice, chanted a no less monotonous song. He continued his search almost because "it was written."

Until on a dull afternoon he came to Mequinez, with its palaces of dead kings, which rise up one behind the other, draped in golden lichens, vast roofs stretching away into the distance, green and grey with the whipping of rains, tower overtopping tower, crumbling crenellations of wall, silent, oppressive. Each palace shut and barred after its master was dead, and left so, to frown into decay and make a habitation for the storks.

To this city Charnock tracked the merchant, and taking up his abode in the Mellah with a Jew to whom M. Fournier had recommended him, he walked out through the streets beneath the walls of the palaces, neither inquiring for the merchant nor scanning the faces of the passers-by, but wrapped in his burnous, careless of any cry, impenetrable, unobservant, until he came out of the darkness of a bazaar, and saw, right before his eyes, a door.

The door was set in a wall perhaps sixty feet high. Charnock could not see the top for the narrowness of the street. Blank, and menacing in the sinister light, the wall towered up before his eyes, and reached out to the right and to the left. And at the foot of the wall was the door—a door of walnut wood, studded with copper nails, and the nails were intricately ordered in a geometrical figure, impossible for the eye to unravel.

That Charnock already knew; he had made trial before now to unravel those geometrical figures, once, very long ago, and very far away in the white sunlit street of a Spanish town. Charnock stood and stared at the door, and the Spanish town loomed larger before his vision, drew nearer, moved towards him, first slowly, then quickly, then in a rush. Ronda! Ronda! The town, as it were, swept over him. He seemed to wake; he seemed to stand again in the street. To his right was the chasm of the Tajo, and the bridge, and the boiling torrent; behind that door lived—and these two years slipped from him like a cloak. With an unconscious movement of his hands he pushed the hood back from his forehead, and stood bare-headed and alert. He was again one of the hurrying, strenuous, curious folk who live beyond the Straits.

He gazed at the door. Behind that door's fellow Miranda lived and waited. Even as the thought burned through his mind, the door opened. For a moment Charnock imagined that Miranda herself would step out; but only a Moor came forth from an interview with the Basha, and a ragged, decrepit greybeard of a servant attended on the Moor and made his path. Charnock was in an instant aware of a grey light filtering between the squalid roof-tops, of the filth of the streets, of the tottering walls of Mulai Ismail. He was in Mequinez.

And at Mequinez the long two years should end, and in ending bear their fruit. That door, on which his eyes were set, augured as much, nay promised it. "Not a sparrow shall fall. . ." Just for this reason, centuries ago, a Moorish conqueror had taken these slabs of walnut wood in Spain, and brought them back upon the shoulders of his slaves and made his door from them and set it in his wall at Mequinez; just that Charnock coming to this spot centuries afterwards might be quickened in his service towards a woman, and gird himself about with the memory of things which were growing dim, and be assured the service should not fail! Charnock was uplifted to believe it.

He drew the hood again about his head, and the voice of the Mueddin called the world to prayer. Through the open doors of the mosques, from the white walls glimmering in the dimness within those doors, from the streets, from the houses, the high-pitched tremulous prayer rose and declined in an arc of sound.

Charnock felt his whole being throb exultantly. At Mequinez, yes, and to-night, his search would end. Surely to-night! For the hour after the evening prayer was the hour for the selling of slaves.

Charnock walked to the market and sat himself down in the first dim corner. He did not choose a place prominent and visible, inviting whosoever had wares to sell; he took the first seat which offered— certain that wherever he sat Ralph Warriner would be brought to him. He sat down and looked about him.

Some half a dozen men were grouped about the market talking; a young negress from the Soudan, a white Moorish girl, a young negro from Timbuctoo, were brought to them in turn. They examined their teeth, their arms, their feet. The Moorish girl was bought; the others passed on, each with the owner. They were followed by the Moor whom Charnock had seen step from the Basha's door. He wished to sell his decrepit greybeard, and was met with laughter wheresoever he turned. These were all the slaves in the market.

Charnock did not lose heart. At any moment within the next few minutes the narrow entrance to the market might darken, and Ralph Warriner's owner thrust Ralph Warriner in—at some moment that would happen.

Did Warriner still shuffle in the Moorish slippers as he walked? Charnock found himself asking the question with a curious light-heartedness. The negress was offered to him, and then the negro; he refused them with a gesture. He lent an ear to the rustling whispering traffic of the streets outside. He listened patiently, confidently, for the sound of a shuffling footstep to emerge, and grow distinct and more distinct. The Moor brought his greybeard to Charnock's corner. Charnock held his head aside and listened for the loose slap-slap of the slipper upon the mud. The Moor spoke, was importunate; Charnock waved him aside impatiently.

But as he waved his arm he turned his head; and then he suddenly reached out a hand, while his heart leaped in his throat. "Ten dollars," he said. The Moor began to expatiate on the merits of his slave; he was still strong; he could carry heavy loads, and for far distances. Charnock was impatient to interrupt, to pay the price. When he had turned his head, suddenly, for an instant, he had looked straight into the greybeard's eyes—and they were the blue eyes which had stared into his—once, how many centuries ago?—through the window of a hansom cab in a noisy street of Plymouth. Charnock had no doubt. Other Moors had blue eyes, and in no other feature of this wizened, haggard creature but his eyes could he trace a resemblance to Ralph Warriner; but he had no doubt. All the intuitions of the last half-hour came to his aid. He remembered the door, the call to prayer. This was Ralph Warriner, and he had almost let him pass! Had he not turned by mere accident just at the one moment when the greybeard's eyes were raised, he would have lost his chance now and forever. Warriner would have perished in his servitude, would have dropped somewhere on the plain under a load too heavy, and lain there until nightfall brought the jackals.

The thought took Charnock at the throat, left him struggling for his breath. So near had he been to failing when he must not fail! He began to fear at once that another purchaser might step in, while the Moor was still exaggerating his goods. Yet he must not interrupt; he must give no sign of anxiety lest he should awaken suspicion; he must bargain with extreme indifference while a fever burnt in all his blood.

"Thirty dollars," the Moor proposed.

Charnock shrugged his shoulders and shook his head. The Moor turned away; the slave followed the master. Charnock clenched his hands together under the folds of his sleeves to prevent them reaching out and clasping the man. The merchant walked slowly for a few yards. At the entrance of the market there was a sudden obscurity; a tall man blocked the way, entered, and stopped before the merchant and his slave. Charnock's heart died within him; but the man only laughed and passed on.

Charnock felt all his muscles relax, as his suspense ended. For now surely the slave would be brought back. The merchant turned slowly; Warriner turned obediently behind him, and the obedience went to Charnock's heart. It spoke of a discipline too hideous. Slowly the owner returned to Charnock; it seemed that he would never speak.

"Twenty-five dollars," he said.

With an effort Charnock mastered his face and controlled his body. "Twenty," he returned, and spoke of the slave's age, and how little need he had of him. He heard the newcomer across the market haggling over the negro from Timbuctoo. And at last,—at last the word was spoken, the man he had come to search for was his, and his inalienably, so long as he remained in any corner of Morocco.

Charnock paid the money; he did not so much as glance again at his slave. He rose from his seat. "Follow me," he said to Warriner in Moghrebbin; and one behind the other, Miranda's lover and Miranda's husband, master and slave, passed out of the market and down the street towards the gate of Mequinez.

XX

CHARNOCK, LIKE THE TAXIDERMIST, FINDS WARRINER ANYTHING BUT A COMFORTABLE COMPANION

On the way Charnock stopped at the *fondak* where Hamet slept, and bade the lad saddle the mules and bring them out of the town. Hamet looked surprised, for nightfall was an ill time to start upon a journey near the country of the Lemur tribes, but he was accustomed to obey. Charnock's new slave did not even show surprise. Leaving Hamet to follow him, Charnock passed through the gate. He dreaded to remain in the town lest by some misfortune he might lose his slave; and, besides, a nausea for its smells and its dirt began to gain upon him. He walked down the slope of the hill to the olive trees and the mossy turf. Lepers, of an unimaginable aspect, dragged by the side of the beaten track and begged; robbers, who for their crimes had had their eyes burnt out, kept pace with him, their eyelids closed upon red and empty sockets; dead horses, mules, and camels were scattered by the way, their carcases half devoured; everywhere were ruins, and things decaying and things decayed; and over all was a sky of unbroken cloud, and a chill lugubrious light.

Charnock observed his surroundings with newly-opened eyes and hurried on till he reached the olives. Then he stopped and turned to watch for Hamet's coming. He turned a trifle suddenly and his slave instinctively shrank away and stood submissive and mute, stilled by a long companionship with despair. And this was a captain of Her Majesty's Artillery, who had sailed his yacht in and out of Gibraltar Bay!

"My God, how you must have suffered!" cried Charnock, and he spoke in the English tongue.

Warriner raised a dazed, half-witted face. "Say that again," he said slowly, and he spoke in Arabic.

"My God, how you must have suffered!"

Warriner listened with one forefinger uplifted; he moved his finger backwards and forwards sawing the air. "Yes," he answered, and this time in English; but his mouth was awkward and the English came rustily from his tongue. "Yes, it has been a hell of a time."

He spoke in a quite expressionless voice. But whether it was that the forgotten sound of the tongue he used awoke in his dim mind faint associations and a glimmer of memories, of a sudden he dropped upon the turf amidst the olive trees and, burying his face in the moss, sobbed violently like a child.

Charnock let him lie there until he saw Hamet leading the mules down the beaten way from the town-gates. Then he bent down and touched Warriner on the shoulder. "Here is my servant—do you understand?—my servant."

The white man's pride answered the summons. Warriner got quickly to his feet and drew a ragged sleeve across his face. Then he looked round between the withered olives at that grey cruel ruin of a city looming through the falling desolate light, and shivered. His eyes lighted upon Hamet, and suddenly opened wide. "Those mules," he said almost fiercely. "They are yours?"

"Yes!"

"Let us ride! O dear God, let us ride!" And until Hamet reached them, his head darted this way and that, while his eyes searched the trees. "Mind, you bought me," he said. "I belong to you; to no one else. How far from here to the sea?"

"Nine days."

"Nine days," and he counted them over on his fingers.

Hamet brought up the mules. Charnock unrolled a burnous and a turban. Warriner plucked off his rags and put on the dress. Then the three men rode out between the olive trees, past the outer rampart of breached walls, into the open plain.

"Shall we camp?" said Charnock.

Warriner cast a look across his shoulder. Mequinez was still visible, a greyer blot upon the grey hillside. "No," said he.

They rode forward over carpets of flowers, between the hills. The light fell; the marigolds paled beneath their mules' feet; the gentians became any flower of a light hue. At last a toothed savage screen of rock moved across Mequinez.

"Here," said Warriner. He tumbled rather than dismounted from his mule, stretched his limbs out upon the grass, and in a moment was asleep. Hamet gathered a bundle of leaves from a dwarf palm tree and a few sticks, lit a fire, and cooked their supper. Charnock woke Warriner, who ate his meal and slept again; and all that night, with a Mouser pistol in his hand, Charnock sat by his side and guarded him.

The next morning they started betimes; they passed a caravan, farther on a tent-village, and towards evening, from the shoulder of a hill they looked down upon the vast plain of the Sebou. Level as a sea it stretched away until the distinct colours of its flower-patches merged into one soft blue.

"Eight days," said Warriner; and that night, as last night, he asked no questions of Charnock, but ate his supper and so slept; and that night again Charnock sat by his side and guarded him.

But the next morning Warriner for the first time began to evince some curiosity as to his rescue and the man who had rescued him. The two men had just bathed in a little stream which ran tinkling through the grass beside their camp. Warriner was kneeling upon the bank of the stream and contemplating himself in the clear mirror of its water, when he said to Charnock: "How in the world did you know me?"

"By your eyes."

"We are not strangers, eh?"

"I hailed you from a hansom cab once outside Lloyd's bank in Plymouth. You expressed an amiable wish that I should sit in that cab and rot away in my boots. Lucky for you I didn't!"

"You were the man who jammed his finger? I remember; I thought you had got a warrant in your pocket. By the way," and he lifted his head quickly, "you never, I suppose, came across a man called Wilbraham?"

"Ambrose?"

"Yes, yes; when did you come across him?"

"He was blackmailing your wife."

"Oh, my wife," said Warriner, suddenly, as though it had only just occurred to him that he had a wife. He turned his head and looked curiously to Charnock, who was scrubbing himself dry some yards behind him. "So you know my wife?"

"Yes."

"Ah!" Warriner again examined his face in the stream. "I think I might walk straight up from the Ragged Staff," said he, wagging his grey beard, "and shake hands with the Governor of Gibraltar and no one be a penny the wiser." Then he paused. "So you know Wilbraham," he said slowly, and paused again. "So you know my wife too;" and the pair went to their breakfast.

Warriner walked in front of Charnock, and the latter could not but notice how within these two days his companion had changed. His back was losing its timid differential curve; there was less of a slink in his walk; he no longer shrank when a loud word was addressed to him. Moreover, his curiosity increased, and while they were at breakfast he asked "How did you find me?"

And that morning as they rode forwards over the marigolds and irises, Charnock told him of his first visit to Tangier and of Hassan Akbar. "So when I came again," he said with perhaps a little awkwardness and after a pause, "I had a clue, a slight one, but still a clue, and I followed it."

"It was you who shouted through Fournier's shop-door, was it?" said Warriner. "That's the second time a cry of yours has fairly scared me. So you know Wilbraham," he added in a moment; "so you know my wife too."

They halted at noon under a hedge of cactus, and Charnock, tired with his long vigils, covered his head and slept. Through the long afternoon, over pink and violet flowers, under a burning sun, they journeyed drowsily, with no conversation and no sound at all but the humming of the insects in the air and the whistle of birds and the brushing of their mules' feet through the grass. That evening they crossed the Sebou and camped a few yards from the river's bank in a most lucid air.

It was after supper. Charnock was lying upon his back, his head resting upon his arms, and his eyes upturned to the throbbing stars and the rich violet sky. Warriner squatted cross-legged beside a dying fire, and now and then, as a flame spirted up, he cast a curious glance towards Charnock.

"How long have you been searching?" he asked.

"Two years," replied Charnock.

"Why?"

The question was shot at him, in a sharp challenging voice. Charnock did not move from his position; he lay resting on that vast plain under the fresh night sky and the kindly stars; but he was some little while silent before he answered, "Your wife asked me to come."

Warriner nodded his head thoughtfully, but said no more. That night Charnock did not keep watch, for they were across the Sebou and out of the perilous country. The next morning they rode on towards Alkasar with few words between them. Only Charnock noticed that Warriner was continually glancing at him with a certain furtiveness, and it seemed with a certain ill-will. Charnock grew restless under this surveillance: he resented it; it made him vaguely uneasy.

They rode with no shadows to console them until the afternoon brought the clouds over the top of the Atlas. Towards evening they saw far ahead of them the town of Alkasar amongst its gardens of orange trees and olives.

"We shall not reach it to-night," said Charnock, looking up at the sky.

"No, thank God," answered Warriner, fervently. "No towns for me! What if it does rain?"

So again they camped in the open, under a solitary wild fig tree, and the rain held off. They talked indifferently upon this subject and that, speculated upon news of Europe, and Charnock heard something of Warriner's comings and goings, his sufferings and adventures. But the talk was forced, and though now and again Wilbraham's name, and now and again Miranda's, recurred, it died altogether away.

Warriner broke it suddenly. "You are in love with my wife," he said.

Charnock started up on his elbow. "What the devil has that got to do with you?" he asked fiercely.

The two men eyed one another across the leaping flames of the fire. "Well, you have a right to put it that way, no doubt," said Warriner.

Charnock sank down again. He felt resentment throbbing hot within him. He was very glad that there were only five more days during which he and Warriner must travel together alone, and during which he must keep ward over the man he had rescued.

But the next day was one of peace. The mere proximity of a Moorish town had terrors for Warriner. His eyes turned ever towards it, scared and frightened. His very body shrank and took on a servile air. Besides, it rained.

"We might sleep in Alkasar. There is a Jew I stayed with coming up; you will be safe there," said Charnock.

"I would sooner shiver to death here," replied Warriner, and they skirted the town.

But a little distance from the gates Charnock called a halt, and taking Hamet and a mule he went up into the town. He sought out his Jew, and bought a tent, which he packed upon the mule, and so returned to where Warriner crouched and hid amongst the orange trees. Beyond Alkasar they passed through a long stretch of stubble, whence acres of wheat had been garnered, and at night the two men sat in the opening of their tent, while the lad Hamet drew weird melancholy from his pipe.

Warriner was silent; he was evidently turning over some thought in his mind, and his mind, rusted by his servitude, worked very slowly. A man of great vindictiveness and jealousy, he was not grateful for his rescue; but he was brooding over the motives which had induced Charnock to come in search of him, and which had persuaded Miranda to send him in search. Warriner had never cared for his wife, but his wife had never till now given him any cause for jealousy, and out of his present jealousy there sprang and grew in his half-crazy and disordered mind a quite fictitious passion.

He revealed something of it the next morning to Charnock. For after he had waked up and yawned, after he had watched for a moment the busy shadow of Hamet upon the tent-wall and heard the light crackle of the breakfast fire, he roused Charnock with a shake of the shoulder and resumed the conversation at the point where it had been broken off when they sat by the camp-fire.

"But I'll tell you a question which has to do with me, Charnock," he said. "Is my wife in love with you?"

"You damned blackguard!" cried Charnock.

"Thanks!" said Warriner, with a chuckle. "That's answer enough."

"It's no answer at all!" exclaimed Charnock, hotly, and he sat up amongst his blankets and took refuge in subterfuges. "If what you say were true, is it likely that your wife would have asked me to find you out and bring you back?"

"That's the very point I have been considering," returned Warriner; "and I think it uncommon likely. Women have all sorts of underground scruples which it's difficult for a man to get upside with, and I can imagine a woman would send off her fancy man on this particular business as a kind of set-off and compensation. See?"

Charnock dared not trust himself to answer. He got up and walked to the door of the tent, unfastened the flap, and let the sunlight in.

"Funny thing!" continued Warriner, "I never took much account of my wife. She was a bit too stately for me. It was just as though someone played symphonies to you all day when you hankered after music of the music-hall type. But somehow,—I suppose it's seeing you doing the heroic and all for her, don't you know?—somehow I am getting very fond of her."

Charnock seemed to have heard not a single word. He stood at the door of the tent, looking indifferently this way and that. His silence spurred Warriner to continue. "I tell you what, Charnock," he said, "you had better run straight with me. You'll find out your mistake if you don't. I'll tell you something more: you had better let me find when I get back to Ronda that you have run straight with me." He saw

Charnock suddenly look round the angle of the tent and then shade his eyes with his hand. It seemed impossible to provoke him in any way. "Mind, I don't say that I shall take it much to heart, if the affair has stopped where you say it has." Charnock had said not a word about the matter, as Warriner was well aware. "No," he continued, "on the contrary; for no harm's actually done, you say, and my wife steps down from her pedestal on to my level. Understand, sonny?—What are you up to? Here, I say."

Charnock had stridden back into the tent. He stooped over Warriner and roughly plucked him up from the ground. "Stand up, will you!" he cried.

"Here, I say," protested Warriner, rather feebly; "you might be speaking to a dog."

"I wish I was."

At that Warriner turned. The two men's faces were convulsed with passion; hatred looked out from Warriner's eyes and saw its image in Charnock's.

"Get out of the tent," said Charnock, and taking Warriner by the shoulder, he threw rather than pushed him out.

"Now, what's that?" and he pointed an arm towards the east.

"That's a caravan."

"Quite so, a caravan. Perhaps you have forgotten what you said to me outside the walls of Mequinez. You belong to me, you remember. You're mine; I bought you, and I can sell you if I choose."

"By God, you wouldn't do that!" cried Warriner. His years of slavery rushed back on him. He saw himself again tramping, under the sun, with a load upon his back through the sand towards Algiers, over the hills to the Sus country; he heard again the whistle of a stick through the air, heard its thud as it fell upon his body, and felt the blow. "My God, you couldn't do that!" And seeing Charnock towering above him, his face hard, his eyes gloomy, he clung to his arm. "Charnock, old man! You wouldn't, would you?"

"You'll fetch half a dozen copper *flouss*," said Charnock.

"Look here, Charnock, I apologise. See, old man, see? I am sorry; you hear that, don't you? Yes, I'm sorry. It's my cursed tongue."

Charnock shook him off. "We left your rags behind, I believe, so you can keep those clothes. The caravan will pass us in an hour." Then Warriner fell to prayers, and flamed up in anger and curses and died down again to whimpering. All the while Charnock stood over him silent and contemptuous. There was no doubt possible he meant to carry out his threat. Warriner burst out in a flood of imprecations, and Moorish imprecations, for they came most readily to his tongue. He called on God to burn Charnock's great-grandmother, and then in an instant he became very cunning and calm.

"And what sort of a face will you show to Miranda," he said smoothly, "when you get back to Ronda? You have forgotten that."

Charnock had forgotten it; in his sudden access of passion he had clean forgotten it. Warriner wiped the sweat from his face; he did not need to look at Charnock to be assured that at this moment he was the master. He stuck his legs apart and rested his hands upon his hips. "You weren't quite playing the game, eh, Charnock?" he said easily. "Do you think you were quite playing the game?"

From that moment Warriner was master, and he was not inclined to leave Charnock ignorant upon that point. Jealousy burnt within him. His mind was unstable. A quite fictitious passion for his wife, for whom he had never cared, and of whom he certainly would very quickly tire, was kindled by his jealousy; and he left no word unspoken which could possibly wound his deliverer. Charnock bitterly realised the false position into which he had allowed passion to lead him; and for the future he held his peace.

"Only one more day," he said with relief, as they saw the hills behind Tangier.

"And what then, Charnock?" said Warriner. "What then?"

What then, indeed? Charnock debated that question during the long night, the last night he was to spend under canvas in company with Ralph Warriner. Sometime to-morrow they would see the minarets of Tangier—to-morrow evening they would ride down across the Sôk and sleep within the town. What then? Passion was raw in these two men. It was a clear night; an African moon sailed the sky, and the interior of the tent was bright. Warriner lay motionless, a foot or two away, wrapped in his dark coverings, and Charnock was conscious of a fierce thrill of joy when he remembered Miranda's confession that she had no love left for her husband. He did not attempt to repress it; he hugged the recollection to his heart. All at once Warriner began softly to whistle a tune; it was the tune which he had whistled that morning at the gates of Tangier cemetery, it was the tune which Miranda had hummed over absently in the little parlour at Ronda, and which had given Charnock the clue—and because of the clue Warriner was again

A.E.W. MASON

whistling the tune in the same tent with himself—a day's march from Tangier.

Charnock began hotly to regret that he had ever heard it, that he had charged Hamet to repeat it, and that so he had fixed it in his mind. He kicked over on his rugs, and he heard Warriner speak.

"You are awake, are you? I say, Charnock," he asked smoothly, "did Miranda show you the graveyard in Gib? That was my youngster, understand?—mine and Miranda's."

Charnock clenched his teeth, clenched his hand, and straightened his muscles out through all his body, that he might give no sign of what he felt.

"Bone of my bone," continued Warriner, in a silky, drawling voice, "flesh of my flesh,—and Miranda's." Perhaps some deep breath drawn with a hiss through the teeth assured Warriner that his speech was not spoken in vain; for he laughed softly and hatefully to himself.

Charnock lay quite still, but every vein in his body was throbbing. He had one thought only to relieve him. Warriner had said the last uttermost word of provocation; he had fashioned it out of the dust of his child, when but for that child he would still be a slave; and out of the wifehood of Miranda, when but for Miranda Charnock would never have come in search of him. *Rupert Warriner, aged two.* The gravestone, the boy looking out between the lattices, was very visible to Charnock at that moment. He was in the mind to give Warriner an account of how and why he was brought to see it; but he held his peace, sure that whatever gibes or stings Warriner might dispense in the future, they would be trifling and inconsiderable compared with this monumental provocation.

He was wrong; Warriner's malice had yet another resource. Seeing that Charnock neither answered him nor moved, he got up from his couch. Charnock saw him rummaging amongst the baggage, hopping about the tent in the pale moonlight; the shadow of his beard wagged upon the tent-wall, and all the while he chuckled and whispered to himself. Charnock watched his fantastic movements and took them together with the man's fantastic words, and it occurred to him then for the first time to ask whether Warriner's mind had suffered with his body. He had come to this point of his reflections when Warriner, stooping over a bundle, found whatever it was for which he searched. Charnock heard a light snick, like the cocking of a pistol, only not so loud. Then Warriner hopped back to Charnock's side, knelt down and thrust something into the palm of Charnock's hand. Charnock's fingers closed on it instinctively and gripped it hard; for this something was the handle of a knife and the blade was open.

"There!" said Warriner. "You have to protect me. This is the last night, so I give you the knife to protect me with."

He hopped back to his rugs, twittering with pleasure; and turning his face once more towards Charnock, while Charnock lay with the open knife in his hand, he resumed, "My boy, Charnock—mine and Miranda's—mine and Miranda's."

The next evening they rode over the cobblestones of Tangier and halted at M. Fournier's shop.

XXI

Completes the Journeyings of this Incongruous Couple

M. Fournier received the wanderers with an exuberant welcome. He fell upon Warriner's neck, patted him, and wept over him for joy at his return and for grief at his aged and altered looks. Then he grasped Charnock with both hands. "The deliverer," he cried, "the friend so noble!"

"Yes," said Warriner, pleasantly; "*ce bon* Charnock, he loves my wife."

Within half-an-hour the two travellers were shaved and clothed in European dress.

"Would anyone know me?" asked Warriner.

"My poor friend, I am afraid not," answered Fournier, and Warriner seemed very well pleased with the answer.

"Then we will go and dine, really and properly dine, at a hotel on champagne wine," said he.

They dined at a window which looked out across the Straits, and all through that dinner Warriner's face darkened and darkened and his gaze was sombrely fixed towards Gibraltar.

"What are your plans?" asked Fournier.

"The first thing I propose to do is to walk up to the cemetery and astonish my friend Hassan Akbar."

"You will not find him. The Basha thought it wise to keep him safe in prison until you were found."

"He has been there two years then?" said Warriner. "He had no friends. Then he is dead?" For the Moorish authorities do not feed the prisoners in the Kasbah.

M. Fournier blushed. "No, he is not dead. He would have starved, but,—you will forgive it, my friend? After all he had no great reason to like you,—I sent him food myself every day,—not very much, but enough," stammered M. Fournier, anxiously.

Warriner waved his hand. "It is a small thing; yes, I forgive you."

"And he may go free?"

"Why not? He will not catch me again."

M. Fournier's face brightened with admiration.

"Ah, but you are great, truly great," he exclaimed; "my friend, you are *magnanime!* Now tell me what you will do."

M. Fournier's magnanimous friend replied. "The boat crosses to Algeciras to-morrow. I shall go up to Ronda. And you?" he asked, turning to Charnock.

"I shall go with you," said Charnock.

"*Ce bon* Charnock," said Warriner, with a smile. "He loves my wife."

"But afterwards?" Fournier hurried to interpose. "Will you stay at Ronda?"

"No."

Warriner's eyes strained out across the water to where the topmost ridge of Gibraltar rose against the evening sky. Since his rescue two thoughts had divided and made a conflict in his mind; one was his jealousy of Charnock, his unreal hot-house affection for Miranda; the other had been represented by his vague questions and statements about Wilbraham. He was now to speak more clearly, for as he looked over to the Rock, Wilbraham was uppermost in his mind.

"You did not know Wilbraham," he resumed. "Charnock did, *ce bon* Charnock. I have a little account to settle with Wilbraham, a little account of some standing, and now there's a new item to the bill. The scullion! Imagine it, Fournier. He blackmailed my wife; blackmailed Miranda! Do you understand?" he cried feverishly. "Miranda! You know her, Charnock. Fournier, how often have I spoken of her to you? Miranda!" And words failed him, so inconceivable was the thought that any man should bring himself to do any wrong to his Miranda.

M. Fournier stared. As he had once told Mrs. Warriner, Ralph had spoken to him of Miranda; but it had not been with the startling enthusiasm which at present he evinced.

"I shall settle my accounts with Wilbraham first," continued Warriner, "after I have seen Miranda. Did you know it was Wilbraham who sold the plans of the Daventry gun?"

"Was it?" exclaimed Charnock.

"It was," and the three men drew their chairs closer together. "Wilbraham was a moneylender's tout at Gib. I had borrowed money and renewed; I borrowed again, and again renewed. You see," he argued in excuse, "I would not touch a penny of my wife's estate; that of course was sacred. It was Miranda's—"

"And settled upon Miranda," Charnock could not refrain from interposing.

"Don't you call my wife by her christian name, else you and I will quarrel," exclaimed Warriner, banging his fist violently upon the table, and M. Fournier anxiously signed to Charnock to be silent.

"It was a slip," said Fournier, and soothingly he patted Warriner on the shoulder. "Here! have one or two fine champagne, eh? Now go on; we are all of us good friends. You borrowed twice from Wilbraham and did not pay; you would not, of course. Well?"

"I tried to borrow a third time," continued Warriner; "but Wilbraham refused unless I could offer him good security. He himself suggested the plans of the Daventry gun. He swore most solemnly that he would not use them; he would keep them as a security for three weeks, and I wanted his money. I had debts to pay, debts to my brother officers, and I agreed. He lent me the money; I gave him the plans, and he went off to Paris and sold them. I received a hint one afternoon that the mechanism of the gun was known, and I ran out of Gibraltar that evening. So, you see, I have an account with him; and it grows and grows and grows upon me each time that I see that." He pointed a shaking finger to where the sharp ridge of Gibraltar cut the evening sky. "Now that I can go where I will and no one will know me, I will get the account paid, and cut a receipt in full with a knife right across Wilbraham's face."

His voice rose and quavered with a feverish excitement, his eyes shone and glittered; it seemed to Charnock there was madness in them. M. Fournier's eyes met his and they exchanged glances, so M. Fournier, who was engaged in assiduously soothing Warriner, shared the conjecture. Indeed, as M. Fournier took his leave, he said privately to Charnock: "My poor friend! what will be the end of it for him? His wife does not like him and he will follow this Wilbraham, and he is not himself."

Charnock was lighting his candle at the hall-table.

"Yes," said he, slowly. "There is his wife, there is Wilbraham, there is himself; what is to be the end of it all?"

He went up the stairs to his room. His room communicated with Warriner's, and taking the key from the door, he left the door unlocked. More than once as he tossed upon his bed vainly reiterating the question, what was to be the end, he heard the latch of the door click, he saw the door open slowly, he saw a head come cautiously through the opening; and then, as he lay still, Warriner came hopping across the room to his bed. Warriner came to assure himself that Charnock had not stolen a march upon him during the night; he was possessed by a crazy fear lest Charnock should see Miranda before himself.

On the following afternoon they crossed together to Algeciras, through a rough sea in a strong wind.

"It's the Levanter," said Warriner; "there'll be three days of it." He looked earnestly at Gibraltar as the boat turned into the bay. "Wilbraham, Wilbraham," he muttered in a voice of anticipation. Then he turned to Charnock. "Mind, we go up to Ronda together! We shall have to stay the night at Algeciras. Mind, you are not to charter a special and go up ahead while I am asleep."

Charnock was sorely tempted to secure an engine, as he could have done, but Miranda had asked to see him "once when he brought Ralph back," and so the next morning they travelled together.

At noon Charnock saw again the walnut door encrusted with the copper nails, and Warriner was already hammering upon it with his stick. The moment it was opened he rushed through without a word, thrusting the servant aside.

Charnock followed him, but though he followed he had the advantage, for while Warriner gazed about the patio into which for the first time he entered, Charnock ran across to the little room in which Miranda was wont to sit. He opened the door.

"Empty," said Warriner, from behind his shoulder, and he pushed past Charnock into the room. From the balcony above them Jane Holt spoke. She spoke to Charnock as she ran down the stair.

"It's you at last! Miranda is at Gibraltar. She expected to hear of you, and thought she would hear more quickly there. She has been ill, besides; she needed doctors."

"Ill?" exclaimed Charnock.

"Who is that?" asked Miss Holt, glancing across Charnock's shoulder.

"Ralph."

"Ralph!" cried out Miss Holt. "But he's—"

"Hush!"

They followed Warriner into the room, and Charnock closed the door.

"Didn't you know?" he asked. "I went to find him."

"No," she replied, utterly bewildered. "It seems strange; but Miranda is very secret. A little unkind, perhaps," and then her voice went up almost in a scream as Warriner turned towards her. "Ralph! Is that Ralph?"

A.E.W. MASON

"Yes, yes, it's Ralph," said Warriner, and all the time he spoke, he trotted and hopped and danced about the room. "Ralph Warriner, to be sure; a little bit aged, eh, Jane Holt? Little bit musty? Been lyin' too long in the churchyard at Scilly—bound to alter your looks that,— what?" He skipped over to the writing table and began with a seeming aimlessness to pull out the drawers. "Where's Miranda? Does she know her lovin' husband's here? Why don't she come? Tell me that, Jane Holt!" He made a quick, and to Charnock an unintelligible, movement at the writing table, shut up a drawer with a bang, and the next moment he had a hand tight upon Jane Holt's wrist. "Where's Miranda? Quick!" and he shook her arm fiercely, but with a sly look towards Charnock; his other hand he thrust into his pocket. Charnock just got a glimpse of a sheet of paper clenched in the fist. Warriner withdrew his hand from his pocket empty. He had stolen something from the writing drawer. But what it was Charnock could not guess, nor did he think it wise, in view of Warriner's excitement, to ask.

"Miranda's at Gibraltar," said Miss Holt, quite alarmed by the man's extravagance. "I told you, she is ill."

Warriner waited to hear no more. He dropped her arm. "At Gibraltar," he said, and ran out of the room across the patio. Charnock followed him immediately. "He must not go alone," he cried over his shoulder to Miss Holt, but the excuse was only half of his motive. Passion, resentment, jealousy,—these too ordered him and he obeyed.

Charnock came up with Warriner at the railway station. The train did not leave Ronda until three, as Charnock might have known and so behaved with dignity before Miss Holt; but he was beyond the power of argument or reflection. He hurried after Warriner and caught him up, and during the two hours of waiting, the two men kept watch and ward upon each other. Together they walked to the hotel, they lunched at the same table, they returned side by side to the station, and seated themselves side by side in the same carriage of the train. The train which takes four hours to climb to Ronda runs down that long slope of a hundred miles in two hours. Charnock and Warriner took their seats in a *coupé* at the end of the last carriage; they rushed suddenly into the dark straight tunnels, and saw the mouths by which they had entered as round O's of light which contracted and contracted until a mere pin's-point of sunshine was visible far away, and then suddenly they were out again in the daylight.

There were certain landmarks with which Charnock was familiar,—a precipitous gorge upon the right, an underground river which flooded out from a hillside upon the left, a white town far away upon a green slope like a flock of sheep herded together, and finally the glades of the cork forest with the gleam of its stripped tree-trunks. The train drew up at Algeciras a few minutes after five.

Charnock and Warriner were met with the statement that the Levanter of yesterday had increased in force, and by the order of the harbour-master the port of Algeciras was closed. It was impossible to make the passage to Gibraltar—and Miranda was ill. She had needed doctors, Jane Holt had said. Charnock's fears exaggerated the malady; she might be dying; she might die while he and Warriner waited at Algeciras for the sea to subside. "We must reach Gibraltar to-night," he cried.

"And before gunfire," added Warriner. "But how?"

Charnock went straight to the office of the manager of the line. The manager greeted him with warmth. "But, man, where have you been these two years?" he exclaimed.

"There's a station at San Roque half-way round the bay," said Charnock. "I must get into Gibraltar to-night. If I can have a special to San Roque, I might drive the last nine miles."

Gibraltar is before everything a fortress, and the gates of that fortress are closed for the night at gunfire, and opened again for the day at gunfire in the morning.

"You will never do it," said the manager. "The gun goes off at seven."

"What's the month?" cried Warriner.

"July," answered the manager, in surprise.

"And the day of July?"

"The fifth."

"Good," cried Warriner. "You are wrong; on the fifth of July the gun goes off at eight—from the fifth of July to the thirty-first of August."

The manager uncoupled one carriage and the engine, coupled them together and switched them on to the up-line. Meanwhile Charnock telegraphed to the station-master at San Roque, to have a carriage in readiness; but time was occupied, and it was six o'clock before the engine steamed into San Roque.

San Roque is a wayside station; the village lies a mile away, hidden behind a hill. Charnock and Warriner alighted amongst fields and thickets of trees, but nowhere was there a house visible, and worst of all, there was no carriage in the lane outside the station. The station-master had ordered one, and no doubt one would arrive. He counselled patience.

For half-an-hour the incongruous companions, united by a common passion and a mutual hate, kicked their heels upon the lonely platform of San Roque. Then at last a crazy, battered, creaking diligence, drawn by six broken-kneed, sore-backed mules, cantered up to the station with a driver and a boy upon the box, whooping exhortations to the mules with the full power of their lungs.

Charnock and Warriner sprang up into the hooded seat behind the box, the driver turned his mules, and the diligence went off at a canter, along an unmade track across the fields.

It was now close upon a quarter to seven, and nine miles lay between San Roque and the gates of Gibraltar. Moreover, there was no road for the first part of the journey, merely this unmade track across the fields. The two men urged on the driver with open-handed promises; the driver screamed and shouted at his mules: "Hi! mules, here's a bull after you!" He counterfeited the barking of dogs; but the mules were accustomed to his threats and exhortations; they knew there were no dogs at their heels, and they kept to their regular canter.

Charnock longed for the fields to end and for the road to begin; and when the road did begin, he longed again for the fields. The road consisted of long lines of ruts, ruts which were almost trenches, ruts which had been baked hard by the summer suns. The mules stumbled amongst them, the diligence tossed and pitched and rolled like a boat in a heavy sea; Charnock and Warriner clung to their seats, while the driver continually looked round to see whether a wheel had slipped off from its axle. At times the boy would jump down from the box, and running forward with the whip in his hand, would beat the mules with the butt-end; the lash had long ceased to influence their movements.

"The road's infernal," cried Warriner.

"It will be when we get to the sea," replied the driver, and Charnock groaned in his distress. There was worse to come, and Miranda was ill.

The diligence lurched between two clumps of juniper trees, swung round a wall, and instantly the wheels sank into soft sand. The huge, sheer landward face of Gibraltar Rock towered up before them as they looked across the mile of neutral ground, that flat neck of land between the Mediterranean and the Bay. They saw the Spanish frontier town of Linea; but to Linea the sand stretched in a broad golden curve, soft and dry, and through that curve of sand the wheels of the diligence had to plough. The mules were beaten onwards, but the Levanter blew dead in their teeth. The driver turned the diligence towards the sea, and drove with the water splashing over the wheels; there the sand bound, and the pace was faster.

It was still, however, too slow; Gibraltar seemed still as far away. The travellers paid the driver, leaped from their seats, and ran over the soft clogging sand to Linea. They reached Linea. They passed the sentinel and the iron gates, they stood upon the neutral ground. They had but one more mile to traverse.

A cab stood without the iron gates. They jumped into it and drove at a gallop across the level; but the gun was fired from the Rock, while they were still half-a-mile from the gate, and the cabman brought his horses to a standstill.

"What now?" said Warriner.

"We might get in," said Charnock.

"The keys are taken to the Governor. There would be trouble; there always is. I know there would be questions asked; it would not be safe. I might slip in when the gates are open, but now it would not be safe. And mind, Charnock, when you go in I go in too."

There was no doubt that Warriner meant what he said, every word of it. For Miranda's sake Charnock could not risk Warriner's detection. They must remain outside Gibraltar for that night, even though during the night Miranda should die.

"Can we sleep at Linea?" said Charnock.

"No, Linea is a collection of workmen's houses and workmen's pot-houses." The two men made their supper at one of these latter, and for the rest of the night paced the neutral ground before Gibraltar.

A scud of clouds darkened the sky, and one pile of cloud, darker than the rest, lowered stationary upon the summit of the Rock. All night the Levanter blew pitilessly cold across that unprotected neck of land between sea and sea. With their numbed hands in their pockets, and their coats buttoned to the throat, Charnock and Warriner, accustomed to the blaze of a Morocco sun, waited from nightfall until midnight, and from midnight through the biting, dreary hours till dawn.

The gates were opened at three o'clock in the morning. Together the two men went through; they had still hours to wait before they could return to the hotel. They breakfasted together, and they let the time go by, for now that they were within reach of, almost within sight of,

Miranda Warriner, they both began to hesitate. What was to be the end? They looked at one another across the table with that question speaking from their eyes. They walked down to the hotel and faced each other at the door, and the question was still repeated and still unanswered. They turned away together and strolled a few yards, and turned and came back again. This time Charnock entered the hotel. "Is Mrs. Warriner in?" he asked.

The waiter replied, "Yes."

Charnock drew a long breath. Surely if much had been amiss with her the waiter would have told them; but he said nothing, he merely led the way upstairs.

XXII

IN WHICH CHARNOCK ASTONISHES RALPH WARRINER

The waiter threw open the door, the two men entered, and Warriner shut the door. Miranda rose from a chair and stood looking from Charnock to Warriner and back again from Warriner to Charnock; and as yet no word was spoken by anyone of them. Charnock had time to note, and grieve for, the pallor of her face and the purple hollows about her eyes. Then she moved forward for a step or two quite steadily; she murmured a name and the name was not Ralph; and then suddenly, without any warning, she fell to the ground between Charnock and her husband, and lay still and lifeless.

"My God, she's dead!" whispered Warriner. "We should have sent word of our coming. We have killed her," and then he stopped. For Charnock was standing by the side of Miranda and talking down to her as she lay, in a low, soft, chiding voice.

"Come," he was saying, "it's what you wished. You will be glad when you have time to think over it and understand. There is no reason why you should—"

This intimate talking with the lifeless woman came upon Warriner as something horrible. "Man, can't you see?" he whispered hoarsely. "She's dead, Miranda is. We have killed her, you and I."

Charnock slowly turned his head towards Warriner and looked at him steadily with his eyebrows drawn down over his eyes. Somehow Warriner was frightened by that glance; he felt a chill creep down his spine; he was more frightened than even on that morning when Charnock threatened to sell him outside Alkasar. "She's dead, I tell you," he babbled, and so was silent.

Charnock looked back to Miranda, sank upon one knee by her side, and bending his head down began to whisper to her exhortations, gentle reproaches at her lack of courage, and between his words he smiled at her as at a wayward child.

"There is no reason to fear," the uncanny talk went on; "and it hurts us! You don't know how much. You might as well speak, not be like this—pretending." He reached over her and took her hand, cherished it in his own, and entwined his fingers with her fingers and then laughed, as though her fingers had responded to his own. "You are rather cruel, you know."

Warriner moved uneasily. "Charnock, I tell you Miranda's—"

Charnock flung his other arm across her body and crouched over it, glaring at Warriner like a beast about to spring.

"And I tell you she's not, she's not, she's not!" he hissed out. "Dead!" and suddenly he lifted up Miranda's head, held it in the hollow of his arm and kissed the face upon the forehead and the lips. "Dead?" and he broke out into a laugh. "Is she? I'll show you. Come! Come!" He forced his disengaged arm underneath her waist, and putting all his strength into the swing lifted himself on to his feet, and lifted Miranda with him. "Now don't you see?" Warriner was standing, his mouth open, his eyes contracted; there was more than horror expressed in them, there was terror besides.

"Don't you see?" cried Charnock, in a wild triumph. "Perhaps you are blind. Are you blind, Ralph Warriner?"

He held Miranda supported against his shoulder, and swung her up and tried to set her dangling feet firm-planted on the ground; but her limbs gave, her head rolled upon his shoulder. He hitched her up again, her head fell back exposing the white column of her throat. The heavy masses of her hair broke from their fastenings, unrolled about her shoulders, and tumbled about his. He tried again to set her on her feet, and her head fell forward upon his breast, and her hair swept across his lips. "There, man," he cried, "she can stand. . . Can a dead woman stand? Tell me that!" He held her so that she had the posture, the semblance, of one who stands, though all her weight was upon his arm. His laughter rose without any gradation to the pitch of a scream, sank without gradation to a hoarse cry. "Why, she can walk! Can a dead woman walk? See! See!" And suddenly he dropped his arm from her waist, and stood aside from her, holding her hand in his. Instantly her figure curved and broke. She swung round towards him upon the pivot of his hand, and as she swung she stumbled and fell. Charnock caught her before she reached the ground, lifted her up, strained her to his breast, and held her so. One deep sob broke from him, shook him, and left him trembling. He carried Miranda to a couch, and there gently laid her down. Gently he divided her hair back from her temples and her face; he crossed her hands upon her breast, watched her for a second as she lay, her dress soiled with the dust of his journeyings; and then he dropped on his knees by the couch, and with a set white face, with his eyelids shut tight upon his eyes, in a low, even voice he steadily blasphemed.

Some time later a hand was laid upon his shoulder and a strange voice bade him rise. He stood up and looked at the stranger with a dazed expression like one who comes out of the dark into a lighted room. Warriner also was in the room. Charnock caught a word here and there; the stranger was speaking to him; Charnock gathered that the stranger was a doctor, and that Warriner had fetched him.

"But she's dead," said Charnock, resentfully. "Why trouble her? she's dead." And looking down to Miranda, he saw that there was a faint flush of pink upon her cheeks, where all had been white before. "But you said she was dead," he said stupidly to Warriner, and as the doctor bent over her, it broke in upon him that she was in truth alive, that she had but swooned, and the shame of what he had done came home to him. "I was mad," he said, "I was mad."

"Go," said the doctor, "both of you."

"I can stay," said Warriner. "This is Mrs. Warriner; I am her husband, Ralph Warriner." The doctor looked up sharply. Warriner simply nodded his head. "Yes, yes," he said; "and this is Charnock. *Ce bon* Charnock. You see, he loves my wife."

Warriner spoke slowly and in an inexpressive voice, as though he too was hardly aware of what he said. The conviction that Miranda was dead had come with equal force to both of these two men, and the knowledge that she was not brought an equal stupefaction. Warriner remained in the room; Charnock went outside and down the stairs.

He came to his senses in the streets of Gibraltar, and looking backwards, seemed to himself to have lost them weeks ago somewhere between Mequinez and Alkasar, in a profitless rivalry for a woman who could not belong to him. In the present revulsion of his feelings he was conscious that he had lost all his enmity towards Warriner. He walked down to the landing-stage at the Mole. The Levanter had spent its force during the night; the sea had gone down; a steamer was dropping its anchor in the bay. Charnock was in two minds whether or no to cross the harbour to Algeciras, where Warriner and himself had left their traps the day before, gather together his belongings, and sail for England in that steamer. He had done all that he had been enjoined to do; he had brought Warriner back; he had even, as he had promised, paid the one last visit to Miranda. But,—but, he might be wanted, he pleaded to himself, and so undecided he wandered about the streets, and in the afternoon came back to the hotel.

The waiter was watching for his return. Mrs. Warriner wished to speak with him. There was no sign of Warriner. Charnock mounted the stairs. There was no sign of Warriner within the sitting-room. Miranda was alone, and from the frank unembarrassed way with which she held out her hand, Charnock understood that she knew nothing of what had passed in the morning.

XXIII

Relates a Second Meeting Between Charnock and Miranda

"I Was afraid you had gone without my thanks," she said; "and thanks are the only coin I have to pay you with."

"Surely there needs no payment."

"I should have thanked you this morning; but your return overcame me, I had hoped and prayed so much for it."

The scream of the P. and O.'s steam-whistle sounded through the room. They both turned instinctively to the window, they saw the last late boat-load reach the ship's side, and in a moment or so they heard the rattle of the anchor-chain.

"And Ralph?" asked Charnock.

Miranda pointed to the steamer. Already the white fan of water streamed away from its stern.

"He has sailed?"

"Yes. He could not stay here. His—" she paused for a second and then spoke the word boldly, "his crime was hushed up, but it is of course known here to a few, and all know that there is something. He told his name to the doctor. It was not safe for him to stay over this morning."

"He has gone to England?"

"Yes, but he will leave England immediately. He promised to write to me, so that I may know where he is."

More of Warriner's interview with his wife, neither Charnock nor anyone ever knew. Whether he asked her to come with him and she refused, or whether, once he saw her and had speech with her, his fictitious passion died as quickly as it had grown—these are matters which Miranda kept locked within her secret memories. At this time indeed such questions did not at all occur to Charnock. As he watched the great steamer heading out of the bay, and understood that he must be taking the same path, he was filled with a great pity for the lonely woman at his side. The thought of her home up there in the Spanish hills and of her solitary, discontented companion came to him with a new and poignant sadness. Ronda was no longer a fitting shrine for her as his first fancies had styled it, but simply a strange place in a strange country.

"Why don't you go home to your own place, to your own people?" he suggested rather than asked.

Miranda was silent for a while. "I have thought of it," she said at length; "I think too that I shall. At first, there was the disgrace, there was the pity—I could not have endured it; besides, there was Rupert. But—but—I think I shall."

"I should," said Charnock, decidedly. "I should be glad, too, to know that you had made up your mind to that. I should be very glad to think that you were back at your own home."

"Why?" she asked, a little surprised at his earnestness.

"Of course, I wasn't born to it," he replied disconnectedly; "but now and then I have stayed at manor-houses in the country; and such visits have always left an impression on me. I would have liked myself to have been born of the soil on which I lived, to have lived where my fathers and grandfathers lived and walked and laughed and suffered, in the same rooms, under the same trees, enjoying the associations which they made. Do you know, I don't think that that is a privilege lightly to be foregone." And for a while again they both were silent.

Then Miranda turned suddenly and frankly towards him: "I should like so much to show you my home." She had said much the same on that first evening of their meeting in Lady Donnisthorpe's balcony, as they both surely remembered.

"I should like much to see it," returned Charnock, gently; "but I am a busy man." Miranda coloured at the conventional excuse, as Charnock saw. "But it was kind of you to say that. I was glad to hear it," he added.

It was not to the addition she replied, but to his first excuse. "As it is, you have lost two years. I have made you lose them."

"Please!" he exclaimed. "You won't let that trouble you. Promise me! I am a young man; it would be a strange thing if I could not give two years to you. Believe me, Mrs. Warriner, when my time comes, and I turn my face to the wall, whatever may happen between now and then, I shall count those two years as the years for which I have most reason to be thankful."

Miranda turned abruptly away from him and looked out of the window with intense curiosity at nothing whatever. Then she said in a low voice: "I hope that's true; I hope you mean it; I believe you do. I have been much troubled by an old theory of yours, that a woman was a brake on the wheel going up hill, and a whip in the driver's hand going down."

"I will give you a new theory to replace the old," he answered. "There are always things to do, you know. Suppose that a man has cared for a woman, has set her always within his vision, has always worked for her, for a long while, and has at last come surely, against his will, to know that she was. . . despicable, why then, perhaps he might have reason to be disheartened. But otherwise—well, he has things to do and memories to quicken him in the doing of them."

"Thank you," she said simply. "I think what you say is true. I once met a man who found a woman to be despicable, and the world went very ill with him."

It was of Major Wilbraham she was thinking, who had more than once written to Miranda during these two years, and whose last letter she imagined to be lying then in a drawer of her writing-table at Ronda.

XXIV

A Mist in the Channel Ends, as it Began, the Book

B ut that letter was in Ralph Warriner's pocket, as he walked the deck of the P. and O. It was dated from a hotel at Dartmouth, whence, said the Major, he was starting on a little cruise westwards in the company of a young gentleman from Oxford who owned a competence and a yacht. The Major would be back at Dartmouth in some six weeks' time and hoped, for Mrs. Warriner's sake, that he would find a registered letter awaiting him. The Major was still upon his cruise, as Ralph Warriner was assured from the recent date of the letter.

Warriner disembarked at Plymouth and took train to Dartmouth, where he learned the name of the yacht by merely asking at the hotel. He tried to hire a steam launch, for sooner or later in one of the harbours he would be sure to come up with Wilbraham, if he only kept a sharp eye; but steam launches are difficult to hire at this season of the year, and in the end he had to content himself with chartering a ten-ton cutter. He engaged one hand, by whose testimony the history of Ralph's pursuit came to be known, and sailed out of Dartmouth to the west. He sailed out in the morning, and coming to Salcombe ran over the bar on the tail of the flood, but did not find his quarry there, and so beat out again on the first of the ebb and reached past Bolt Head and Bolt Tail, across Bigbury Bay with its low red rocks, to Plymouth. Wilbraham had anchored in the Cattwater only two days before; the yacht was a yawl, named the *Monitor*; and was making for the Scillies. Warriner laughed when he picked up word about the destination of the yacht, and thought it would be very appropriate if he could overhaul the *Monitor* somewhere off Rosevear. As to what course he intended to pursue when he caught Wilbraham, he had no settled plan; but on the other hand he had a new revolver in his berth.

He put out from Plymouth under a light breeze, which failed him altogether when he was abreast of Rame Head. Through the rest of the day he drifted with the tide betwixt Rame Head and Plymouth. The night came upon him jewelled with stars, and a light mist upon the surface of the water; all that night he swung up and down some four miles out to sea within view of Plymouth lights, but towards morning, a fitful wind sprang up, drove the cutter as far as Polperro, and left it becalmed on a sea of glass, in front of the little white village in the wooded cliff-hollow, while the sun rose. Warriner opened the narrow line of blue water which marks the mouth of the Fowey river at eleven o'clock of the morning, and anchored in Fowey harbour about twelve. It was a Sunday, and though the *Monitor* was not at Fowey, Warriner determined to stay at his anchorage till the morrow.

The Brixham fisherman who served him upon this cruise relates that Warriner displayed no impatience or anxiety at any time. Of the febrile instability which had set his thoughts flying this way and that during the days of his companionship with Charnock, there was no longer any trace in his demeanour. Perhaps it was that he was so certain of attaining his desires; perhaps the long lesson of endurance which he had been painfully taught in Morocco now bore its fruit; perhaps too he had acquired something of the passive fatalism of the Moorish race. During this Sunday afternoon, his last Sunday as it proved, he quietly sculled the dinghy of his cutter, when the tide was low, through the mud flats of the Fowey river to Lostwithiel; and coming down again when the river was full, lay for a long time upon his oars opposite a certain church that lifts above a clump of trees on the river-bank. There he remained listening to the roll of the organ and the sweet voices of the singers as they floated out through the painted windows into the quiet of the summer evening; when the service was over he bent to his sculls again and rowed back between the steep and narrowing coppices, but it was dark before he turned the last shoulder of hill and saw the long lines of riding-lights trembling upon the water.

Warriner raised his anchor early on the Monday morning, and having the wind on his quarter, made Falmouth betimes. At Falmouth he learned that the *Monitor* had put out past St. Anthony's light only the day before and had sailed westwards to Penzance.

Warriner followed without delay, and when he was just past the Manacle rocks, the wind dropped. With the help of the tide and an occasional flaw of wind, he worked his cutter round the Lizard Point and laid her head for Penzance across the bay; and it was then that the fog took him. It crept out of the sea at about four of the afternoon, a thin grey mist, and it thickened into a dense umber fog.

The fog hung upon the Channel for thirty hours. The cutter swung into the bay with the tide. The Brixham fisherman could hear all along, to his right hand, the muffled roar as the groundswell broke upon the Lizard rocks, and the sucking withdrawal which told that those rocks were very near. The Lizard fog-horn, which sounded a minute ago abreast of them, sounded now quite faintly astern. The boat swung with the tide and would not steer; yet Warriner betrayed no alarm and no impatience at the check. He sat on the deck with a lantern by his side and drew, said the fisherman, a little flute or pipe from his pocket, on which he played tunes that were no tunes, and from which he drew a weird shrill music of an infinite melancholy and of infinite suggestions. Once the Brixham man crouched suddenly by the gunwale and peered intently over the boat's side. At a little distance off, something black loomed through the fog about the height of the mast's yard,—something black which rapidly approached.

"It's not a squall," said Warriner, quietly interrupting his music. "It's a rock. I know this coast well. We had better get the dinghy out and row her head off."

When that was done, he squatted again upon the deck by the side of the lantern, and played shrilly upon his pipe while the light threw a grotesque reflection of his figure upon the fog.

After a while they heard the Lizard-horn abreast of them again.

"The tide has turned," said Warriner, and the Brixham man dived hurriedly into the well for the poor fog-horn which the boat carried. The cutter drifted out stern-foremost past the Lizard rocks, and in a little, from this side and from that, ahead of them, astern, they heard the throb of engines and the hoarse steam-whistles of the Atlantic cargo-boats and liners. They had drifted across the track of the ocean-going steamers. The Brixham man blew upon his horn till his lungs cracked. He relates that nothing happened until three o'clock in the morning, as he knows, since Warriner just at three o'clock took his watch from his pocket and looked at the dial by the lantern-light. He mentions too, as a detail which struck him at the time, that the door of the lantern was open, and so still was the heavy air that the candle burnt steadily as in a room. At three o'clock in the morning he suddenly saw a glimmering flash of white upon the cutter's beam. For a fraction of a second he was dazed. Then he lifted the horn to his mouth, and he was still lifting it—so small an interval was there of time—when a huge sharp wedge cut through the fog and towered above the cutter out of sight. The wedge was the bows of an Atlantic liner. No one on that liner heard the despairing, interrupted moan of the tiny fog-horn beneath the ship's forefoot; no one felt the shock. The Brixham man was hurled clear of the steamer, and after swimming for the best part of an hour was picked up by a smack which he came upon by chance. Warriner's body was washed up three days later upon the Lizard rocks.

This history did not reach Charnock's ears for a full year afterwards; for within a week of his arrival in London, where his unexplained disappearance had puzzled very few, since he was known for a man of many disappearances, he had started off to Asia Minor, there to survey the line of a projected railway. The railway was never more than projected, and after a year the survey was abandoned. Charnock returned to London and heard the story of Warriner's death from Lady Donnisthorpe's lips at her last reception at the end of the season. Lady Donnisthorpe was irritated at the impassive face with which he listened. She was yet more irritated when he said casually, without any reference whatever to a word of her narrative, "Who is that girl? I think I have seen her before."

Lady Donnisthorpe followed the direction of his eyes, and saw a young girl with very pale gold hair. Lady Donnisthorpe rose from her chair. "Perhaps you would like me to introduce you," she said with sarcastic asperity.

"I should," replied Charnock.

Lady Donnisthorpe waved her hands helplessly and brushed away all mankind. She led Charnock across the room, introduced him, and left him with a manner of extreme coldness, to which Charnock at this moment was quite impervious.

"I think I have seen you here before," said Charnock.

"Yes," said the girl, "I remember. It was some while since. Why have you quarrelled?"

The meaning of that question dawned upon Charnock gradually. The girl with the gold hair smiled at his perplexity, and laughed pleasantly at his comprehension.

Charnock looked round the room.

"No," said she.

He looked towards the window, and the window was open.

"Yes," said the girl.

Charnock found Miranda upon the balcony.

THE END

A Note About the Author

A.E.W. Mason (1865–1948) was an English novelist, short story writer and politician. He was born in England and studied at Dulwich College and Trinity College, Oxford. As a young man he participated in many extracurricular activities including sports, acting and writing. He published his first novel, *A Romance of Wastdale*, in 1895 followed by better known works *The Four Feathers* (1902) and *At The Villa Rose* (1910). During his career, Mason published more than 20 books as well as plays, short stories and articles.

A Note from the Publisher

Spanning many genres, from non-fiction essays to literature classics to children's books and lyric poetry, Mint Edition books showcase the master works of our time in a modern new package. The text is freshly typeset, is clean and easy to read, and features a new note about the author in each volume. Many books also include exclusive new introductory material. Every book boasts a striking new cover, which makes it as appropriate for collecting as it is for gift giving. Mint Edition books are only printed when a reader orders them, so natural resources are not wasted. We're proud that our books are never manufactured in excess and exist only in the exact quantity they need to be read and enjoyed.

Discover more of your favorite classics with Bookfinity™.

- Track your reading with custom book lists.
- Get great book recommendations for your personalized Reader Type.
- Add reviews for your favorite books.
- AND MUCH MORE!

Visit **bookfinity.com** and take the fun Reader Type quiz to get started.

Enjoy our classic and modern companion pairings!